The Emperor's Woman

An Akitada Novel

I. J. Parker

I · J · P Books

Published 2013 by I.J.Parker and i·J·P Books
428 Cedar Lane, Virginia Beach VA 23452
http://www.ijparker.com
First published electronically 2012.

Cover design by I. J. Parker.
Cover image byOgata Gekko.

Publisher's Note: This is a work of fiction. Names, characters, places,
and incidents are a product of the author's imagination.

The Emperor's Woman/I.J.Parker – 2nd edition
ISBN 978-1492260134

Praise for I. J. Parker and the Akitada series

"Akitada is as rich a character as Robert Van Gulik's intriguing detective, Judge Dee." *The Dallas Morning News*

"Readers will be enchanted by Akitada." *Publishers Weekly* Starred Review

"A brisk and well-plotted mystery with a cast of regulars who become more fully developed with every episode." *Kirkus*

"Parker's research is extensive and she makes great use of the complex manners and relationships of feudal Japan." *Globe and Mail*

"The fast-moving, surprising plot and colorful writing will enthrall even those unfamiliar with the exotic setting." *Publishers Weekly,* Starred Review

". . .the author possesses both intimate knowledge of the time period and a fertile imagination as well. Combine that with an intriguing mystery and a fast-moving plot, and you've got a historical crime novel that anyone can love." *Chicago Sun-Times*

"Parker's series deserves a wide readership." *Historical Novel Society.*

Characters

Sugawara Akitada   senior secretary in the Ministry
of Justice

Tamako   his wife

Yasuko, Yoshitada his children

Akiko   his married sister

Tora   his longtime retainer, a former
soldier

Genba   another retainer, a former
wrestler

Saburo   a severely disfigured servant and
former spy

Fujiwara Kaneie   his superior, Minister of Justice

Kobe   Superintendent of the Imperial
Police

Nakatoshi   Akitada's friend in the Ministry
of Ceremonial.

Persons Connected with the Death of the Emperor's Woman:

Prince Atsuhira   son of an emperor

Fujiwara Kishi   his senior wife, daughter of the
Regent

Fujiwara Kosehira   Akitada's friend and Kishi's cousin

Minamoto Maseie   Lord of Sagami, powerful provincial nobleman

Minamoto Masanaga   his son, officer in the Imperial Guard

Minamoto Masako   his daughter, the emperor's "woman"

Nagasune Hiroko   her attendant in the palace

Persons Connected with the Case of the Murdered Brothel Keeper:

Ohiro	Genba's love, a prostitute
Shokichi	her roommate, another prostitute
Tokuzo	owner of the brothel Sasaya
His mother	
Miyagi and Ozuru	two dead prostitutes
Bashan	a blind masseur
Kenko	chief of the Beggars' Guild
Jinsai	a beggar
Mrs. Komiya	a landlady
Sosuke	a rice merchant
Abbot Raishin	abbot of a small mountain temple

Pronunciation of Japanese Words

Unlike English, Japanese is pronounced phonetically. Therefore vowel sounds are approximately as follows:

> "a" as in "father"
>
> "e" as in "let"
>
> "i" as in "kin"
>
> "o" as in "more"
>
> "u" as in "would."

Double consonants ("ai" or "ei") are pronounced separately, and ō or ū are doubled or lengthened.

As for the consonants:

> "g" as in "game"
>
> "j" as in "join"
>
> "ch" as in "chat".

Remember well
Those promises of love
That bring my end—
Clouds of yesterday dispersed
By the cold breath of the mountain wind.

(Fujiwara Teika, "A lady's final reproach to her lover")

1

Snow

It started snowing heavily as he made his way uphill with his burden. At first he took little notice, except that the drifting flakes cooled his skin. She was infernally heavy and awkward to hold because of her pregnancy. Besides, her long hair and parts of her clothing swept the ground and kept getting caught on branches. He would have taken her clothes off, but he needed to make this look like suicide.

He paused a moment to shift his load and use the silk of her full sleeve to mop his face. The snow was falling more heavily. He glanced up the stony path leading to the cliff. Already the dirt between the stones was turning white. He realized that this sudden snowfall was a very good thing and smiled. If he left any tracks, the snow would soon hide them. There would be nothing to show that she had not walked this steep path by herself before jumping off the cliff. Luck was with him. In the end, it was always so. He started climbing again. Best do this quickly and be on his way.

When he reached the promontory, out of breath and tired, he let his burden slide down and looked around. He was well above the villa, whose roof he could not see from here. He liked the loneliness of the spot. A hermit would have built his hut here to meditate in solitude on the Buddha. On all sides rose forested hills, hazy and immaterial behind the veil of falling snow, and the rock outcropping before him jutted over an abyss. Some fifty feet below him, a small brook splashed over and around rocks toward the valley. The sound of the waterfall that fed the brook blotted out all other small noises, even his heavy breathing.

This made him look back nervously, but all was empty except for him, the woman on the ground, and the drifting snow. Already snowflakes clung to her hair and turned the deep blue of her silk gown pale. Her face—what he could see of it—was as white as the snow. There was a little blood in her hair, not much. He had been lucky to hit her so as not to break the skin and leave stains in the house.

Her eyelids fluttered. He gasped. She was coming round. He must hurry. Moving cautiously up to the edge on the slippery rocks, he peered over. He had to make sure she would not catch on something on the way down and survive the fall. Having selected the best spot, a sheer drop fifty feet to the bed of the brook, he turned back, grasped her under the arms and dragged her to the edge. When he released her, she gave a small moan and raised one arm. Shifting her body, he got ready to give it a hard push. At that moment, she opened her eyes and looked up at him.

If she was pleading, it was too late. He was frightened into sudden action; she slipped forward and was gone.

Stunned by the momentary eye contact, he crouched near the edge. When she hit the rocks below, the sound was very small, almost lost in the rushing of the waterfall.

Then there was only the sound of the water and the silent falling of the snow. Cold crept up his hands and knees.

He shivered and slowly crawled backwards, then straightened up, and stood. The snow fell thickly, in large wet flakes. With darkness, it would become cold, and by morning the world would be covered with in a blanket of purest white.

He wiped the sweat from his face and found that his hands were shaking. That look she had given him. They said the ghosts of the murdered pursued their killers. With a muttered prayer, he started back down the path, slowly at first, and then faster, until he was running, slipping on the wet stones, brambles ripping at his clothes and hands.

2

A Deadly Conspiracy

Akitada's day began quite pleasantly. The sun had made its appearance, the children had woken them early, and now Akitada stood on the veranda, watching as they chased his wife and each other around the garden. Birds chirped and the cherry tree's branches were thick with buds. From the front of the house came the sound of barking.

Tamako, raising her long gown and showing smooth legs and bare feet, passed him. She was rosy with exercise and called out, "The wisteria is alive. And I think it will bloom," then squealed as Yasuko snatched at her long hair. Yoshitada, who was still too slow to be a real contender, burst into loud giggles and toddled after them.

Akitada strolled over to the wisteria, so pregnant with significance for their marriage, and studied it attentively. Tamako was right. A good omen.

He had presented her with a blossom from the an-
cestor of this plant on the morning after their marriage
night. It had come from her own home which had
been destroyed by the fire that took her father's life.
Years later, when they lost Yori, their first son, to
smallpox and grew apart and bitter, the transplanted
wisteria had declined and stopped blooming. Since
then, both Tamako and Akitada had checked it every
spring for signs of new life on the gnarled old trunk.

Whistling softly to himself, Akitada walked to his
study, where Saburo awaited him with tea and hot rice
gruel. Saburo, a disfigured ex-monk, had taken over
many of Seimei's functions after the old man had died.

Akitada thanked him and received in return the gro-
tesque grimace that was Saburo's smile. Saburo was
indefatigable in his efforts to make himself useful and to
prove a faithful servant. In spite of his unsavory past,
Akitada had not regretted taking him on.

When his workday at the ministry began, Akitada
was still in an excellent mood. He managed to finish a
thick stack of dossiers before he was called to the minister's office. Gathering them up, he went to see Fujiwara
Kaneie.

Kaneie was a privileged member of the ruling clan
and had managed to obtain his lucrative assignment
without much effort or talent for it. The upper positions in the government were riddled with such men,
while the actual work of the government was carried out
by underlings or a few career officials in the lower
ranks. Kaneie was one of the better senior officials in
that he readily admitted his shortcomings and left the

work to abler people like Akitada. He was also a friendly and affable man.

This day he seemed abstracted. He signed and stamped the last document with his seal, then handed the sheaf of papers back to Akitada. "Have you heard the news about Prince Atsuhira?" he asked.

Akitada searched his memory for Atsuhira and found, hazy by the distance of years, a rather pleasant young man he had met at one of his friend Kosehira's parties. But, no, there had been a more recent incident. It had involved the prince's love affair and a case of blackmail. He said, "I haven't heard anything recently. I believe we met many years ago." He paused, adding a little doubtfully, "I liked him then."

The minister nodded. "Yes, he's a very pleasant man. Married to one of the Fujiwara daughters. I cannot believe the tale. Nobody thought he had it in him."

"Had what in him?"

"The kind of ambition that makes men overreach themselves. We all assumed he'd given up any hopes of succession, but here his name is linked to a very unsavory business. It may also involve his wife's father and uncle. And several other high-ranking men as well. A major conspiracy, if one can believe it."

Akitada tried to recall what he knew of the prince's marriages. As a potential heir, he had taken one of the daughters of the present chancellor to wife. He said, "He seemed unambitious when I first knew him. But that was a long time ago, and his name has come up once before. Is he in serious trouble?"

It had been six years ago when the prince's uncle, Bishop Sesshin, had contacted Akitada because he had feared one of the prince's love letters had fallen into the wrong hands. The letter had contained some very incautious remarks about His Majesty.

The minister said, "Oh, yes. Exile perhaps. And he won't be going alone." The minister shook his head. "There are always the innocent who suffer along with the schemers." He looked at Akitada. "I should hate to lose this post."

Akitada was startled. "But surely not you, sir? Did you know the prince well?"

The minister gave a weak chuckle. "No, not really. But I do know his wife. The way these things go, once the censors have their teeth into a conspiracy, they make a wide sweep. I recently attended a party with him." He paused. "Speaking of parties, I think you know Fujiwara Kosehira."

"Yes, he's my friend." Akitada smiled. "And you're right. He used to give some famous parties, but Kosehira hasn't been in the capital for years. He has estates in Yamato and has been serving as governor of Omi Province for two years now."

"Oh, then I regret to tell you he has been recalled to explain his role in the affair. It seems there was correspondence between him and the prince."

"Kosehira is involved? I cannot believe it. He's the most apolitical of men. It must be a mistake."

"Possibly. But they used to say the same of the prince. Perhaps they kept their intentions from the world?"

"No. Kosehira would never do such a thing." But that would not matter to his enemies. Akitada clutched the documents to his chest. "Forgive me, sir, but I think I should go to him. I hope I can give you more reassuring news when I get back."

"I don't think that's very wise, Akitada."

Akitada did not wait for any more. He rushed from the minister's room to his own and flung the documents on the desk, telling his clerk, "Please have these delivered to the appropriate persons." Then he dashed from the building.

What puzzled him was that Kosehira had not contacted him. That did not bode well. Perhaps he had already been arrested and was under guard somewhere.

Hurrying through the palace grounds, he was soon out of breath and a sharp pain in his side forced him to slow down. Years of paperwork had made him an old man.

He felt miserable and helpless about Kosehira. What could he do in a case of high treason? Guilt for not keeping up with the friend who had stood by him all his life shamed him. Kosehira had defended Akitada in his university days, when the unpopular Sugawara heir had been mocked by the sons of high-ranking nobles. Later, throughout Akitada's career, whenever trouble had befallen him, he had interceded for him. And what had he done in return? Less than nothing. He had forgotten his friend, or very nearly so. Since the odd memory had invariably brought uncomfortable guilt feelings, he had banished thoughts of Kosehira quickly.

And now Kosehira was in serious trouble.

Fujiwara Kosehira's residence occupied a large corner in the best quarter of the capital and was impressive enough to have served on two occasions as the temporary home of an empress and a crown prince. Kosehira was generous, and the house had never really been closed during the years he was absent. Akitada, still out of breath, was relieved to find no soldiers at the open gates or in the courtyard. All looked quiet enough in the spring sunshine.

His arrival was noted, however. A servant appeared, bowed, and asked his purpose.

"I understand Lord Kosehira is in residence. Please let him know that Sugawara Akitada has come to see him."

The servant bowed again and left, Akitada following more slowly. He saw now that there were a few people about. The stables seemed unusually quiet, though. His heart grew heavy again. Surely such a lack of activity was unnatural with Kosehira in residence.

He had reached the steps to the main residence when the servant reappeared, followed by Kosehira himself.

"Akitada," his friend cried. "I'm so glad to see you. How did you know? It's very good of you to come so quickly when I've only just arrived myself." The smile was the old Kosehira's, but there was something drawn and tense about him. His slightly corpulent figure seemed to have shrunk, become less buoyant and bouncy.

Akitada ran up the steps and they embraced. For a moment emotion nearly choked Akitada. He made up for it by clasping Kosehira very tightly to himself. They hugged, laughed a little, and patted backs, then finally parted to study each other's faces.

Kosehira had lost weight and looked older. There were lines in his face and a few gray hairs in his mustache. Akitada felt a surge of affection for him, stronger perhaps because of having neglected him.

"How is the family?" he asked.

Kosehira chuckled. "Thriving. There seem to be more children running around every year. Mind you, I'm very fond of them all, but I've been known to mix up their names. And their mothers." He rolled his eyes. "Not advisable, my friend. You're lucky you have only one wife to worry about."

"You used to urge me to take more."

"I know. And I love all my ladies. Come in. I think we can get something to eat, but I only just got here."

The news had spread quickly if Kaneie already knew. That was ominous.

They settled down in Kosehira's study, which looked dim and smelled unused, but two servants appeared quickly with a brazier of glowing coals and trays with snacks and wine.

Akitada waited until they had left again and Kosehira had poured their wine before saying, "I just heard a strange story from the minister. I still cannot believe it, but I rushed over so fast that I was out of breath. Is it true? Kaneie thinks you're in danger of arrest for treason."

Kosehira made a face. "No, no. There is some confusion. Don't worry, Akitada. All will be well. I came up to straighten out a few things, that's all. It's nothing . . . or rather, it affects someone else. But drink your wine and let's catch up on family news. How is your lovely lady? And the little ones?"

Kosehira hardly touched his wine, and Akitada was not at all satisfied, but since his friend seemed eager to hear about Akitada's new little son—well into his third year by now—he complied. Kosehira then recited the names and ages of his own large brood, his face softening as he recounted their achievements and amusing tricks.

Happy children, thought Akitada, to have such a father who doted on them and had the leisure to spend time with all of them. He never seemed to have enough himself.

When they ran out of family matters, Akitada said, "Kosehira, something is wrong. Will you not tell me about it?"

His friend's smile faded, and he looked away. "It's nothing I want you to become involved in, Akitada. The last thing you need is more enemies among those in power."

Akitada smiled wryly. "You don't think my reputation is sufficiently good yet to keep me out of trouble?"

Kosehira did not smile. He said bluntly, "No, I don't. Not for something like this. And I won't be able to do anything for you."

Taken aback, Akitada sat silent for a moment, but their long friendship overcame the slight resentment. "I expect you're right. I've relaxed because things have been quiet lately. I like Kaneie, and he likes me, but I tend to forget how dispensable I am and what long memories some people have."

"Forgive me for speaking harshly, Akitada." Kosehira reached across to touch his hand. "I don't want to be the one to bring you more trouble."

"I know that. But I've just been told that you're involved in some conspiracy with Prince Atsuhira, so there's no point in keeping things from me. I will try to find out what I can whether you take me into your confidence or not."

Kosehira sighed. "Akitada, I tell you, this is not for you. Think of your family. And you with a new little son. I would never forgive myself—."

"Tell me, Kosehira!"

"Did you ever meet the prince?"

"Yes. Here, in your house. I thought him a nice man . . . in spite of his imperial blood."

A weak chuckle greeted that. "A very nice man. I got to know him well over the years. He's married to one of my cousins, the regent's daughter. Kishi prefers to use her Chinese name, even though Atsuhira is no longer considered for the succession. That will tell you how proud she is. Those girls were all raised to be empresses someday. The disappointment that he didn't want the succession weighs heavily on her."

So possibly, Atsuhira's wife was behind this. Perhaps her aspirations had suggested the plot. Women could be very fierce when they fought for their families. He wondered if there were children.

Kosehira sighed again and went on. "There was an affair. I knew about it because we corresponded. He was very deeply in love and planned to take the young woman to wife. I suspect Kishi found out. In her anger, she must have made some allegations, and that's why Atsuhira has been charged. I'm involved because of our correspondence. There you have the whole story. There's no truth to the conspiracy rumor. It's all due to the fabrication of a passionate woman with enough power to destroy her husband."

Akitada digested the information. The prince was an inveterate womanizer and clearly it had got him in trouble again. And once again, there was a letter trail. Though this time, Akitada was too late to fix the problem.

He said, "There must be more to it than that. They would not move against him otherwise. He's the son of the last emperor. What of his father? Can't he do something to protect him?"

Kosehira grimaced. "The retired emperor is in ill health and has forsaken the world rather more completely than most. He resides like a hermit in the wilderness of Mount Hiei, hoping for sainthood. Such men have truly abandoned their families."

"That's both ridiculous and reprehensible!" snapped Akitada.

His passion brought a slight smile to Kosehira's drawn face. "Irreverent as always. You know, Akitada, part of your troubles come from the fact that you don't behave as you ought to. It upsets people."

"I know. I try to curb my tongue as best I can." Akitada smiled, then sobered. "What does Atsuhira say? You say you corresponded. Do you recall any comments in his letters to you that could be called treasonous?"

Kosehira did not answer right away. He looked down at his hands folded on his lap. After a long moment, he said, "We would occasionally pass an observation on events. That's only natural and didn't mean anything. As for the prince's reaction to the charges against him, I don't like betraying a confidence, especially of this kind, but he's in dire straits and does absolutely nothing to defend himself. Perhaps you can at least advise me how to get through to him." He gave Akitada a pleading look. "For the past three months he hasn't answered my letters, and he refuses to see me. His personal servant is frantic. He fears that Atsuhira will take the dark path. He hardly eats and spends hours staring straight ahead with tears pouring down his face. I'm at my wits' end. I write—no answer. I go to see him—no admittance. I'm turned away from his house like an enemy. I cannot find a single man who was once his friend and will now speak for him or about him. I tell you, Akitada, if it weren't so infernally dangerous, I would have turned to you long ago."

"Well, I'm here now. And since the prince's troubles are also yours, I suppose, they become mine as well. You describe a man who seems to be in mourning. And you mentioned a woman."

Kosehira nodded. "Very astute of you. Yes. Oh, the affair is still officially a secret, but you're right. Her death accounts for the fact that he doesn't seem to care what happens to him." Kosehira paused in indecision and searched Akitada's face. Heaving a deep breath, he said, "Perhaps I'll be forgiven this indiscretion. Atsuhira fell deeply in love with a ... er ... very highly-placed young woman, and she returned his passion. Apparently, they met secretly in his summer place in the mountains. One day last winter, he got there late and found her gone. She'd left behind her cloak and veiled hat, her box of cosmetics, and her horse." Kosehira paused to drink some wine.

"Do you mean to tell me that a young gentlewoman rode alone into the mountains to meet her lover? At night? And in winter? I find that somewhat hard to believe."

"I expect it was still day time. Besides, the lady was unusual. Still, the whole situation is highly reprehensible and very secret. Oh, well, I see I'll have to be totally frank. Just keep it to yourself. The prince's beloved was the Lady Masako."

Akitada's jaw dropped. Even he, who paid no attention whatsoever to court gossip, knew about Lady Masako, daughter of Minamoto Masaie, lord of Sagami. Her reputation had preceded her to the capital when she arrived to serve the emperor. Her father had raised her like a son. She rode horses and was rumored to wear male clothing. She allegedly had greater skill with bow and arrow or a sword than most men. And she was said to be very beautiful. Her father had intended her to catch the young emperor's eye. Shocked, Akitada asked, "I recall hearing something about her death."

"Not the truth. The court suppressed details because of the scandal. They gave out she succumbed to an illness while visiting her aged nurse."

"What happened?"

"Apparently she threw herself off a cliff near the villa. He found her the next morning. It's this that has deranged him."

Akitada frowned. "If he stopped speaking to you, how did you find out?"

Kosehira gave him a fond look. "I was in the capital on provincial business that week. We spent some hours together the very evening it happened and chatted long over wine. That was what made him late that night. I'd never seen him so happy, so excited to see her. The next day, he was a changed man, wild-eyed and shaking, frantic because he didn't know what to do. I didn't either, and you were out of town. In the end I went to Kobe. A good man! He handled everything most discreetly."

This time, astonishment left Akitada speechless. He sat staring at Kosehira, trying to comprehend how a police investigation had been managed without a word getting out.

Kosehira seemed to find nothing remarkable in it, for he continued after tossing down another cup of wine. "Before you get suspicious again, there was never any doubt about it being suicide. She was alone. The old couple, who look after the villa during the winter months, were asleep in their own house, and the prince thinks she was distraught. He told me about her state of mind because I asked him how he found her. She had written him that they could not meet again, and that she could not live without him. They searched for her all night, he and the caretaker. It snowed that night, so it wasn't until the following morning that he found her. He went to the cliff, half afraid, and looked over. That's when he saw an odd pile of snow in the creek below and a bit of her blue robe showing. Some animal had disturbed it." Kosehira shuddered and rubbed a hand over his face. "Horrible! Can you imagine what the poor man must've felt? Filled with happiness one day, and losing her the next. What a night he must have spent. And to find her at the bottom of the cliff, all broken." Kosehira's voice shook.

Akitada was silent. Yes, it was unimaginable. He thought of Tamako and how he would feel if she killed herself like that, leaving him to find her broken body. No, she would never do that to him. This couple had not been happy lovers before this happened. There must have been a reason for her sudden decision.

He asked, "Is her suicide in some way connected with this charge of conspiracy against His Majesty?"

Kosehira looked surprised. "I don't see how it could be. She died almost four months ago, long before the present troubles."

"Perhaps the charges were trumped up in order to punish the prince for seducing one of the emperor's women and causing her to take her life."

"Masako wasn't one of the emperor's women. His Majesty did not care for her at all. Her reputation of mannishness repelled him."

"I see." Akitada pondered this. The story seemed unsatisfactory. "And because the prince is distraught over his lover's suicide, he refuses to defend himself, and that puts you and others in danger of arrest and punishment?"

Kosehira squirmed uncomfortably. "Well, it may seem that way but, Akitada, you must feel for the man. What an absolutely horrible thing to have happen! It was all I could do to convince him that he wasn't responsible for her death."

"Oh? Why *did* she jump off the cliff?"

Kosehira bit his lip. "Well, umm, she was expecting their child. It would have made a fine scandal for both of them. Maybe someone found out."

"It's a shocking story, but I'm not going to let you sacrifice yourself and your family because your good nature keeps you from speaking out. I'll go see Atsuhira and get him to face the situation. Once we have a clearer account of what the charges are, we can surely clear you."

"You can't see him. I tried early this morning. He's under guard in his palace."

Akitada grimaced. "You forget that I work in the Ministry of Justice. I'll get in somehow."

"No, I won't let you do that. You'll lose your position."

Akitada gave Kosehira a smile. "I owe my career to you. You have interceded for me many times, so you have nothing to say in the matter." He got to his feet.

Kosehira rose also, looking miserable. "I shouldn't have told you. You mustn't, Akitada. Think of Tamako and the children."

"Tamako would agree with me, and the children, I'm convinced, would do so if they were old enough. I'll be back when I've learned more."

3

Genba's Sweetheart

Tora and Saburo were amusing themselves throwing coppers at an old target when Genba left his quarters in the stables and strode quickly across the courtyard.

Saburo whistled.

Tora paused in mid-toss, narrowed his eyes, and called out, "Off to see the girlfriend again? And in a new jacket? How fine you've become, brother!" He burst into laughter.

Genba flushed and sent him an angry glance, hurrying toward the gate.

"When may we expect you back?" Tora called. "Or will you spend the whole night in her arms?"

The shouting attracted the attention of the cook and Tamako's maid, who stood chatting outside the kitchen.

Both laughed. Genba dashed the last few steps and slammed the small gate behind him.

Laughter and assorted ribald shouts followed him.

Genba's resentment faded quickly. He knew he made a ridiculous figure, a man his age, his hair already gray, and his body fat and ungainly. He had never given them occasion to laugh at him before, having conducted himself with the greatest circumspection on his rare forays into the city for the services of a prostitute.

But this was different. This was Ohiro. He thought he must really be in love this time. It was a strange emotion, as unfamiliar and uncomfortable as it was exhilarating. All he knew was that he needed to see her and protect her, that lying with her arms around him was a bliss he had never felt with other women. He wondered what she saw in him. It made him humble.

Ohiro was pretty. She had a wonderful smile that caused dimples in her cheeks. Her eyes were the softest brown he had ever seen. And her body! Oh, she was shapely, with curves that invited exploring. A tiny waist, but oh, such hips. He got warm just thinking about them.

His sweetheart shared a room with another of Tokuzo's girls. They lived in a poor area on the opposite side of the capital and almost as far south from the Sugawara residence as you could go. Genba walked fast. He wanted to spend as much time as possible with Ohiro. It was her day off. He hoped she would like his new jacket. A passing comment by the master about his threadbare clothing had caused Genba to purchase it. He had begrudged every copper.

In the western market, he passed a stand selling sweets and stopped to buy a honey-filled rice cake. Ohiro was very fond of them. He liked them too, but seeing her pleasure was much better than tasting the sweet himself. Besides, he must save his money.

The tenement where Ohiro and Shokichi roomed was poorly built and worse maintained even though the rents were very high. It belonged to Tokuzo's mother, and all of Tokuzo's women were expected to live there. Genba looked around, saw no one, then knocked three times softly on one of the doors.

She opened immediately and pulled him inside, closing the door very quickly. The girls were not supposed to have male visitors without passing the fees on to Tokuzo.

Genba knew right away that something was wrong. Ohiro kept her face averted.

"What happened, love?" he asked.

She walked away from him and mumbled, "It's nothing. Please don't make a fuss."

He frowned. "Ohiro, turn around."

When she did not respond, he went after her and took her gently by the shoulders to turn her around. "Amida!" He dropped his hands and stared in shock at her swollen face. One eye was closed and surrounded by red and black bruises, there were traces of blood in her nostrils, and she had a badly cut lip. "He did that to you?" he asked hoarsely. "I'll kill him!"

"Please, Genba," she said, her good eye filling with tears.

A faded curtain parted on the inner doorway, and Shokichi came in, a thin girl—almost scrawny, he thought—who moved quickly and laughed a lot. She was not laughing now. "He's an animal," she said sharply. "No, I lie. Animals don't do that to each other. He's an *oni*, a true devil. He raped her, too. Beating women gives him a hard-on."

"Oh, Shokichi, you promised not to tell," wailed Ohiro.

Genba swallowed down the sickness that rose in his throat. Opening his arms, he drew Ohiro against his wide chest and belly and laid his head on hers. "My love," he said softly, "you must come with me. I cannot bear it any longer. He'll kill you next time."

She gave a small sob and put her arms around his waist. "Just a little longer," she said. "Be patient, my love."

He groaned. "How much do we still need?"

She slipped from his embrace and went to a trunk that held her clothes. Opening it, she dug down and brought out a small sandalwood box.

Genba glanced at Shokichi, who flushed and ducked back into the other room. He felt embarrassed, but these girls were so very poor and led such miserable lives that they would do anything to free themselves from Tokuzo's hold.

Ohiro upended the box on the floor. A small pile of coins, some gold, quite a few silver, and a large number copper, lay on the dirt floor. She crouched down and sorted through them, counting under her breath. Then she looked up, disappointment on her swollen face. "We need another ten pieces of gold," she said in a small voice.

A fortune.

Genba knelt beside her and helped her put the money back. "I'll get it," he said. "Meanwhile, lock your door and don't go back to work. Maybe tomorrow I can get you."

"No, no. I have to work tonight, but it will be all right. He always feels sorry for what he did and leaves us alone afterward."

"Ohiro, please don't. I cannot bear it . . . I love you."

She reached for him, and they embraced. He wanted to kiss her but was afraid of hurting her, so he stroked her back instead. She twitched a little, and he muttered a curse. "Take off your clothes," he commanded, pulling her up with him.

She giggled weakly and started to undo her sash. He reached for it with impatient fingers, took it off, pulled open her gown, and slipped it off her shoulders. Then he lifted her undergown over her head. She submitted, blushing furiously. Ohiro had a very nice body, with full hips and a small waist.

But instead of admiring and fondling her breasts and pulling her hips toward him, he moved around her and lifted her long hair. She gave a little cry. Turning, she started to reach for his trouser ties, but he stopped her.

"I'll kill him!" he growled, looking at the red welts that criss-crossed her back. "I'll kill the filthy bastard."

Shokichi stuck her head through the door to take a look. She gasped. "Tokuzo did that? Why? What did you do?"

Ohiro snatched up her clothes and covered herself. "You shouldn't have looked, Genba," she said. "I wanted you to make love to me. Now you've spoiled it." She burst into tears. "I cooked your favorite food, too. Sea bream with new herbs and fiddleheads. Ohhh!" With a long wail, she cowered down, drew up her knees, and buried her face in her arms.

Genba stood helpless at such a flood of tears. Shokichi went to Ohiro and put her arms around her.

"Look," she said, glancing up at Genba, "if you really love her, you've got to understand what her life's been like. Her parents died when she was nine, and she went to live with an aunt and uncle. When she was ten, the uncle started raping her. Her aunt found out and sold her to Tokuzo to be rid of her. Ohiro was okay until you came. That's when she started balking at what customers wanted, and that's when she got beatings. I bet this thing today happened because Tokuzo found out about you. He thinks she's been holding back money."

Ohiro made sounds of protest at this bald telling of her life. She moved away from Shokichi and looked at Genba with swimming eyes. "Don't hate me, Genba," she pleaded. "I have to work for him. I'm sorry."

Genba finally woke from his stupor. He went to kneel beside her. "Ohiro, I love you," he said. "I think you should run away and hide. I'll find the money somehow and pay the bastard. Then, when all is settled, you'll come home with me as my wife."

Both women gasped at that.

"Your wife?" Ohiro asked, stunned. "You want me to be your wife?"

He nodded, then glanced at Shokichi, who got up.

She said, "I'll tell the bastard you've had the doctor and can't work. He'll believe it." She left, a smile on her face.

They made love. He was gentle so as not to hurt Ohiro, but both felt passionate. Then they ate what Ohiro had cooked, and Genba remembered the sweet he had bought.

Ohiro received it like a jewel. "I've never been so happy before, Genba. I love you. Thank you." She gave him a melting glance.

And after a little while, they made love again.

It was near the middle of the night, the hour of the rat, when Genba left Ohiro. He was worried. Would the master permit him to bring another hungry mouth into the family? He was not Tora, had not served with such distinction, had, in fact, not yet lived down the fact that he had left the house unguarded three years ago when armed men had forced their way in and caused Seimei's death. And then there was Ohiro. Tora had tried to keep his wife Hanae a secret because she was a singer in the amusement quarter. And now here he was, bringing a prostitute into the family.

And how was he to raise the money? Even if he could borrow the rest of the money to buy Ohiro out, how would he be able to face the man who had done such things to the woman he loved?

At the memory of her bruised face and lacerated back, his anger rose again. Without thinking, he turned his steps toward the amusement quarter and the Sasaya, Tokuzo's brothel.

It was still well lit, and one of Tokuzo's bruisers, a man who had once been a wrestler like Genba and who now kept quarrelsome customers in line, stood outside the door with a few of the girls. They looked well-worn already, but greeted Genba with eager cries of welcome. The bruiser gave him a friendly wave. Genba glared at him and quickly faded into the next dark alley where he collided with another man.

They both grunted. The other man fumbled around in the dark, and Genba realized he might have a knife, that he had surprised a footpad. He carried no money, but he did not relish a knife in the belly, and his pent-up anger over Tokuzo's assault on Ohiro erupted in a furious attack on the dimly perceived person near him. He roared and lashed out, heard a metallic clinking, then seized an arm and brought the other man into his crushing embrace. He was not an ex-wrestler for nothing. He started to drag the stranger out into the street, to get a good look at him. At this point, the other man twisted suddenly, punched him in the groin, and slipped away when Genba doubled over.

Genba took a minute for the pain to ease, then he left the alley and looked up and down the street. The scene before the Sasaya was the same, and he saw no one who could have been the footpad.

He went back into the alley and searched the ground for the object that had made the clinking sound. He found it quickly near the house wall. It was not a knife but something smaller and far more wicked. Taking it out into the street, he saw it was a thin metal pin, a little less than a foot long and sharpened at one end.

A strange implement, but quite as deadly as a knife. Still, it was an unusual weapon for a footpad. Perhaps it was some sort of tool he used in his trade. Or someone else had dropped it, and they had kicked it in their struggle.

He tucked the pin in his sleeve and looked again at the brothel. His fury had abated. He decided to go home and sleep.

The bruiser at the door approached him with a couple of girls in tow. "Why not pay us a visit?" he said with a smirk. "We're still open for business. Tokuzo provides the best service in the quarter—right, girls?" They nodded and pressed themselves against Genba.

Genba pushed them away. "I'd like to put that bastard Tokuzo in hell," he snarled and stalked off.

4

A Strange Case of
Suicide

From Kosehira's house, Akitada headed straight for the *kebiishi-cho,* the police headquarters, where Superintendent Kobe's office was.

The story Kosehira had divulged appalled him on so many levels. And Kosehira had been right: it was dangerous to meddle in this. Becoming involved in either the court lady's suicide or Prince Atsuhira's conspiracy could damage his career permanently.

Lady Masako was not only the favorite daughter of a powerful lord, but she had been very close to the young emperor. Even if His Majesty had not been attracted to her, her person was taboo, and so were the activities prior to her death and the circumstances of that death.

The political intrigue was potentially even more explosive. And in this case, the ruling Fujiwara lords had no reason to suppress public knowledge or to protect

Atsuhira and his friends. In fact, if they wanted to make their point, they would act openly and quickly.

But Akitada owed Kosehira a great deal, and the truth was that Kosehira's story had intrigued him. He did not like coincidence, and to his mind the suicide of one of the emperor's ladies and the arrest of her imperial lover for conspiracy were not separate events. He meant to get to the bottom of the puzzle.

But to do so, he must find out why Kobe had decided to cover up the "alleged" suicide. Akitada suspected that all was not as Kosehira had told it. He did not suspect Kosehira of lying, but Lady Masako's action seemed too sudden. The prince had apparently not expected her action. Besides, Akitada felt she would not have acted in this fashion if she had loved the prince.

He found the superintendent inspecting the adjoining jail. Few ranking officials in his post would have troubled themselves with such a depressing and disgusting chore. Prisoners came from the dregs of humanity and were not treated very well. They were dirty and crawled with vermin, and their cells stank in spite of frequent cleanings. Kobe felt strongly that the situation would become intolerable if he did not walk through both jails at least once a week and unannounced.

He broke off his inspection when he saw Akitada. They returned to his office, where they took the bad taste out of their mouths with a cup of wine.

"What brings you?" Kobe asked, after smacking his lips and setting his cup down. He was usually abrupt and got to the point quickly.

"Prince Atsuhira," Akitada said, equally blunt.

Kobe's face fell. "No. You can't. Believe me, that's not for you."

"I have to disagree. My best friend is involved."

"Your best friend?" Kobe looked hurt.

"My other best friend." Akitada smiled. "Kosehira."

"Oh, him." Kobe pursed his lips. "If this is about the conspiracy charge against Atsuhira, I have nothing to do with it. And that business is definitely not a good thing to meddle in."

"I'm really here about Lady Masako's so-called suicide. But I think the two cases are connected."

Kobe's eyes widened, and he sat up. "You can't be serious. That's ridiculous! You're really reaching this time. And how do you come to know about her? Never mind. I see Kosehira told you. He's another meddler. He should know better than to talk about it."

"How much of an investigation did you do before shuffling the body off to her family?"

The superintendent flushed. "Are you accusing me of a cover-up?"

Akitada wished he had been more circumspect. Kobe was thin-skinned when it came to his work, and he had a notorious temper. "Sorry. I know there were good and sufficient reasons to protect her reputation and that of Prince Atsuhira."

"Not to mention His Majesty's feelings."

"That too. But the point is, was there anything peculiar about her death?"

"Peculiar? If one of His Majesties women jumps off a cliff, I'd call that peculiar."

"You know what I meant. She could have been thrown over."

"What? You think this was murder?" Kobe flushed with anger. "Why do you always assume the worst? And why do you still have no confidence in my methods after all these years?"

Awkward.

Akitada thought of Kosehira. Whatever had happened to the dead lady, it was the living who must be protected. "You're my friend and I trust you," he said in a soothing tone. "Please bear with me. I'm just trying to understand the connections. Kosehira is innocent of conspiracy. I know him. He's simply not political. He's always stood up for me, and I was never a popular man. I cannot let this happen because he was good-natured enough to be a friend to the prince."

Kobe grunted. Then he said, "There's not much to tell. Your friend asked to speak to me privately. Naturally, I accommodated him—because of his rank, but also because he came as your friend. His story was shocking. It involved an affair between an imperial prince and one of His Majesty's women. Furthermore, this lady was lying dead in Atsuhira's summer villa, where he'd been meeting her. I used discretion and went to see Atsuhira. He was in a terrible state. Together we rode to his villa where I inspected the corpse, was told of the letter she'd written the prince, retraced her path to the cliff, and climbed down to the streambed where he'd found her. Then I spoke with the old couple who were the caretakers. They knew only that the lady had arrived and gone into the house to await the prince. In other words, there was nothing whatsoever to indicate that she hadn't committed suicide." Kobe stopped and looked at Akitada as if he dared him to challenge his findings.

Akitada thought about it. "The letter," he mused. "It hinges on that letter. Anything odd about it?"

Kobe frowned. "No. Why should there be? The prince told me what it said. It seemed a bit flowery, but you know how emotional women get. All about taking the dark path alone and meeting again in paradise."

"Hmm. Did she say why she was taking such a step?"

"I asked the prince, who wasn't altogether rational. He burst into tears, then confessed she was expecting their child, and perhaps her condition had made her unstable. He seemed to think women do strange things at such a time, but he insisted she'd been happy about the child and that he'd planned to take her to wife. Then he started moaning, and I couldn't get another sensible word out of him."

"And the body? What injuries did you find?"

"What you'd expect with a fall from that height. She fell at least fifty feet onto a rocky streambed. Broken limbs. Bleeding from the mouth, nose, ears. Badly broken skull." Kobe frowned. "She must have hit head first," he added.

"Head first? Surely that's strange. You would expect her to step off and fall straight down. You'd expect her lower limbs to take the brunt of the impact. Or, if

I. J. Parker

she let herself fall forward, she'd hit flat and face down. Was her face damaged?"

Kobe's frown deepened. "No. I doubt anyone would dive down a precipice. But Akitada, what does it matter? She died from the fall. All the bleeding proves that. If she'd been dead already and then tossed over, she wouldn't have bled so much. Besides, there was no sign that anyone helped her to her death. Remember, she'd been alone. The two old people couldn't have managed such a thing."

But his voice sounded less certain. Akitada asked, "You checked for tracks?"

"Yes. But it snowed that night, and later the prince and the old man searched for her. They both say they saw no tracks."

"Ah. Not even hers. The snow was expected?"

"Perhaps it was, but I still don't see how that matters."

"Come, Kobe, what do you really think?"

Kobe shook his head. "That it's far too dangerous to investigate this case. Think of all the people we would offend. The emperor first of all. Then Lady Masako's father and her family. And Prince Atsuhira. And finally whoever was behind it." He added quickly, "If someone did, in fact, stage it."

"Yes," said Akitada. He felt an inner satisfaction. So Kobe had some doubts after all.

Kobe gave him a look, and silence fell.

"But that doesn't make it right," Akitada said.

"No."

"Then you're with me on this?"

Kobe glared. "Let's say I'm dissatisfied with the whole situation." He paused. "And I'm resentful that I've been dragged into it by your friend." Throwing up his hands, he protested, "What good is it to expect me to investigate and tell me that no one must know about it?"

"Yes, that's a problem. What did you do with Lady Masako?"

"We—the prince and I—carried her to a nearby monastery. The monks are very holy, and it's a small community. They prayed and read sutras over her. The prince attended the services, while I hurried back to the capital and sent an overnight messenger to her father. Minamoto Masaie arrived immediately in a state of grief and fury. He and the prince huddled behind closed doors. In the end, Lord Masaie took Lady Masako's body home to Sagami with him. End of story."

"I see. But it isn't really the end, is it? I wish I knew more about the relationship between Masaie and Prince Atsuhira. The prince seems to have calmed down the father's anger. I wonder how." Akitada got up. "Thank you, my friend. I'll try to find out what the prince thinks of all this."

Kobe frowned. "He won't talk to you. They say he's in retreat, preparing to forsake the world. Whatever you do, will you keep me informed?"

Akitada smiled at him. "Certainly. You may wish to reopen the case of Lady Masako's death after all."

Kobe just shook his head and looked unnerved.

Akitada left the compound of the *kebiishi-cho* with a lighter step. He had managed to shake Kobe's conviction that he was dealing with a simple, if dangerously scandalous, suicide. The thought that it must have been a murder was strangely energizing. It seemed better than such a pathetic end to the love affair.

He had also worked up a great anger at what had been done to the poor young woman and her unborn child. He burned to find out who and what was behind it

5

Murder
in the Willow Quarter

Genba did not sleep well that night. He kept seeing Ohiro's bruised face. By morning he had decided he must take Tora into his confidence, even if it would bring him more mockery.

He found Tora in his quarters with his wife Hanae and their little son. They greeted him and offered to share their breakfast gruel, but Genba had no appetite. He sat down, glanced at Tora's full bowl, swallowed down a bout of nausea, and said, "Thanks, no. But please finish. I'll wait to talk with Tora." He saw Hanae's surprise and had an idea. "And you, Hanae."

Now they both looked at him with concern, but they finished their meal without comment and sent Yuki out to play.

"So, what is it, Brother?" Tora asked when they were alone.

"You know I've met someone." Genba felt himself blushing.

To his relief, Tora did not grin or mock him. "What's wrong?" he asked. "You look upset."

Genba shot Hanae a glance. "It's as wrong as it can be. I, well, I met Ohiro. Ohiro's a working girl." He blushed more deeply. "She works for a bastard called Tokuzo. He owns a wine house in the Willow Quarter. His waitresses . . . well, they do whatever the customers pay for. Yesterday Tokuzo beat Ohiro brutally, and then he raped her. He'd found out she'd been seeing me." He paused to swallow again. "Ohiro and I, we've been saving for six months to buy out her contract, but we still don't have enough. I almost killed the swine last night. Please tell me what I should do." Against his will, tears rose to his eyes. He blinked them away. "Tora, Hanae, I love this girl. She's a good, gentle girl. I want her to be my wife. You two know how it is."

Clearly shocked, they looked at each other.

Hanae said, "Tokuzo? That's bad. I know of him."

"How much money do you need?" Tora asked. "We have some saved."

"Thanks, Brother. It's too much. Twenty pieces of gold."

Tora made a face. "We can scrape together ten. Maybe." He and Hanae looked at each other again.

"Tokuzo will raise the price," Hanae said.

Genba stared at her. "How can he do that? It's in the contract."

"He'll find ways to charge her for things she's used over the years. Maybe he'll fine her for not having collected from you."

"Amida!" Genba clenched his fists and hung his head. Then he looked up. "I'd go to the master, but you know how he is about women like Ohiro."

They nodded gravely.

"I don't know what to do. And even if I could buy her out, how can we be together?" Now the tears started again, and Genba choked up. "I'll have to leave here. Maybe Ohiro and I should just run away together and hide out some place."

"You can't do that," Tora said. "The master would be hurt. You'd better tell him about it."

Hanae put a hand on her husband's arm. "Wait. Tora, can't you do something first? Maybe you and Saburo and Genba could go and frighten the man into being cooperative?"

"Saburo?" Genba looked shocked.

"He's one of us." Tora smiled at his wife. "If I have your permission to go to the Willow Quarter, we'll do it."

"Anytime," she said with an airy wave and got up to remove the bowls. "Though maybe you'd better go in the daytime. Before he gets busy with his customers and the girls."

Tora nodded. "Good thinking. Come, brother, let's talk to Saburo."

Genba and Saburo shared quarters in a spacious room adjoining the stable. Saburo had been offered Seimei's room in the main house, but had humbly declined.

When they walked in, Saburo was getting ready for his duties in the main house. He had dressed as usual in a neat blue robe with a black sash. He had also taken pains with his hair, making sure the knot and loop were perfectly centered on top of his head and tied with the black silk ribbon. His disfigured face looked even more incongruous with his very neat and proper appearance.

Saburo heard Genba's story without much surprise, but he glanced at Genba as if reassessing his character in light of this new information. When Tora and Genba had finished, he was matter-of-fact. "You said you changed your mind about killing this man. Was that because you're opposed to killing on principle, or for some other reason?"

Genba frowned. "Does it matter?

Saburo made one of his unreadable grimaces. "I like to know how other people solve their problems. It's been useful in the past."

Genba thought about it. Saburo was an ex-spy and an ex-monk. That made him a far more unpredictable and mysterious person than Genba knew himself to be. On the other hand, his curiosity was probably part of his training. The spy wanted no surprises from allies or opponents, and the monk was opposed to killing. Suddenly curious himself, he asked. "Have you ever killed anyone, Saburo?"

Saburo scowled. "Don't ask me such things."

"Well, I have," Genba said heavily. "I swore to my-self that I would never do such a thing again. It's not because I'm very religious. It's because I felt sick and dirty and because it almost destroyed me. If the master hadn't taken us on, me and my best friend Hitomaro, I'd be dead today. We were both wanted for murder. But yesterday was different. Yesterday it was because someone hurt the woman I love. I felt like killing the man."

Tora said loyally, "I'd kill anyone who lays a hand on Hanae. I almost did once, but she got away from the bastard, and then an earthquake flattened him per-manently."

Genba said, "There was something odd, though. I bumped into a man outside Tokuzo's. I thought he was a footpad. We struggled and he dropped an object. Or I think he dropped it. It's a bit like some of those strange weapons you have, Saburo. Wait a moment." He went to his trunk and returned with the long metal pin or needle.

Saburo almost snatched it from his hand. "An as-sassin's needle! I haven't seen one in years. This is a fine one. Look at the workmanship." He held it up. It gleamed a dull charcoal gray from thickened shaft to long and narrow point. He touched the point. "It's as fine as a sewing needle. A master smith made this."

Tora peered at it. "Looks vicious. What do you mean 'an assassin's needle'?"

Saburo still handled the needle lovingly. "There are men—a very few—who can kill without leaving a trace.

They're expensive, but when they're good, they're worth their weight in gold. They're paid very well to remove certain people who are a trouble to others. When they use this, not even the best physician can prove it was murder."

Shuddering, Genba said, "You can keep that thing. I can't believe I had a run-in with an assassin." He brightened a little. "Maybe someone else dropped it."

Saburo looked at him. "Not likely. Whoever dropped it would have gone back for it."

Genba turned pale. "He could've killed me easily by shoving that in my eye or belly."

"No," said Saburo, inserting the needle carefully into the lining of his sleeve. "That way people would know you've been murdered. He would have inserted it into your ear when you're asleep. Or into your skull in the back of your head where your hair would hide the small puncture wound. Mind you, it takes skill. Maybe the assassin didn't get a chance to use it on you."

Genba thought back to the dark alley and shuddered again. He had caught the man's arm and then hugged him hard against himself with a wrestler's hold. He had heard the clinking sound then. "Amida, he had it in his hand!" He shook his head in horror. "And I thought he'd just been relieving himself."

Tora laughed. "Maybe he was. What did he look like?"

"I didn't get a good look at him."

"Probably wouldn't have helped. They look ordinary," said Saburo. "It's part of their disguise." He paused. "I've heard it said they don't kill unless the victim is guilty of some crime and can't be brought to justice. There's a code of honor about it. It makes them pretty decent in my estimation."

Tora looked at Saburo with a frown. "People who sneak up on others when they're asleep and shove needles in their ears are not decent men. Give me an honest thug and a knife-fight any day."

Genba, got impatient. "Stop arguing, you two. The assassin has nothing to do with my problem. He's gone, and Ohiro and I are still desperate. What am I going to do?"

"We'll all go have a talk with that bastard Tokuzo." Tora started for the door.

Saburo looked down at his neat blue robe with its black sash and then at Tora, who wore the same clothes. Their master insisted that they dress properly at all times because they might have to accompany him on ministry business. Genba, in charge of the stables, wore his work clothes of short pants, a tunic of brown hemp, and leather boots.

"Better change our clothes first, Tora," Saburo said. "I doubt the master wants us to represent him in the amusement quarter."

They set out a short while later in clean but ordinary outfits. Tora and Genba both wore their boots with long trousers tucked into them and loose jackets over their shirts. Saburo had on a dark brown robe, somewhat patched, and sandals on his feet. All three were armed but their weapons were concealed by their jackets or hidden in Saburo's full sleeves.

As Genba had completed his chores in the stables, they left word in the main house that they would be back in time for the midday rice. At the last moment, Cook pressed a basket on Genba, with instructions to purchase a bream, some cabbages, bean paste, and onions while he was in town. He tried to refuse, but she prevailed.

They attracted stares in the streets. Genba was huge and strode along with enormous strides, while Tora had the sort of looks young women got weak knees over. And Saburo? Well, when their eyes reached Saburo, they gasped and looked away quickly. Children stared at him wide-eyed and sometimes burst into tears. Unhappily, Saburo had a great fondness for children, but when he tried to smile at them, they tended to shriek and hide their faces in their mothers' skirts.

Genba shifted his basket uncomfortably. He was not at all certain the coming interview with the bastard Tokuzo would end happily.

Saburo looked at the basket. "Why do you always run that kitchen woman's errands for her, Genba? In most houses, such women do the shopping themselves."

Genba flushed. "Well, she's got a lot of work. I don't mind normally."

Tora shot him a pitying glance. "The dragon has her claws into poor Genba and enjoys giving him orders. He doesn't like to offend women. He thinks of them as weak creatures who must be cared for and protected."

Genba snapped, "They *are* weak, Tora. They do need our help and protection. What good is a man in this world if he doesn't look after women and children?"

"Some women don't deserve such devotion," Saburo said darkly. "The kitchen woman is such a one. She's ugly and ill-tempered and her voice grates on my ears."

The others refrained from pointing out that Saburo was not exactly easy on the eyes either. Tora said, "Exactly! The evil witch used to be after me until she got hold of Genba." He paused to chuckle. "What do you think will happen when Genba brings home his bride? Will our cook leave her comfortable home and seek a man elsewhere, or will she go after you, Saburo?"

Saburo cursed. "I've no time for women. Especially not that fat slug."

Genba raised his brows. Tora was not so delicate. "I meant to ask you about that, Saburo. Are boys more to your taste? They say that sort of thing is very common in monasteries."

Saburo gave him an ugly look. "You're a very stupid man," he snapped.

"No offense, Saburo. I have a blunt tongue, as you know."

"I know. And the answer is I don't like boys that way. But that doesn't mean I run after women."

"In some ways you're a lot like Seimei," Genba offered. "He was afraid of women. Cook made him shudder whenever she smiled at him." He laughed.

"Seimei's a hard man to live up to." Saburo sounded a little resentful. "The man must've been a saint."

"He was," Tora and Genba said together. Genba added, "The master thought of him as his father. You see, Seimei raised him, his own father being mostly too busy."

"Ah, yes. Still, I get depressed every time one of you cites Seimei to me."

They turned in at the gateway into the Willow Quarter. At this time of day, the place looked a little shabby, the lacquer and gilding on the gate was patched, and the people in the quarter were mostly menials like street sweepers and restaurant porters delivering hot food to overnight guests. The willows, however, showed the first pale green of spring. A few people in loose kimonos were on their way to the bathhouse, carrying their clean clothes rolled up under their arms.

They passed through several streets, Genba leading the way, and turned the final corner. The Sasaya wine house and brothel lay halfway down the street. A small crowd had gathered at its door. Notable among their drab attire were several red coats.

Police.

They halted. Genba, suddenly fearful for Ohiro, said, "Something's happened," and started forward.

Saburo snatched at his sleeve to pull him back, but Genba was already halfway to the Sasaya, calling out, "What's happened? Is someone hurt?"

Heads turned to stare.

Tokuzo's bully recognized him. He called out, "It's you again! You were here last night." He turned to a policeman. "He made threats against my master. He said he wanted to see him in hell."

The policeman approached. "You were making threats? What's your name?" He raised himself almost on tiptoe in an effort to look the huge Genba in the eye.

Genba glanced down at him. "What happened?"

The watchers now gathered around them. One said, "Tokuzo's been murdered. It's a blood bath in there."

"Murdered?" Genba's jaw sagged. He looked across at the gaudy flags and curtains decorated with bamboo and the name Sasaya. His first thought was one of gratitude to the killer. He had done to Tokuzo what should have been done long ago. Men who abused women and forced them to work for them like slaves did not deserve to live. He breathed, "May the Buddha be praised! So that bastard is finally dead."

"And you're pretty happy about that, are you?" demanded the policeman, his voice becoming shrill with excitement. He grabbed Genba's arm, then realized he was hardly the man to hold on to it and called to his colleagues, "Over here! I've got a suspect. Quick!"

They were quick, five of them. Two redcoats and three neighborhood constables. The bruiser volunteered his assistance, too. Genba was too surprised to make a move. He looked blankly at the men who had taken hold of him and then back at the Sasaya. "When did it happen?" he asked. His interest in the answer was not great, but it seemed the right thing to say. Part of his mind was busy working out who would now claim ownership of Ohiro's contract, and whether they might be inclined to take less gold for it.

Tora walked over. "You're making a mistake, fellows," he said, flashing his big smile. "Genba's my friend, and we just got here. I'm Tora, in case you've forgotten my handsome face and charming manners."

"I remember you." The policeman looked sour, perhaps having less than pleasant memories of his run-in with Tora. "Your friend's been recognized by a witness as having been here last night near the time of the murder. He was making threats against the victim. And just now he admitted it. He's under arrest."

Genba said, "But I didn't see Tokuzo last night. I was just passing. Besides, if you ask around, most people in the quarter hated that bastard. He was not a good man, officer. He beat and raped the women who worked for him."

"So?" The policeman looked unimpressed. "That's true of about half the brothel owners in the quarter, the male ones anyway. Though the aunties have been known to enjoy their girls also." He gave a hoot of laughter. "Who knows what goes on after the customers leave, eh? A girl has a contract, she works it out any way she can. And most of them cheat their aunties and uncles at a horrible rate. What would you do if you're a businessman and your employee sells your goods on the side and pockets the money?"

Genba opened his mouth to argue, but Tora put his hand on his arm. "Look," he said to the policeman, "we both belong to Lord Sugawara's household. You've heard about him, I'm sure. Let Genba go in

peace. He's got the marketing to do, and you can always find him when you want him. As he says, this
Tokuzo's got enemies and you may be missing the real
suspect if you don't keep looking."

There was a pause, during which the policeman
glanced at Genba's empty marketing basket and his
round, friendly face. Then he relented. "All right.
Since I know your names and where to find you, you
can go, but make sure he's available or you'll be sorry."

Tora and Genba departed speedily around the next
corner and stopped.

"Where's Saburo?" Tora asked, looking around.
"Let's wait to give him a chance to catch up."

Genba was lost in thought. What about Ohiro?
Would she be suspected? "What do you suppose happened to Tokuzo?" he asked. "The policeman said he
was killed last night when I was there."

"He was lying to scare you. Still, I wish we could
have hung about to find out a little more."

Saburo appeared so suddenly between them that
they jumped apart. Tora said irritably, "I wish you
wouldn't do that. It's spooky. If you have to walk silently, at least clear your throat."

"Sorry." Saburo took each of them by an elbow and
pulled them away. "No sense in staying here. That
policeman may regret letting you get away so easily. As
for finding out more, Tokuzo's had his throat slit. He'd
gone to bed, because they found him in it this morning.
The bedding was soaked in blood. No sign of the
knife, but it must've been a sharp one. The doctor they

called said it was a clean, deep cut. It isn't easy cutting a throat. You need a very sharp blade."

Genba shook his head in wonder. "Who could have done it? A woman, do you think?"

Saburo pursed his lips. "Not very likely. As I said, it isn't easy. Not when it's a deep cut. And he was lying down, remember? The killer must've been covered with blood."

"How do you know so much about cutting throats?" Tora asked suspiciously.

Saburo gave him another of his quelling looks. "Don't ask stupid questions, Tora."

"Amida!" breathed Tora. "You must've led quite a life. Does the master know? I'm not sure we're safe in our beds at night."

Saburo stopped, his face working. "Tora," he said, his voice cracking with emotion, "I've never killed an honest man or woman, and the master has a better opinion of me than you do. That's because he's a good man who still believes in the goodness of others. *You*, I don't know about."

Genba said quickly, "Tora didn't mean it. He jokes sometimes. You've been with us long enough to know that."

Saburo looked at Tora, clearly trying to decide if he should be offended. The struggle did not last.

Tora grinned. "You'll learn in time." He slapped the bony back of the ugly man. "Didn't mean to offend you, Saburo. It's just that your mysterious past makes me curious. You can understand that."

Saburo nodded. "Maybe I'll tell you things some day, but give me time. My memories are very bad, and I don't like being reminded."

Genba would have enjoyed his peace-making role—he was by nature a man who abhorred arguments and confrontations—but his mind was again on his own problem. "Do you think the police will tell the master about the murder?" he asked anxiously. "Do you think he'll tell me to leave this time?"

Tora snorted. "You know better than that. After all these years, he'd never show so little faith in you. Besides, you didn't kill the bastard. If things turn really bad, the master will step in and solve the crime. That's what he'll do."

Genba sighed. There was still Ohiro to be considered. He was impatient to see her and to warn her about talking to the police. She needed to stay home and keep away from prying eyes. "Well, there's no point in you tagging along with me. Why don't you go back home. I can go to the market by myself."

They nodded. There were chores waiting.

Genba walked on and quickly made his purchases at the market. Avoiding the lengthy contest with women bargaining shrilly for their purchases, he made no effort to find the freshest fish or the largest cabbages. He even ignored the mouth-watering smells of fried foods and the sounds of slurping and lip-smacking from the noodle soup vendor's customers. Cook would complain about his purchases and call him a big ox, but she did so anyway. From the market, he went on to Ohiro's tenement.

To his relief, she was still home and had heard the news.

"Oh, Genba," she cried, flinging her arms around him. "I've been so worried. Shokichi's been to the Sasaya. She said Tokuzo's been murdered and the police think you did it."

"They made a mistake, love. But it's best that you stay away as long as your face looks like that. If someone asks, say you're sick. And if someone sees you, tell them you fell in the dark."

She nodded. "Will you come every day so I know you're all right?"

He smiled at that. "I'll try, love. I'm glad that animal is dead, and you don't have to put up with him any longer. Maybe now we can wait until we've saved up the money." He was not happy about it, but as long as they had no other way of raising the money, he would have to let other men touch her and make love to her.

Her face fell. She turned away. "Yes, Genba," she said softly. "I'll wait."

His heart ached, but he did not know what to say. "I've got to go now. Cook's waiting for this food." He picked up the basket he had set down to embrace her. "I'll get back as soon as I can."

When she looked at him, her eyes were filled with tears. "Good bye, Genba. Thank you."

As he had expected, Cook was irate at his lateness and cursed him when she inspected his purchases. Tora was out, exercising one of the horses, and Saburo sat in the master's study, catching up on the family accounts.

"The master's out?" Genba asked unnecessarily. The room was empty of anyone but the ugly man, who had changed back into his blue robe.

Saburo raised his eyebrows. "He never comes home before sunset when the ministry does its monthly reports. You've talked to your girlfriend?"

Genba blushed. "How did you know I was going to see her?"

"You're not a stupid person, Genba. You may look slow and move like a turtle, but you've got a good head. Of course, you went to see her. That's why you wanted to get rid of us. What did she say?"

"She'd heard the news. I told her to stay home. Her face looks terrible."

Saburo nodded. "Did she have any idea who might have killed her master?"

"No. I wish I could find out. I know our master could do it, but I really don't want him to know about my troubles. Now that Tokuzo's dead, we have a bit more time to save the money we need."

"You told her that?" When Genba nodded, Saburo said dryly, "I bet that made her happy."

Genba recalled the tears in Ohiro's eyes and hung his head. "What else can I do?"

"Talk to the master. You can ask to borrow the money and let him take it out of your wages."

"Saburo, she's a prostitute. He won't want her in his household." Genba sat down abruptly and buried his face in his hands. "There's no hope for us," he mumbled indistinctly.

"Look at me!" snapped Saburo.

Genba did and saw the fierce look in Saburo's good eye. "What?"

"Look at my face, you dolt. If there was hope for someone like me, what reason do you have to sit there whining about your hardships? Even a starving warrior will hold his toothpick high."

Genba smiled at that. "Sorry, Saburo. You're a good man. I'll think about it."

"Tell the master what's happened. As for Tokuzo, I've got a good mind to do a little snooping there."

"Thank you." Genba hesitated, then said in a rush, "I'm glad you're one of us," and left quickly before he got maudlin.

6

Scattered Blossoms

Prince Atsuhira resided with his family in the Tsuchimikado Palace, the property having been given to him by his father, the ex-emperor when there was still a hope that he would become crown prince and succeed to the throne. But the late chancellor Michinaga and his sons had other plans and shifted the succession to one of Michinaga's grandsons instead.

Atsuhira had submitted with very good grace. To his credit, he only wished for a peaceful life and was not adept at court politics. Still, he had his supporters, men who liked him as a friend as well as men who hoped to advance themselves by throwing in their lot with him.

Of late, the prince had withdrawn from social life and even from appearances at court, much to the regret of many ladies. He had the sort of good looks and elegant manners that had caused them to call him "Shining Prince" after Genji, that famous romantic hero in Lady Murakami's book.

When Akitada was finally admitted to his presence, there was little left of the brilliant aura that once surrounded him.

Their meeting was possible only after some planning. Akitada had prepared for it by going back to the ministry where he dispatched one of the junior clerks to the archives for documents relating to the prince's property holdings. The young man dashed off eagerly and returned somewhat dusty, with a huge stack of bound maps and rolled scrolls.

Akitada selected a reasonable number of these and sent the rest back. The young man then accompanied Akitada, carrying the documents and a small writing box.

They arrived at the Tsuchimikado Palace with a proper air of importance and demanded to speak to the prince. A guard at the gate denied them access. The prince was apparently under house arrest.

"I'm here on official orders from the Ministry of Justice," snapped Akitada. "Send for your superior this instant."

After a short wait, a senior officer, wearing the uniform of the outer palace guard, appeared, a captain by his insignia, and a member of a family in power at court. He frowned and drawled, "What is all this? I have not been informed. You're Sugawara, are you? What business does the Ministry of Justice have with His Highness?"

Akitada made the man a slight bow—received with a mere nod—and said stiffly, "It has been thought proper at this time to confirm the extent of His Highness's holdings, since they are likely to play a part in the legal proceedings."

The captain's face cleared. In fact, he looked positively eager. "Ah! Is that the case? My apologies. They must be moving more quickly than we thought. Still, rules are rules. May I check the documents?"

Akitada waved the clerk forward, and the captain investigated each scroll and volume before nodding.

"Yes. Quite correct," he said cheerfully. "Well, I have no objection, of course, but I don't think he'll see you. He won't talk to anyone. A bit mad, if you ask me. There have been outbursts. Even his ladies are afraid to go near him."

"I see. Please tell him that I must see him urgently. Umm, perhaps you should say it is in his best interest."

The captain smirked at this and showed them to a very elegant reception room. Akitada paced nervously. Much depended on his seeing the prince, and seeing him alone. He became aware of soft sounds—silken rustlings and whispers. Behind the dais a series of screens with painted scenes of mountain landscapes hid an adjoining room. No doubt, eyes were glued to the narrow gaps between the panels. The prince's household was curious about his purpose here. He could not blame them. Their own lives and fates were tied to those of their husband and master.

To his relief, it was not the captain who returned, but an elderly man in a sober brown silk robe. He introduced himself as the prince's majordomo and led the way to an inner apartment past several courtyards where cherry trees bloomed. True to their poetic meaning of impermanence, they had scattered their petals like snow across the gravel.

Happiness had indeed been short-lived for Prince Atsuhira.

There were no guards at the door to the prince's room. This, too, made things easier. Apparently, the prince was allowed a certain amount of privacy out of respect for his person.

"Wait here," Akitada said to the young clerk, taking the documents but leaving the writing utensils with him. "I'll call when I need you."

The majordomo opened the door, announced, "Lord Sugawara," let Akitada walk in, and then closed the door behind him.

The room was dim. The green reed shades to the outside had been lowered, and the bright sunlight outside left only faint golden patterns on the polished wood floor. The prince sat hunched over a scattering of books and papers. Akitada was shocked to see how much he had changed from the cheerful young man he used to know. They were nearly the same age, but Atsuhira's sagging figure had nothing in common with the athletic young man who had liked riding, sports, and hunting in the mountains.

Atsuhira's face was pale and drawn. He raised listless eyes to Akitada.

"I remember you," he said in a flat voice. "You used to be at Kosehira's parties."

"Yes, Highness." Akitada looked around the room and back at the solid door. They seemed to be alone, and the apartment was self-contained, without those screens and temporary walls that could be erected in large spaces to divide them into many smaller rooms. Still, he lowered his voice when he said, "Kosehira has told me of your difficulties."

The prince frowned. He looked at the documents under Akitada's arm. "I'm confused. Are you here because Kosehira sent you, or because my enemies are already dividing up my lands?"

"The former." Akitada set the documents down and bowed. "I'd like to be of service if you will allow me." Seeing the prince hesitate, he added, "You may recall that I was once able to intercede in the matter of a stolen letter."

The prince flushed, then gestured to a cushion, and Akitada sat.

"Very good of you to come," the prince said, sounding listless again, "but I need no help this time."

"Surely, Highness, you must defend yourself against the false charges of insurrection and treason."

"My enemies are posturing. They have no case. They want to frighten me into flight. As it is, they have nothing to fear from me. I shall take the tonsure soon, and if they try to prevent me, I shall make an end of my miserable life. You may tell Kosehira of my decision." He took up one of his scrolls and began to read, a signal that he considered the conversation over.

Akitada sought for words to reach the prince, who now seemed to be reciting a sutra. Finally, he said the only thing that came to his mind.

"Your Highness, the Lady Masako may have been murdered."

He regretted his words instantly, because he had no proof. In truth, all he really had was a vague suspicion—and a fervent wish that the young woman had not stepped off the cliff that snowy night four months ago.

The prince dropped the sutra scroll. "What? Are you serious?"

"Yes, there are aspects to the case that look suspicious. I came to ask you about them."

The prince's brows contracted. "Kosehira had no right." He looked angry.

"Kosehira is your friend, as he is mine."

"Do you have anything to support your extraordinary charge?"

Atsuhira was nothing if not intelligent. That distinguished him from most of the imperial offspring and perhaps accounted for the fact that his enemies had started their ugly campaign against him again. They preferred sovereigns who were easily led and took no interest in government. The current emperor, the prince's first cousin, was still very young and, from all accounts, totally engrossed in his women and games. It was Atsuhira's bad luck that he was much admired by the people who wanted him to be reinstated as crown prince.

Akitada said cautiously, "I have spoken with Superintendent Kobe. He described the injuries on the body.
They have raised some questions."

The prince buried his face in his hands. "I found
her," he said hoarsely. "She lay at the bottom of the
cliff, covered with snow. There was blood in the snow.
Kobe said it proved she was alive and died from the
fall." He raised his head to look at Akitada with bleak
eyes. "Is that what you came to hear?"

"No. I knew it already." Akitada hesitated, seeing
the pain-racked face of the prince. "You see, her skull
was badly damaged," he ventured as gently as he could,
"but there was little damage to her legs. I would have
expected the opposite if she had stepped off the cliff."

The prince slowly shook his head from side to side.
"What does it matter? She's dead."

"Someone may have pushed her and caused her to
fall head first. If Lady Masako was murdered, don't
you want the guilty person punished?"

"No!" The word was an agonized shout. The
prince was very upset. His eyes flashed. "Why do you
force your way into my solitude to talk to me of things
that churn up my insides and bring back the nightmares
that are with me day and night? Are you so unfeeling
and lacking in understanding that you cannot see that
nothing matters now? *She is gone!* Nothing will bring
her back. How much better to accept that she took the
fatal step because she wanted to than to imagine her in
the hands of a brutal killer, unable to save herself?" He
gave a small sob and clenched his hands. "She was
alone! Alone because I was not there to protect her.

How do you think that makes me feel? I was passing the time in idle chatter with your friend Kosehira instead. If you came here to help me, I don't want your help. And if you're here to help your friend, you've come to the wrong man. I have cursed Kosehira for delaying me that night. I don't care what happens to him . . . or me . . . or you. *Go!*"

With that final shout, the prince turned his back on Akitada.

Akitada sat frozen. How could he have been so stupid? He should have considered the prince's feelings. He had wasted his time and made things worse. The anger at Kosehira for delaying the prince on that fateful night had probably lain dormant until this moment.

After a long time, he said humbly, "Forgive me, your Highness. I was truly insensitive and should have spared you this. I hope you will believe that my first thoughts were for Lady Masako. I have seen many crimes in my life, and always my thoughts have been for the victims. But I also think about preventing more grief and death among the living by apprehending the murderer."

He got to his feet. The prince did not turn or give any indication he had heard. Akitada made his deep bow anyway and, picking up the documents, left quietly.

Outside the door waited his clerk. Akitada passed the stack of papers back to him. Had the boy been listening? The doors of the palace were solid enough, but Akitada could not be sure they blocked all sound, and the prince had shouted in his anger. The young face was expressionless, and Akitada turned to go.

In the courtyard, the captain met him. "Ah, back already?" he asked, his eyes bright with curiosity. "I hope you got what you needed."

"No, I'm afraid not." Akitada did not have to pretend disappointment. "His Highness refused to discuss the matter."

The captain scowled. "I thought so. It's time he learned that he's no better than the rest of us and has no special rights. Never mind. It won't be long and he'll be very glad to cooperate."

And that perhaps was another thing Akitada would regret. The last thing he wished on that broken man was for his life to be made even more unbearable than it was already.

7

Tokuzo's Brothel

During the night following their visit to the Sasaya, Saburo got up very quietly and left the room he shared with Genba.

It was not the first time he had done so. Since he had entered Lord Sugawara's service, he had sacrificed a few hours' sleep every night in order to explore the capital and hone his old skills. His duties were not particularly onerous, and he needed little sleep. But he was uncomfortably aware that he lacked Seimei's gift of making himself indispensable to the family in areas other than bookkeeping and letter writing. His knowledge of medicine, for example, had been sadly neglected at the monastery in favor of spying skills. He was quite fond of children, but since his disfigurement frightened most of them

, he had kept his distance. His master's children were used to him by now, but he had long since become awkward at talking to the young.

He also stayed away from the women in the household, but for different reasons. He distrusted women, even hated them at times. His Buddhist teachings had painted women as mindless, soulless, corrupt, and corrupting. His rare encounters had proved they were also cruel and greedy.

He had laid ready his black shirt and long black pants. These two items had cleverly sewn seams that held small useful implements of metal and bamboo. As soon as Genba's snoring assured him he was soundly asleep, Saburo seized the bundle of clothes and his old brown jacket, and left the stable.

He changed outside, under the eaves, tucking his regular clothes behind a barrel. Then he left the compound by climbing over the back wall. The dog Trouble raised his head briefly, gave a few muffled slaps with his tail, and went back to sleep.

As Saburo walked the dark streets, he looked no different from most of the poor who were out after a late night at a wine shop or brothel. He kept his face tucked into the collar of his brown jacket and moved along purposefully on the soft grass soles of his sandals.

Tonight he was going to try to help Genba. He liked the big man; you could not help liking him. But Saburo was also jealous of his placid good nature that made people like him; there were even times when he almost disliked him. This always made him feel guilty, because Genba in his cheerful innocence went out of his way to be a friend to the friendless Saburo.

Genba's success in having found love surprised and dismayed him. The big man with his paunch, his round, plain face, and his awkward rolling gait was hardly the type to be attractive to women. In fact, Genba should have experienced female cruelty much like Saburo had, yet the man was still capable of falling madly in love with one of the creatures. Only Cook, both ugly and fat, had ever shown any interest in Genba.

Of course, Genba's woman was a harlot. In Saburo's experience, harlots were rapacious and hid their cruelty only when they planned to fleece the customer. He had learned that bitter lesson after his disfigurement, and had it confirmed on the rare occasions when he tried to buy sexual services.

So he had laughed at Genba, along with Tora.

And felt guilty again.

The night was dark and sweet-scented. Clouds had moved in and covered the sky with black silk. Saburo loved the dark. In the dark, people could not see his face. In the dark, it was even possible to lie with a woman and pretend he was normal.

For a little while.

Yes, he was jealous of Genba's happiness. And because he was ashamed, he hoped to discover Tokuzo's killer and clear Genba. Perhaps he could also help the romance along a little.

The hour was late, but in the pleasure quarter, a few women still walked the street or peered from the small windows of their brothels. They called out invitations to Saburo or tried to pull him inside by his sleeve until he raised his face out of the collar of his jacket and scowled at them, baring his teeth and rolling his eyes, taking small satisfaction from their gasps.

The Sasaya was closed and appeared to be dark—whether from respect for the death of its owner or because Tokuzo's harlots were out celebrating their temporary freedom was not clear.

Saburo passed the brothel slowly a few times, then slipped along its side wall to the back. Like many businesses in the quarter, it had a walled yard formed partially by a kitchen building on one side and a storage shed on the other. Here, too, all was dark and still. Luckily there were no dogs about, for the animals would have detected him by now. He took off his brown jacket and laid it on the ground. Now dressed from head to foot in black, he melted into the darkness.

From the narrow footpath that ran behind the block of businesses, Saburo swung himself up onto the rear wall and, after a quick look around, dropped down silently on the other side. He verified that kitchen and shed were deserted, then studied the two-storied main house. Rickety stairs led up to a balcony that ran along the entire back of the building. Apparently it formed the access to rooms above where the harlots could take their customers.

Tonight, those rooms were unlikely to be occupied, but he drew in his breath when he detected a very faint chink of light behind one of the closed shutters below. Someone was here. Given the owner's recent murder, this was interesting.

Saburo considered the problem. Two-story houses without exposed ceiling beams were difficult to enter when occupied. He could not get in through the roof to cross the building on the beams. Still, perhaps all was not lost. He eyed the stairs and balcony and decided both were so poorly built that they would give away his presence by creaking.

In the end, he climbed on the low roof of the kitchen building, and from there he leaped to the corner post of the balcony. He almost did not make it and cursed himself for having become so clumsy. His grip had been somewhat desperate, and he had slid a foot or so before wrapping his legs and arms around the post and shimmying back up. For a moment, he listened. When all remained peaceful, he lifted a leg over the railing and stepped cautiously on the boards near the wall. They were solid and silent. Then he slowly slid open the nearest door and slipped inside.

Intense darkness and stench. The smell of the room disgusted him. Dirt, sweat, spilled wine, and sex. Motionless, he listened. Nothing. The faint light from the half-opened door showed sparse furnishings: a smallish grass mat and a bundle of bedding. He grimaced. Little enough was needed to bring a half-drunk man up here, take his money, and lie with him for some brief groping and sex.

There was a faint sound, and he listened. He thought he could hear voices from below. Slipping back out on the balcony, he walked along the wall until he reached the room next to the last. Here the voices were clearest.

A man and a woman.

He entered this room on his hands and knees, exploring the boards with his fingertips before putting his weight on them. The planking was cheaply made. In one corner, it had not been nailed down properly. Very slowly and silently, he raised the loose board and propped one of his sandals under it. Lying down next to the narrow opening, he could not only hear what the two below were saying, but he also saw a part of the room they sat in.

A lantern lit the scene inadequately. The two people sat near an open money chest. Saburo saw the top of the man's head, his shoulders, and his hands as he took coins and bars from the chest. The man counted softly as he put the money into a bag. Saburo was amazed at the sums. For a brothel keeper, Tokuzo had been very successful. The man who handled Tokuzo's wealth so efficiently wore the clothes of a low-ranking official. He was hatless, and his balding scalp and thick neck proved he was middle-aged and fat.

The woman, whom Saburo could not see at all, spoke with the cracked voice of the elderly and in a tone that suggested they were related. She was apparently watching the man. From their comments, Saburo decided these two were Tokuzo's mother and brother.

"Hurry up," the old one said in a querulous tone. "This could've waited till morning."

"I'm not leaving my brother's wealth unguarded in this house," he said. "You forget the people he associated with. Besides, you could've stayed home."

"I want to know how much you're taking. There's your sister's future to be considered."

He snorted. "Don't be ridiculous. She's almost as old as I am. Who'll marry someone like her?" He tied the heavy bag and stuffed it inside his robe. The chest he simply slammed shut. Then he got to his feet, a little awkwardly with the heavy bulge under his clothes. "Looks like I'll have to take care of both of you for the rest of your lives," he said. "Come on, Mother. It's getting late."

The mother grumbled a little, and the son bent forward and pulled her to her feet. Saburo caught a glimpse of a gray robe and a twist of white hair on a small and thin woman. Then they disappeared from view, though he could still hear them arguing.

"What about the contracts?" the old woman protested.

"They're safe enough until tomorrow. Let's go."

The light receded, steps moved away, arguments faded, a door closed, and it got quiet.

Tokuzo's brother had sounded unpleasant. Saburo scowled to himself. The whole family apparently lacked common decency. The brother had come for the gold Tokuzo had made as a brothel keeper. It was money earned by the women he had treated worse than animals. But his brother considered himself too good to become identified with the brothel business.

Saburo thought about the money chest, emptied of its treasures and left unlocked. It still held the contracts, probably worth a good deal if sold to other brothel owners. Worth a great deal more to the women who were forced to sell their bodies every night.

His experiences with harlots had been painful. Most had refused him; the rest had collected the fee, submitted with a shudder, and run from the room.

But there was Genba.

He had no way of getting into the lower part of the building. No doubt, the greedy pair who had just left had made sure all the doors were secured.

But on second thought, it was worth checking. He went downstairs, taking fewer precautions than before, but moving with his customary stealth.

He made a circuit of all the doors and found them all securely locked. Only the side door closest to the kitchen had a loose hinge that might be loosened further. He considered, then set to work. His other errand could wait.

With the help of one of his clever tools, he managed to loosen the hinge until he could lift the door up and prop it open. No one was likely to pass through the courtyard at this hour and notice the farthest door standing slightly ajar, and he would be quick, get back out, and reattach the panel.

It was pitch dark inside, but Saburo moved by instinct and touch in the direction of the room where he had watched Tokuzo's mother and brother. The smells in this part of the house were of *sake*. Here the guests were rendered drunk enough that the whores could march them upstairs. His nose eventually identified the smell of fresh candle wax and led him to the right room. Feeling for the sliding door, he found it and pushed it open. Yes, this must be it. He might have risked looking for a lamp and lighting it, but memory took him to the money chest, and touch found the papers in its bottom. He scooped them out and shoved them inside his shirt, then made his way back to the door he had left open.

But something had changed. There was a smell he had not noticed before. He paused and sniffed. Sweat and scented oil, he decided. Odd!

He could make out the narrow rectangle of the door. In spite of the clouded sky, the outside was lighter than the thick blackness of this hallway. It struck him that he had left it nearly closed.

Listening, he took a cautious step forward and brushed up against fabric. When he reached out a hand to feel what it was, he touched a face.

The next moment, the paler rectangle of the world outside disappeared, and pain exploded in his head.

8

The Trouble with Women

In the morning Akitada found Genba waiting outside his study. He was in a cheerful mood because
he had just left Tamako's rooms, where he had
played with the children again. Genba's face promised
that would not last.

"Come in, Genba," he said, opening the door. "Is
something wrong?"

"Yes, sir." Genba stopped in the middle of
Akitada's study, clenching and unclenching his huge
hands and looking about helplessly.

"Well, sit down." Akitada missed his customary
morning tea and the bowl of gruel. Apparently, Saburo
was late. He seated himself and watched as Genba lowered his heavy frame to sit, then rearranged his body to
kneel instead and touch his forehead to the floor.

"Don't do that," Akitada said. "We've never been formal with each other."

Genba nodded and looked at his master. To Akitada's surprise, tears, the big man's eyes were moist. Becoming seriously concerned, Akitada pressed him now. "Come on, speak up, man! You're beginning to worry me."

Genba gulped. "Sorry, sir. Saburo's gone!"

Akitada raised his brows. "Saburo? What do you mean?"

"He wasn't there when I woke this morning. He's gone. I looked everywhere. It's all my fault."

"How so?"

"A man called Tokuzo was murdered yesterday, and the police tried to arrest me. Tora talked them out of it. I think Saburo must've gone there last night. And he hasn't come home. I think something bad happened to him."

Akitada's jaw sagged. "What?" He took a breath. "Who is Tokuzo?"

"He runs a brothel in the quarter, sir. He's an evil man. Even Hanae says so."

"Hanae's also involved, eh? What about Cook and my wife's maid? Does my entire household carry on a secret life outside my home?"

Genba flushed and bowed his head. "No, sir. Just me," he mumbled.

Akitada stared at him. "What do you mean?" He was astonished by the notion that placid, ordinary Genba had been leading a secret life. Only the big man's obvious misery stopped him from smiling at the thought.

"There is . . . someone, sir." Genba' big fists were kneading his huge knees. "A woman, I mean. I . . . her name's Ohiro. And . . . and . . . ."

A woman! Genba, in his comfortable middle years— he was in his mid-forties—, had fallen in love. He seemed ashamed to talk about it, though. Akitada cut the stammering short, and said in a hearty tone, "But this is excellent news, Genba. I'm very happy for you. Will you bring your bride here? We'll have to find you better quarters."

Genba's eyes filled with tears. "Sir, she works in the Willow Quarter." He looked down.

"Oh."

A painful silence fell in which the big Genba seemed to shrink into himself.

When they spoke again, it was at the same time, and both stopped again. Genba gave Akitada a look like a beaten dog. Akitada bit his lip. He owed Genba a great deal. Genba had been loyal and would have died for his master many times over.

"Well," he said, "we cannot always make our hearts obey our heads. I assume she will give up her profession?"

"Oh, yes." Genba's fists started their kneading again. "We've been saving, both of us, to buy her out, but we didn't have enough and now her owner has been murdered." He paused. "That's really how the trouble started, sir. Tora, Saburo, and I went to talk to Tokuzo, but the police were there already, and they wanted to arrest me because one of Tokuzo's bullies told them I threatened Tokuzo the night before. Tora talked them out of it."

Akitada's brows knitted during this tale. His first reaction was irritation that his retainers seemed to have the extremely bad taste of seeking out disreputable females and hanging about in brothels. And now Saburo seemed to have fallen into the same habit. But he suppressed his anger. Perhaps he would not have done so with Tora (in fact, he had been very blunt when Tora had married Hanae), but Tora was better able to take a tongue lashing. Genba suffered from the conviction that Akitada considered him a big useless, greedy lout and merely tolerated his presence in the household.

"Tell me about Ohiro," Akitada suggested. "If she has captured your devotion, she must be remarkable."

Genba was so astonished he gaped at his master for a moment. Then his face lit up, and he said fervently, "She's not like anyone I've ever known, sir. She's sweet and loving and very, very brave. You'd have to be brave to live through the hell that happened to her." Leaning forward a little, he looked at Akitada earnestly. "Sir, she lost her parents when she was young. Her uncle and his wife took her in. But her uncle started raping her when she was ten, and when his wife found out, she sold Ohiro to Tokuzo. Tokuzo's raped her regularly and he beats her, but she never complains. And sir, she's very pretty and could have any man, but she loves *me*." This brought the tears to his eyes again. He sniffed. "I love her. I've promised to take care of her forever."

Akitada gave an inward shudder at the tale. He wanted to point out that nothing is forever, and that such women would say anything to get a man to buy out their contract, and if this Ohiro was really so very pretty, she would leave Genba the moment she had her freedom. He said none of those things, however. He asked, "How much money do you need?"

Genba told him. "I know it's too much. We thought we'd wait and save some more, but now that Tokuzo's dead, she'll be sold again."

Akitada looked outside at his garden, saw that the sun was already high, and got up. "Find out who the heir is. Then arrange to buy her out. I'll give you the money. As for Saburo, I'm sure he'll show up. He knows how to handle himself. Now I must go to work."

Genba was on his knees again, knocking his head against the floor. "Thank you, sir. I'll pay the money back, I promise. If you have extra work, I'll do it gladly. Or, if you permit it, I could find some work outside after I have done the chores here. And Ohiro is a hard worker, too."

Akitada headed out the door. "Nonsense, Genba. You're family."

After taking care of some urgent ministry paperwork, Akitada went in search of the minister.

Fujiwara Kaneie had just arrived and stood at the open door overlooking his private courtyard, hands clasped behind his back. He was watching a pair of swallows building a nest under the eaves.

When he heard Akitada, he turned. "Oh, there you are. How are things going for your friend Kosehira?"

"Very kind of you to ask, sir." Akitada hesitated a moment, then said, "I'm in a quandary. In this situation, taking sides will surely affect a person's career. I'm not concerned on my own behalf but on yours, sir. Had you not better remain in ignorance of the matter?"

The minister chuckled. "I'm quite safe, but it's nice of you to be concerned. No, speak freely . . . unless you're afraid I'll carry tales."

There was always that danger, even though Kaneie was not particularly close to the regent and his brothers and was, in any case, an honorable man. "It's not that, sir, though there are some confidences I cannot divulge. Very well, then. The prince is under house arrest. He will not make any effort to defend himself. He says he doesn't care and will take the tonsure soon. Surely those words should satisfy his enemies?"

The minister pursed his lips. "He still has his supporters, and many a retired emperor has ruled from his monastery. No, in Atsuhira's case I don't think they'd be satisfied."

"Ah. That is difficult indeed."

"But you're only concerned about your friend Kosehira. Can't you clear him and leave Atsuhira alone?"

"No, sir. There were letters. They had no relation to the plot, but Kosehira has destroyed them. Since it was known they had corresponded recently and he would not produce them, it looks very suspicious."

"But why did he destroy them if they were harmless?"

Good question. Akitada could not reveal the affair with Lady Masako to Kaneie. He said, "Why keep them? Surely you and I live with too much paperwork all day long to keep our private correspondence also."

Kaneie nodded. "Yes, I see. Awkward. What are your plans?"

"I want to speak to people who can clear either Kosehira or the prince. A large task, but perhaps I'll find the right person quickly."

"If you don't stay away too long, I can spare you. A few days won't matter. And, Akitada, keep me informed."

"Of course, sir. Thank you."

Akitada returned to his office where he took some time to clear pending matters and write out precise instructions for his clerk and those who were working on current cases. Then he left the ministry.

His next stop was to look in on a friend. Nakatoshi worked in the Ministry of Ceremonial. He had once been Akitada's clerk and was a most able and loyal young man, who had deservedly risen in the government and now occupied the same position in the Ministry of Ceremonial as the one Akitada held in the Ministry of Justice. They had become friends over the years, and occasionally visited each other.

Nakatoshi greeted him with a cheerful, "Working on something new?"

Akitada sat down and accepted a cup of wine. "I suppose I've troubled you so often in the past that you no longer expect just a friendly visit. You're quite right, as it happens. The problem concerns my friend Kosehira. You've met, I think?"

Nakatoshi's smile faded. "Yes. Don't tell me you're meddling in the affairs of Prince Atsuhira again?"

The word "affair" could denote all sorts of complications in a man's life. Akitada said, "In a manner of speaking. This is in confidence, Nakatoshi. It concerns a young woman the prince had been meeting secretly."

"Ah. That's better." Nakatoshi grinned. "I prefer romance to politics. Much safer."

"I don't know about that. She was the Lady Masako."

His friend gaped at that. "Atsuhira's been carrying on an affair with one of His Majesty's women?"

"Yes, but His Majesty had shown no interest in her."

"It makes no difference." Nakatoshi frowned. "Didn't she die a few months back?"

"Yes. It happened near the prince's summer villa, though that story was covered up."

"Naturally. What a fascinating scandal! But what's your part in this? Or Kosehira's?"

Akitada explained, and Nakatoshi was appalled. Being bright, he immediately said, "So this death and the plot about the succession are tied together after all?"

"They shouldn't be, but I'm afraid they are."

"You cannot touch it, Akitada. I know you're Kosehira's friend, but this is too dangerous for you and your family."

"Well, it's not the first time. I've had to decide a long time ago whether to look out for myself and my family or hold on to my convictions. My name and the fact I've made enemies will always put me at risk. Since it can't be helped, it must be managed somehow. But I came, as usual, to get some information. I'd like to know more about Lady Masako's family."

"Ah, yes. Minamoto Masaie. I take it he's under suspicion also?"

"I don't know."

"Masako is his oldest daughter. Masaie is lord of Sagami, a very powerful provincial overlord. They say he used his influence to have Masako enter the royal apartments, no doubt in hopes of becoming grandfather to an emperor." Nakatoshi paused. "Yes, it all hangs together. Now that you mention it, I do have some news you may not be aware of. Maseie has been called to court. In view of what you say about Lady Masako and the prince, it may mean that he's connected with the alleged plot."

Akitada said, "I doubt it, but that doesn't mean much to those who wish to rid themselves of perceived threats."

"Well, it would make sense. Perhaps Masaie found that His Majesty wasn't interested in his daughter and decided to back Atsuhira for crown prince."

It opened up new possibilities and confused the issue of Lady Masako's death. Akitada chewed his lower lip. "It could be revenge, of course."

Nakatoshi looked blank. "You mean the court blames Minamoto Masaie for his daughter's affair?"

"Not the court. I was thinking of the Lady Kishi."

"Kishi? Oh, Prince Atsuhira's wife. And you think her brothers agreed to ruin the prince and anyone connected with him or Lady Masako? Well, that would be shocking."

"From what I hear, Kishi's perfectly capable of acting on her own. And she's likely to have taken serious offense."

"Ah. Women." Nakatoshi shook his head. "What a muddle!"

They both sighed, then chuckled. Thanking his friend, Akitada took his leave.

9

The Beggars

Saburo woke in a ruin, looking up through the broken roof high above him. Blue sky and golden clouds shimmered beyond the age-darkened beams and broken spars. He watched the clouds passing across the blue, and wondered if he was glimpsing a distant paradise.

Gradually, he became aware of his other senses. Unpleasant odors assailed his nose. He tried to analyze them while watching the pretty clouds. Dirt, he thought. I'm smelling dirt and rotten things. Nothing in particular stands out.

His arms were laid across his chest. He was quite comfortable except for an ache in the back of his head. He moved and hissed at the acute stab of pain that brought tears to his eyes.

Somewhere close by, someone cleared his throat of phlegm and spat. Saburo swiveled his good eye as far as he could without moving his head. No good. He saw a dark, stained wall with a doorway into deeper darkness. Nothing else.

The contrast between the golden clouds and this rotten, stinking place where he found himself struck him as ominous. Had he died? And was this his own hell, deserved for a multitude of sins?

A rattling cough and more sounds of spitting.

"Who's there?" he croaked.

"Me."

An old man's voice.

"Where am I?"

A rasping laugh. "Honkoku-ji."

Not hell, then. And not death.

Honkoku-ji was the ruin of an old temple compound. Saburo carefully lifted his head to turn it. This also hurt, but not as much. A strange figure sat near him in a Buddha pose. White-haired and white-bearded, the old man wore a red silk gown, a woman's gown, with a priest's stole over it. Many strands of prayer beads hung about his neck. He looked quite feeble. His eyes were dim with age and his hands resembled the claws of a chicken with their long yellow nails.

Saburo asked, "Who are you?"

"You can call me Kenko, Saburo."

"You know me?"

"Maybe. Maybe not. What's to know?"

Did this mad old man expect an answer? "My head hurts," Saburo said.

"Put it from your mind."

"How did I get here?"

"Too many questions." With the help of a staff lying beside him, the old man got up with much groaning and coughing. He spat again, then, leaning on his staff, he limped away.

Saburo sat up and cautiously felt the back of his head. He encountered a good deal of half-dried blood and a very tender lump. Checking the rest of his body was more reassuring. Memory returned. Some bastard had attacked him inside the brothel.

Who? Tokuzo's mother and brother could not have returned. He would have heard them. No, the attacker in the dark hallway had been someone silent and furtive. A thief.

Or rather, someone like himself, for most thieves would have given themselves away sooner.

But that made no sense whatsoever.

Saburo tested his limbs and turned his mind to another puzzle. He was certain his attacker had not been there earlier. Unless it was an accidental encounter, he must have followed him into Tokuzo's place and waited for him in the hallway. Saburo doubted that their visits had coincided by chance.

Then why had the other man been there? The obvious answer was the gold that Tokuzo's brother and mother had carried away earlier. But a good thief, and this man was very good, would have watched the house and known he was too late for the money.

Perhaps he had wanted something else.

Or someone else. If the stranger had watched carefully, he would have known Saburo had entered the brothel. But what had he wanted?

Frustrated, Saburo dropped the matter and wondered instead how he had got to this place. Had his attacker brought him here? Surely not. It didn't make any sense to knock someone out and then carry him all that far. The distance from the Willow Quarter to the temple was too great.

Saburo was brushing the dust off his clothes when he realized he was missing something. The thick sheaf of papers, the brothel's contracts he had tucked inside his shirt, was gone. And that caused him to check his sleeves.

His tools and the assassin's needle were also gone!

So that had been what the stranger wanted.

The contracts could perhaps be explained. They were valuable. But why take the tools and the needle? And how had the unknown man known where to look for them? They had been inserted into the seams of his shirt. Now those seams were undone and threads hung loose. Unless his attacker had felt them by accident, he must have known where to search.

It began to look more and more as though he had encountered a colleague. Most likely the professional assassin Genba had tangled with the night before. The assassin had a personal interest in the Sasaya.

Saburo got to his feet, fought a bout of dizziness, and looked around him.

In spite of the huge hole in the roof, the floor of the abandoned temple was in partial darkness. It seemed to be strewn with debris and garbage. Fallen columns, leaning walls, piles of broken roof tiles were every- where. So were broken dishes, rags, and rotting food remnants. He was in a section that still had a partial roof over it and walls on three sides. But here, too, a lot of rubble and garbage had collected. Bundles of rags were piled in corners here and there. A charred section showed someone had made a fire on the wooden floor, perhaps to cook, for an iron pot and some other uten- sils stood nearby.

Then Saburo remembered that Honkokuji was the beggars' den.

A bout of dizziness seized him, and a sudden retch- ing took him forward to a corner to vomit.

"Hey!"

The filthy pile of rags disintegrated into two separate segments that flew to either side. The shock stopped his nausea. He swallowed and stared.

Curses assaulted his ears from both sides. Other voices sounded from a distance, and here and there piles of garbage took on substance and life as if they had been magically transformed into creatures.

Saburo apologized to the two old men he had dis- turbed. They grumbled and sat down again. One of them had lost an arm.

"How did I get here?" Saburo asked them. "Did you see who brought me?"

The cripple jerked his head toward the left. There sat a giant of a man with bushy black hair and beard. He was watching Saburo with a wide grin.

Saburo, his head hurting as if it meant to split open, walked over. "Hello," he said, nodding his head in greeting and flinching at the pain. "I'm Saburo. I hear you brought me here last night. Is that right?"

The giant mouthed something incomprehensible. Saburo squatted down before him. "I'm sorry, I didn't hear you. I'm very grateful, though. I wondered where you found me."

One of the old men joined them. "He can't talk. They cut out his tongue. Most people don't know what he's saying."

The giant nodded. His eyes went from Saburo to the old man. He mumbled. Spittle dripped from the corners of his mouth into his beard as he struggled with the words.

The old man translated, "He says you looked like one of us, so he picked you up and brought you here. He says you were in an alley in the Willow Quarter. He works there."

"He works? You mean he isn't a beggar?" Saburo was still trying to understand why this man had carried him all the way across the city.

The old man frowned at him. "We all work," he pointed out. "We got our places, and there we sit or stand every day to pick up a few coppers. Jinsai keeps late hours because the Willow Quarter stays busy till dawn, but he makes good money there. He does odd jobs sometimes."

The giant nodded and grinned.

The old man scowled back. "He needs to," he said snidely. "Look at the size of the beast. He eats his weight in food every day."

The giant smiled more broadly.

"Would you ask him if he saw anyone near me?"

"He can hear you well enough," snapped the old man.

Saburo made the giant an apologetic bow, groaned, and reached for his head.

The big man mouthed something and gestured.

The old-timer nodded. "Nobody near you, but a man was walking away at the end of the alley."

"Did you see what he looked like?"

The giant scratched his head, pointed at Saburo and muttered.

"He looked like you," the old man translated with a grin.

"He looked like me?" Saburo stared at him.

The giant chuckled, gestured some more, and pointed at Saburo's clothes. The old man explained, "He was your size and dressed in black from head to toe. What happened to your face?"

Saburo had to answer this question all the time. He minded, just as he minded the stares, the averted eyes, the expressions of horror and disgust. At least neither the giant nor the old beggar seemed at all bothered by his horrible disfigurement. No doubt they were used to all sorts of horrors. He said, "Some men wanted to know what I couldn't tell them."

"Oh," said the old man and fell silent. The giant leaned across and patted Saburo's shoulder with his huge paw, causing him to tumble sideways and cry out at the sudden pain in his head.

The giant muttered. The old man said, "Jinsai says to let Bashan look at your head. Come, I'll take you."

Saburo protested, but the old man was already limping away. This time, Saburo just waved a hand toward the giant, then followed the old beggar.

The temple had once been very large, and while it offered only partial shelter against the rain, its inhabitants had found their own means of improving it. Here and there, fallen debris and sections of wood flooring or of interior walls had been salvaged and cobbled together to make small huts and lean-tos. There they lived, singly or as small families. The whole formed a village of sorts. He was in the beggars' headquarters. This ruined temple was the location of their *kakibe*, their guild, for they were organized like any other business in the city. And they were untouchable, and therefore outside the jurisdiction of the city. They had their own laws and rules.

The old man headed for the open courtyard. It was still surrounded by partial walls and the remnants of outbuildings. Even parts of the pagoda remained. Near the well of what must have been the kitchen area when monks still lived there, a small group of people had gathered to watch a bald man at his work.

Bashan.

Saburo saw that Bashan was one of the blind masseurs. His head was shaven and he knelt in front of a seated man, probing inside his mouth. Beside him rested an open wooden satchel. Many masseurs were blind men and performed their services by touch only. Some even practiced acupuncture and moxibustion, carrying their tools in a box that could be slung across their shoulder and chest. Such work was possible for the blind, and some became very good at it.

But Saburo did not trust a blind man to touch his head and stopped. "No, wait. I don't need any help. I feel fine."

The old man ignored him and shouted, "Hey, there, Bashan. Got a patient for you. He's had a bad knock on his head. Get your fingers out of Goto's mouth and take a look at him." He chortled at the expression. Seeing Saburo's reaction, he added, "Got magic in those fingers. Don't you worry."

The masseur had turned his face in their direction. His eyes were half closed, and he leaned his head sideways as if to hear better. He called out, "Is that you, Eino? I'm done." He held up a bloody tooth and made Saburo gag again. "Bring him over here."

His patient rose with a wide grin of relief, the gaps in his teeth proving he had lost teeth before and probably more painfully.

The old man seized Saburo by the sleeve and drew him forward.

"Really, I'm fine," said Saburo, hanging back. "Thanks, Bashan, but I don't need any treatment. Besides I've got no money."

Bashan laughed. It was a nice laugh, full-throated and pleasant. Tora saw that the blind masseur was tall and would have been handsome if not for his disability. "Nobody has any money here, friend. Sit down and let me touch your face."

Saburo recoiled. "No!"

Bashan cocked his head. "What's wrong?"

The old beggar explained, "He's got those ugly scars on his face. He says someone tortured him. It's really the back of his head needs looking at." To Saburo, he repeated, "Don't you worry! Bashan's very gentle."

With an inward sigh, Saburo sat down across from the masseur. Bashan washed his hands in a basin and dried them on a cloth attached to his belt. Then he traced Saburo's scars with his fingers. Their touch was cool from the water and soft and very quick. "I see," he murmured. "Did you tell them what they wanted to know?"

"Yes," Saburo said, angry at the man and at himself. "You would've done the same."

"I believe you. Now lean down so I can check your head."

Again Bashan's touch was feather light. Saburo felt only a couple of brief twinges.

"You'll do," pronounced the masseur. "If you permit, I'll wash your hair to keep the wound clean and prevent you frightening people. There's a lot of blood."

"You're very kind, but I don't want to trouble you."

"No trouble. I pride myself on the way I wash hair." Bashan chuckled.

Saburo murmured, "Thank you," and submitted.

Apart from the faint burning when the water and Bashan's fingers came too close to his broken scalp, the experience was pleasant, and when it was over, Saburo felt a good deal better.

"Do you wear your hair in a knot?" asked the masseur.

"Yes, but I didn't tonight. I suppose the knot might have softened the blow."

Bashan smiled. "Perhaps, but I don't think your enemy meant to kill you."

"I don't feel particularly grateful at the moment," Saburo said sourly. "I've worked out that I'm in the temple of the beggars. When I first came to, there was this weird old fellow in women's clothes sitting beside me. He called me by my name and said he was Kenko. It was . . . well, disconcerting. How did he know my name?"

Bashan's eyebrows rose. "A warning, friend. The Venerable Kenko is the chief of the beggars and the temple priest. The people here love and obey him. As for how he knew your name: Kenko knows just about everything. My guess is someone recognized you and told him."

Saburo thought about this. It was possible. His face was not easily forgotten, and beggars were everywhere. He also thought about the priest. Aside from Bashan, the beggars so far had not impressed him. A priest dressed in a woman's red silk gown perhaps least of all. But he knew he had almost made a bad mistake.

"Thanks for your help," he told Bashan. "I owe you. I'm not one of them, so I can pay, only I don't have any money on me. I'll come back. Will I find you here?"

"Only when they need me," Bashan said, packing his tools into his case. "And you owe me nothing. But be careful, Saburo. Next time you may not be so lucky." He got to his feet, slung the box over his shoulder and chest, attached the basin to it, and took up a long staff leaning against the well coping. Giving Saburo a nod, he walked away, tapping the ground before him.

Saburo cast another look around. The beggars had melted away, and he was alone. Never mind. He would return when he felt a bit better. It had struck him that beggars made perfect spies, being everywhere and ignored by all.

10

The Grieving Father

Akitada pondered the character of the prince's wife all the way to the Minamoto residence. He wished he could speak to this powerful woman, but his interview with the prince had not gone well, and he had no way of approaching Lady Kishi.

She would not in any case welcome such a call, even if the problems of visiting another man's wife could be overcome. Lady Kishi was in a peculiar position. As Prince Atsuhira's wife, she was most likely deeply offended by her husband's affair with one of the emperor's ladies, yet, her fate was tied to her husband's, and he clearly was in serious political trouble. Would she have been angry enough to punish him by accusing him of treasonable plotting? It did not seem likely, but perhaps she had acted thoughtlessly in her jealousy and now regretted having taken her vengeance.

Then there was the murder of Lady Masako. Could Lady Kishi have ordered it? The charge of treason did not appear to be related to the murder of his lover, but Akitada did not like the coincidence.

Yes, Lady Kishi was a fascinating character and certainly a suspect in the murder at least.

Minamoto Masaie's house was within a block of the western wall of the Greater Palace enclosure. Many of the provincial lords maintained town residences to conduct business in the capital. Masaie's was a comfortable size and well maintained behind its plaster walls and roofed double gate.

Armed soldiers guarded this gate and were more peremptory than at the prince's palace, but these were Masaie's own retainers.

"I come from the Ministry of Justice and have business with your master," Akitada told them.

The senior man merely shook his head.

Akitada was searching his mind for something that might gain him access when he looked past the warrior and saw a familiar short, round figure inside the compound. His friend Kosehira was coming toward the gate.

He looked glum, but his round face broke into a smile when he saw Akitada. "I'm so glad to see you," he cried. "What are you doing here?"

Akitada glanced at the guard. "I wanted to pay my respects to Masaie, but I don't seem to be welcome. And you?"

"Paying my mother's respects," said Kosehira with a grimace. "Come, I'll introduce you." To the soldier, he said, "He's all right. I know him." And with that he drew Akitada into the compound.

They did not try to stop them. Kosehira's position apparently vouched for both of them.

Still it rankled a little. "Would you mind telling me," Akitada asked, "how you manage to gain access while I, a representative of a ministry, am denied?"

"Oh, it's the same old story. It's not whom you represent but whom you know. Don't forget the regent is my cousin."

Akitada shook his head. They passed into an inner courtyard and walked along an open gallery to a side wing of the main house. Here a servant saw them and ran to tell his master.

Minamoto Masaie was talking to a tall young man as they walked in. Apparently, they had interrupted an argument because both looked thunderous at the interruption.

Masaie glared at the servant, who muttered an apology and ran. "Back again already?" the Minamoto lord said to Kosehira. "What do you want now?"

Not a promising beginning.

And very rude, considering Kosehira's status.

The young man bore a resemblance to Masaie. They were both large with round heads and big limbs. Both wore beards. And both were red-faced with anger. Akitada guessed they were father and son.

Before Kosehira could speak, the son decided to add his own insults, perhaps to deflect his father's anger from himself and curry favor with him. "You lack manners, sir," he snapped at Kosehira. 'How dare you have the gall to trouble my father at such a time? He just lost his daughter. Where is your respect?"

Masaie growled, "Quiet, Masanaga. You may leave us."

The son closed his mouth and glared.

Kosehira didn't bat an eyelid. He smiled at the young man. "Sorry, Masanaga. Didn't know you were with your father."

Masanaga did not acknowledge the apology and walked out.

Kosehira looked after him, then turned to Masaie. "Here's some luck, Masaie," he said. "I was just leaving when I ran into Akitada coming in. Sugawara Akitada. I expect you've heard of him?"

Masaie gave Akitada an unfriendly stare. "He's a troublemaker in the Ministry of Justice."

Akitada opened his mouth to protest, but Kosehira said quickly, "Exactly, and that makes him the very man to help you out of your predicament."

The unfriendly stare was practically frigid now. "I told you there's no trouble, and I'll thank you not to discuss my affairs with everybody you meet on the street."

Akitada cleared his throat, but Kosehira was undisturbed. "Come, let's all sit down," he said, pulling Akitada to one of the cushions near the open doors.

Outside was a small veranda and, as at the prince's house, a cherry tree. Only this one was in a tub and just coming into bloom. Akitada could not help wondering why such a very irate person would arrange for this small tree. And for the sparrows that scratched around in the gravel as if they expected to be fed. But such puzzles were pointless. Masaie normally resided at his country seat. Some servant must have brought the tree here, hoping to please his ill-tempered master.

Masaie did not sit. "You may both leave, Kosehira," he said coldly. "I've said all I'm going to say. I will not help that despicable traitor."

He meant Prince Atsuhira. His anger was understandable. But would he condone the murder of a beloved daughter?

Neither Kosehira nor Akitada sat down. Akitada now said, "Allow me to express my condolences, Lord Masaie. I, too, have lost a child and know the grief."

Masaie turned his face toward him. The light caught his features, and now Akitada saw the deep lines of his face. His heart went out to the man. But Masaie surprised him again.

"My daughter was a slut who shamed me and my house," he snapped. "I welcomed her death. If she killed herself, she only did as she should. If someone did it to her, then let him come to me, and I'll pay him in gold."

At this even Kosehira gasped. "Masaie," he cried, "you should be ashamed. You don't mean that. You cannot mean it. Please consider—"

Masaie took a threatening step toward him. "Out!" he roared.

They left.

Outside, in the open air, Kosehira stopped and took a deep breath. He glanced back at the house. "Whew," he said, "that was about as unpleasant as anything I've ever experienced."

Akitada saw Masaie's son, now armed with a sword, approaching from the direction of the gate. He said, "You may be speaking too soon."

Minamoto Masanaga was taking big steps, even for such a tall man. He crossed the wide courtyard in no time at all and came to a halt before them. His eyes were fixed on Akitada.

"You!" he said, his manner threatening. "You dare to threaten my family. I know what you're about, you infernal busybody. You're in the plot with the rest of them, and you're trying to pin something on us. You will not succeed. I'll see to that." He took a step closer, putting his hand on his sword and leaning into Akitada's face. "I'll see you dead, you and your family, for your insolence. Our people have orders to cut you down."

With that, he flung past them and stalked back to the house. Akitada wiped a trace of spittle from his face. He felt murderous.

"Hmm," said Kosehira. "He doesn't like you, I'm afraid."

"No. He's afraid. And this little temper tantrum has just proved that he and his father have something to hide."

Kosehira shook his head. "Well, I don't see what we can do about it." He looked at the gate, which was now manned by ten armed Minamoto soldiers, all with

their hands on their swords. "Ouch! You don't suppose they'll cut us down on our way out, do you? These provincial lords don't pay much attention to the law."

Akitada was already walking. "Come, we'll test it,"
he said grimly.

They set their faces and strode forward.

The armed men waited until the last moment, then
parted ranks and let them pass. Nobody said a word.

Akitada and Kosehira did not speak until they
turned the corner; then Kosehira stopped. "Heavens!
That was close." He clenched his shaking hands.
"What do you suppose would have happened if they
had cut us down?"

"Do you care what happens after you're dead? It
was very unlikely. I grant you Masaie, and especially his
son, were upset, but we're in the capital, after all. Perhaps they might get away with it in their own fiefdom,
but not here. They would have been arrested, tried,
and sent into exile."

Kosehira looked at him. "How can you be so sure?
Sometimes you're incredibly naïve, my dear Akitada,
You're still under the impression that justice will be
done somehow. Don't forget, in this case you would be
no more. Who would stand up for the victims then?"

Akitada knew Kosehira had a point. The slaughter
of two ranking noblemen by the retainers of another
would raise eyebrows and perhaps even an outcry, but if
political expediency prevailed, Masaie would be briefly
exiled and then recalled. It had happened too often in
the past.

Kosehira peered up at the sun. "Oh well, time for the midday rice, if you still have an appetite for it. Come to my house and let's discuss the case over food."

Akitada accepted. He was hungry, and Kosehira provided elegant repasts and could be trusted to come up with something tasty even when reduced to a skeleton staff.

He was not disappointed. Kosehira had travelled to the capital with his cook, having decided the other services could be performed by the servants left behind to look after his town residence while he served as governor in his province.

They settled down in a pleasant room overlooking a garden with meandering streams, small bridges, pines, and willows in fresh pale leaves. An elderly servant brought some very good wine and bowls of nuts and pickled plums. His manner expressed devotion and concern for his master.

Savoring the wine after the unpleasantness—in retrospect it seemed no more—at the Minamoto house, Akitada decided to find out how things stood with Kosehira. "Do I take it your close connection to the regent has changed your own situation for the better?"

Kosehira grimaced. "Not at all. I had a very uncomfortable meeting with His Excellency and came away cursing such relationships. It's not enough that I must bear the burden of the unpopularity of my powerful Fujiwara relatives, but they seem to think I owe them something. Kinsue reprimanded me for my correspondence with the prince and warned me they would not protect me if I was found to be involved in the plot."

"I asked because you seem to be free to go wherever you wish."

Kosehira refilled their cups and passed the nuts. "Well, at least I'm not under house arrest."

Akitada ate some nuts and sipped his wine. "Do you think it's wise to be seen supporting the prince the way you have been doing? Should you not return to your province and wait out the storm?"

Kosehira shook his head. "I'm angry, Akitada. I will not be treated this way. And I will not abandon a friend." He looked and sounded quite fierce.

It was not an expression Akitada had ever seen on his friend's cheerful round face. Neither had Kosehira ever expressed anything but happy emotions. Kosehira's joyful optimism had always been a great pleasure to the frequently troubled and uncertain Akitada. Now it occurred to him for the first time that he might lose him. Political alliances could be very dangerous.

The same servant returned in the company of a young serving girl, both carrying small trays and dishes. Placing a tray before each, they served Akitada and their master with bowls of a clear soup containing bits of vegetables. The soup was delicious.

When they were alone again, Akitada said, "I haven't made any progress, I'm afraid. What just happened at Masaie's is exactly the same thing that has happened everywhere else I tried to get information. Even Kobe had nothing new. He objects to our meddling and thinks you've behaved very improperly in the matter of Lady Masako's death."

"I had no choice. I couldn't refuse my help to the prince. I think Atsuhira blames me for having kept him that night." Kosehira put down his bowl. He had sipped less than half of it.

Akitada did not mention that the prince had, in fact, cursed him. It would merely add to his friend's guilt and worry, and the prince had spoken out of grief. He said, "In any case, Atsuhira will do nothing to help us. He speaks of forsaking the world. If he's prevented, he says, he'll kill himself."

Kosehira nodded, looking glum.

Akitada finished his soup. "What do you make of Masaie's behavior? And that of his son?"

"Young hothead," muttered Kosehira. "Masaie surprised me. How can a father hate his own child? It's unnatural. I was shocked. These provincial lords are rough and violent men, but I never knew they did not care for their own children."

"Perhaps it was just show. To prove he has reason to hate Prince Atsuhira and cannot therefore be one of his supporters. I don't know the man at all, so I have no idea if it's true."

Kosehira looked thoughtful. "It may be so. He was clearly hoping to make the emperor his son-in-law. You can see how Lady Masako's willfulness destroyed his dream. Of course, it may also be that he switched allegiance once he realized she had chosen Atsuhira instead."

This had been Akitada's thought also, so he nod-ded.

The servants returned to remove the soup bowls. When the old man saw Kosehira had hardly touched his, he shook his head. They substituted an array of small dishes. Delightful aromas rose from them. Akitada saw fried dumplings, a larger dish with a grilled fish, several bowls of pickled vegetables and sauces, an interesting stew, and a splendid mound of white, glisten-ing rice.

The male servant murmured to Kosehira, "Sea bream, sir, very fresh and wholesome, and your favorite rabbit stew. Cook made it especially."

Kosehira said listlessly. "Thank you, Tamori. And thank Cook."

When the servants had left, Kosehira looked at the food before him and sighed. "They worry when I don't eat. I've been a trial to them lately." He glanced up. "Eat, Akitada. I'm sure it's very good. I just have no appetite."

"Nonsense," Akitada said briskly. "You mustn't dis-appoint them. We'll get through this. "Rabbit stew? I haven't had any of that in a long time." He tasted and smacked his lips.

Kosehira chuckled. "It's my favorite. Cook must have ordered the rabbit from home." He reached for his bowl and ate a little. "It *is* good. Do you like it, Akitada?"

"As you see." Akitada showed his empty bowl and reached for a dumpling. "You must cheer up," he said.

"Nothing is to be gained by making yourself ill. We'll unravel the matter soon enough. Eat!"

Kosehira smiled a little and nodded. "Of course. With your help. Thank you, Akitada."

Akitada did not feel at all optimistic, but he returned to their discussion. "I wonder when Masaie found out about the affair."

"I don't know. I still cannot fathom how a man can utter such words about his own child."

"I think he cared, perhaps too much. He did raise her like a son. It shows he favored her, even though she was a mere girl. His effort to raise her to the position of empress shows the same regard. But she bitterly disappointed him. In such a frame of mind, he may well have wished her dead. Not only did she not respect all he had done for her, but her action brought shame to him. She left the imperial apartments to be with another man. If he found out about the affair just before her death, he is a suspect."

Kosehira's eyes widened. "You mean *he* murdered her?" He shuddered. "I hope not. That would be truly terrible."

"Or he paid someone to kill her." Akitada sampled the fish and found it as perfect as the other dishes. Kosehira had eaten most of his stew and was also eyeing the bream.

"Go ahead," Akitada urged. "It's excellent. You must keep up your strength. We need to talk to more people, people who know Masaie and Lady Masako. I feel out of my depth. My connections with the provincial gentry are nonexistent, but perhaps Tora can approach Masaie's servants here. What about you?" An idea struck him. "Do you know Lady Kishi at all well?"

Kosehira nodded. "I told you, she's my cousin. Yes, I'll speak to her. She may say something useful. Oh, Akitada, I'm so grateful to you. I knew I could rely on you. You'll work it all out in no time at all." He reached for the fish and started to eat.

"Perhaps not quite so quickly," said Akitada with a chuckle. "And Lady Kishi had good reason to hate Lady Masako. But surely we'll come across something helpful soon. Can you find out who Atsuhira's alleged co-conspirators are?"

"I'll try, though most of it is just gossip. I'm determined to stay here until Atsuhira's been cleared."

They finished their excellent meal with the fragrant rice and more wine. Kosehira looked almost happy again, and the smile and deep bow of his servant told Akitada he had achieved the same standing as a beneficent deity in Kosehira's household.

11

The Wisdom of Women

Saburo returned to a barrage of questions from Tora and Genba.

"Where had he been?"

"Didn't he know the master would ask where he was?"

"What was wrong with him?"

"Had he been drinking?"

"Why else was he staggering about like this and looking sick?"

Saburo made it to the well coping and sat. The distance from the beggars' temple had seemed endless. He had started feeling faint soon after leaving Bashan's care. His physical weakness was made worse by the knowledge that he had failed most miserably and been bested by someone younger, stronger, and smarter.

The last especially hurt. He was an old man who did not even have the wisdom of experience to count on.

So he sat, and told Tora and Genba what had happened.

"You had the contracts, and this thief stole them?" asked Genba, his eyes round with shock that his salvation had been so close only to be snatched away again.

"Beggars' guild?" asked Tora. "That's going to be very useful. You've made friends, I hope."

Saburo looked at them. They didn't care about him. They cared only about their own concerns. Why should he have expected anything else? "I'll lie down for a while," he said getting to his feet. "Wake me before the master returns."

They protested, wanting more information, but he ignored them and crept into his room, where he slipped into the bedding he had left the night before.

When Akitada walked into his study a few hours later, Tora and Genba were waiting for him. They looked worried.

"What's happened?" asked Akitada, suddenly fearful that the misfortunes of the mighty had already reached his own modest household.

"Saburo was attacked last night."

Tora was always the spokesman. Genba stood beside him, nodding and twisting his big hands.

"How and where?"

"In the Willow Quarter. As to the how—." Tora exchanged a glance with Genba. "Umm . . . it seems he was looking into the murder of the brothel owner, sir."

Akitada frowned.

Genba offered, "It's all my fault, sir. I'm very sorry. I should never have brought our troubles home. And now Saburo's not getting up. He must be badly hurt."

Tora said quickly, "No, Genba. We've been looking in on him all afternoon. He's just sleeping. Genba exaggerates, sir."

Akitada took off his good robe and changed into the comfortable garment he wore at home. Then he went to sit down and told his retainers to do the same. "Am I to understand Saburo went out investigating a murder in the middle of the night?"

They both nodded. Genba said, "I didn't hear him leave, sir. Saburo's very quiet when he goes on his jaunts."

The frustrations of the day made Akitada irritable. "Jaunts? He's done this before?"

Again they nodded, looking a little uneasy.

"You come and go on your own business whenever it pleases you? Day or night?"

Genba shrank, but Tora defended Saburo. "He works here all day and goes out at night because that's his own time, sir. And in this case, he went to help Genba. It isn't his fault this fellow objected to him poking around the brothel. I think Saburo ran into the killer."

Akitada glared. "If Saburo takes his outings during the time when he should be asleep, he won't be much use to me the following day." This was unfair, as Akitada well knew, because Saburo had always been diligent about his chores. "However, I'd better have a look at him. He may need a physician."

There was no need, because they heard slow footsteps approaching, and the door opened. Saburo, dressed in his usual neat blue robe and black sash, his hair arranged in a slightly off-centered topknot, came in. He stopped when he saw Tora and Genba with his master.

"I'm sorry," he said. "I didn't realize you'd come back already, sir."

Tora said quickly, "We told the master that you were having a look at the brothel when you were attacked."

Akitada saw that Saburo's face looked gray and he held on to the door jamb. "Come in and sit down," he said, wondering how bad the injury was. "Tora and Genba told me about your adventure. How do you feel?"

Saburo sat down and looked at the others. "I'm quite well, sir. The rest has done me a lot of good. I'm ready to get to work."

Akitada thought he detected a note of nervousness and wondered. Saburo had always struck him as fearless, or at least unconcerned about danger or death. He said, "There's no work that cannot wait until tomorrow or whenever you are fully recovered. You received a head injury?"

"It was nothing, sir. A little knock on the head. I've had worse."

That went without saying and proved nothing. Akitada decided to check and got up. When his fingers probed his scalp, Saburo shivered, perhaps from pain or simply from the shock of having his master feel around in his hair.

"Hmm. A bad bruise and a scab. Why did you tie up your hair? You made it bleed. Tora, go call my wife and ask her to bring some paste or plaster. We should cut off his hair."

Saburo looked horrified. "Not your lady, sir," he gasped. "I don't want her to bother with me. In fact, you shouldn't have bothered either. It's embarrassing." His voice trailed off as he saw Akitada's bloodied fingers.

"Nonsense. Go, Tora."

Tamako arrived with a jar of ointment, heard part of the story, and peered at Saburo's head. "His hair should be shaved off. And he needs to rest, not work."

Saburo protested weakly, tears of shame on his scarred cheeks.

Akitada relented. "Just some ointment, I think. Is it the stuff you used on Yasuko's skinned knee?"

"Yes," she said. "We can try it. But you cannot wear your hair in a knot, Saburo. And if you don't feel better tomorrow, we will call a physician."

"I'm very sorry," Saburo muttered.

After Tamako left, Tora returned to the subject of the beggars. "About those beggars, Saburo. I've wanted to get to know them for some years now, but they're not likely to let someone like me into the guild. We should go back there together. Beggars are very useful people."

Saburo frowned. "I've thought of that, but it'll be best if I go back by myself first. They're very shy about anyone connected with the law."

"No doubt they have reason," Akitada said drily.

"No doubt, sir." Saburo turned to Genba, who had been sitting by silently and unhappily. "Sorry I wasn't more useful, Genba. I was hoping to help."

"Thank you, Saburo. I meant to tell you how grateful Ohiro and I are. I feel bad you got attacked on our account. If there's ever anything I can do for you, you just have to ask."

"We may find another way," Saburo said, but he did not sound very hopeful.

Saburo went back to bed, and Genba returned to his chores, leaving Akitada and Tora together. Akitada told Tora about his visit to Masaie's home.

"I'd like you to get some information about him from his servants tomorrow," he added. "Don't tell them who you are. Find out if Masaie was in the capital when his daughter was killed and what sort of family life they had. And if there are other children besides the son and daughter."

Tora looked pleased when he left, and Akitada joined his wife and children for their evening meal. His worries about Kosehira and about Genba's problem receded as they always did when he was with the children. Tamako would have questioned him more closely about his activities, but in the presence of the little ones, they both put their daily problems aside.

Tonight, Yasuko delighted her father by reciting a poem she had learned especially for him, and

Yoshitada, who had a distressing habit of upending his bowl to play with the contents, for once behaved perfectly and enchanted Akitada with his knack of producing a wide smile every time their eyes met.

When Tamako's maid had taken them to bed and they were alone, Tamako demanded a full account of events. Over the years, she had taken increasing interest in his work, particularly cases involving crimes. He had resisted her curiosity at first, not wanting to bring the ugly details of his work into his home or to worry her with the frequent danger to himself, but he had realized she deserved to know. Gradually, he had come to enjoy her interest, and once or twice she had been an invaluable source of advice.

But the case of Prince Atsuhira was still too murky. He had no bright ideas to present to her, and Tamako was nothing if not intelligent. Sometimes he had the uncomfortable feeling she could see right through him.

He had that feeling now as he related Kosehira's predicament and the death of the Lady Masako at the bottom of a mountain cliff.

She listened without interrupting and then sat silent for a long time. "Do you think the political plot is real?" she finally asked. "And is the prince aware of it?"

Akitada felt a surge of pride. She had hit on the crux of the matter. He said, "It may be real. There are always discontents, and there are also people who hope to benefit from an alliance with a future emperor. I don't know if it is a serious threat to the regent and his family. As for Prince Atsuhira, I doubt he has had a hand in it, though he may be aware of it. This isn't the first time he's had to deal with such suspicions."

She sighed. "An impossible situation then, unless he can prove to the regent and his brothers that he doesn't support such actions."

"He can do that only by taking the tonsure. He claims he's considering doing so. I don't know if it's due to his grief for the woman he loved or a wish to distance himself from the political wrangling. In any case, he won't make the effort to defend himself or to find his lover's killer."

"I see." She fell silent again.

"I'm sorry," he said, after a moment. "This could affect our lives, but I must try to help Kosehira."

"Yes, of course. But Akitada, there's also that poor young woman. Her killer must be found."

"You think her death is more important than Kosehira's troubles?" he asked uncertainly.

"I do. Kosehira has powerful relatives. He'll survive. Lady Masako is dead and has no one to speak for her. You have always responded to the helplessness of the dead. Surely, you still do?"

And suddenly he saw his way clear. It was all so simple. He must solve the murder. He smiled with relief and reached for his wife's hand. "Yes, I still do, but I'm grateful that you remind me of it." He touched his lips to the inside of her hand, breathing in the familiar orange blossom scent, and finding his thoughts drifting to closer embraces. Controlling his treacherous mind with an effort, he put her hand back in her lap.

"Let's talk about Lady Masako. What do you think happened?"

Tamako smiled a little as if she had guessed his lust. "I don't know, Akitada, but surely the answer must lie in her life before she died. Can you find out about it?"

"Difficult. She was still part of His Majesty's household when she had some of those secret meetings with Atsuhira. How am I to penetrate into the imperial women's quarters?" He made a face and added, "Really, her behavior was thoroughly reprehensible."

"Perhaps. But I think you may learn more about her by talking to her family and friends." He opened his mouth to protest that Masaie would not welcome another visit, but she went on. "She had a mother and sisters perhaps. She also had maidservants and companions. You must speak to the women. This affair touches the hearts of women." She leaned toward him, putting her hand on his knee, and looking at him earnestly. "Akitada, try to put yourself in her place. She grew up, a beloved child, encouraged in all her whims. And then, abruptly, the father who had never shown her anything but indulgence sent her away as a bride to a boy sovereign who took an immediate dislike to her. How must she have felt?"

"You think she took a lover out of rebellion? Perhaps the first man who seemed likely? Prince Atsuhira is a first cousin to His Majesty. No doubt he was a frequent visitor to the inner apartments. She may have seduced him."

Tamako removed her hand. "Nonsense. Prince Atsuhira has a reputation."

He did indeed. But Akitada had seen the man. Atsuhira had been deeply in love with Masako. He said so.

Tamako pursed her lips. "I'm only saying you need to talk to someone who knew her. A woman. At that age, women have friends they confide in. You have only talked to men so far. What can they know about a woman's heart?"

"Oh, come," he protested. "Men aren't incapable of knowing women. I know you."

She smiled.

He did not want to pursue the argument in case it led to a quarrel he wanted to avoid at all cost. "Besides, how am I to approach women who knew her?"

"You must try. I'll speak to your sister Akiko. She knows some of the attendants in the palace. And perhaps you should let it be known you're investigating Lady Masako's death?"

His first thought was that this could bring the combined forces of the palace, the regent's family, and of the irate Masaie and his son down upon him. But word of his interest in the case was probably already out. He could see Tamako was right. It was the logical next move, and the risk could not be avoided in any case. .

He reached for her hand again. "Thank you," he said. "I have married a wise woman . . . and a very desirable one."

That pleased her, and she did not object when he pulled her into an embrace and led her to the bedding her maid had spread out.

12

Tora and the Cook

arly the next morning, dressed neatly but in ordinary clothes, Tora walked to Minamoto Masaie's house. He glanced in through the open gates, noting the armed guards without pausing in his walk. At the next corner, he paused and watched the street for a while, but he saw nobody entering the compound. No doubt, the forbidding presence of Masaie's soldiers discouraged social calls.

He continued along the compound's walls to the rear of the property. Here, in a small side street, the back gate stood open as well, but there were no guards. Instead a large handcart had stopped, and an elderly man unloaded crates and baskets of food from it. These he set down in the dust of the street as a short, round woman berated him.

She gestured at the unloaded goods and pointed inside the compound. The old man shook his head and went on unloading. As soon as the cart's contents were piled on the ground, he took his empty cart and trotted away. The round woman ran after him, shaking her fist.

Tora grinned. Perfect.

The delivery man from the market had refused to carry the goods all the way to the kitchen, and the woman, probably Maseie's cook, had no help at hand. Now she stood there, staring at the pile and muttering to herself.

Putting on his best smile, Tora approached. "Good morning, dear lady. Why so glum on such a pretty spring day?"

She glowered at him, then at the new green leaves on the trees and the pale blue sky above. "It may be a good day for you," she said bitterly, "but some of us have to work." She bent for a bundle, but straightened up again to give him a sharp once-over. "Never mind. Move on. You're in my way."

Her accent sounded familiar to Tora. If he was right, luck was indeed with him. "I think you need to carry all those things inside," he said, "and you don't want to leave them in the street for thieves. Allow me to help. My name's Tora."

She still hesitated, but relaxed a little after giving him another careful look. Tora's handsome face and neat clothing clearly impressed her. Here was a courteous, friendly young man who was certainly strong enough to carry all the abandoned cabbages and turnips, bags of rice and beans, and kegs of *sake* and oil. Well," she said dubiously.

Tora put on one of his dazzling smiles.

She blushed, smoothed her hair back, and straightened the cloth apron covering her blue gown. She was middle-aged, near the same age as the Sugawara's cook, but unlike that shrew she had a pleasant face with apple cheeks and laugh lines at the corners of her eyes.

Tora said, "Look, dear lady, I have some time on my hands, and you cannot be expected to do such rough work. That's for men. I'll gladly give you a hand." He reached for a large basket of vegetables with one arm and scooped up a heavy bundle with the other. "Lead the way, my dear."

"Well, if you'd just take the big stuff inside the gate, that would be a big help. The master doesn't allow strangers inside and makes us keep the gates closed. I'd hate to leave all this outside. There are a lot of thieves in this city."

"It wouldn't last long enough for you to take one basket to the kitchen and come for the next." Tora deposited his vegetables inside the gate in what appeared to be a service yard and turned back for another load.

With both of them moving parcels and bags inside, it was done quickly. Tora had identified the kitchen by the fact that smoke came from the one-story building. "Well," he said, glancing at it, "I think that's still a long way for you to carry all these heavy things."

"It's all right," she said, holding the gate open for him to leave. "I can manage now."

He hung his head. "I see you still don't trust me. I don't blame you. My guess is you're not from here yourself."

She blushed and hesitated. "It's true. I'm from Sagami."

"What if I told you a bit about myself?"

"Well . . ."

"You see, I work for a man called Juntaro. He's a dealer in grass mats and cushions in the fourth ward. This morning, he sent me to drum up some business from your master. He heard his lordship had come to town and he told me to ask the steward if they needed any mats. I tried at the main gate, but they wouldn't let me in."

She nodded. "It's not a good time to sell anything."

"You sound a bit like my people back home. I was born and raised in Shimosa province. My people were farmers."

Her round face lit up. "You're from Shimosa? So am I, from near the coast. Near Chiba. My people were fishermen."

"You don't say! Have you been to Asakusa?"

"Oh, yes. When I was young girl. We went to the beautiful temple there."

They regarded each other happily for a moment, then Tora asked, "So, what do you say? Since our people were practically neighbors, maybe cousins? Back home a dainty female didn't have to lug around heavy things."

She giggled at that "dainty female," then cast a look around. There was no one in sight. "All right, then. But we must hurry so nobody sees us, or I'll be in trouble for letting you in. You're very nice to offer, Tora." She slammed the gate shut.

Tora chuckled. "Least I can do. You remind me of home. I miss it a lot. It was beautiful there. All green woods and fields and the blue sea."

"Yes, not like this big dirty city." She glared at the gate as if it kept out all the filth of the great city. "Let's get everything inside the kitchen over there. I'm Hanishi, the cook. We're short-staffed, because the master rushed up here and left all the servants behind. He only brought soldiers."

"A bit strange, that." Tora loaded up again and started toward the kitchen.

"You'd think he was about to start a war," she grumbled, following him. "And me having to feed the big louts all by myself." They reached the kitchen, and she pointed. "Put those vegetables over there."

Tora sniffed the air. A large iron pot simmered over the open fire, filling the room with the aroma of seafood. He gave her another smile. "I bet you're a great cook, Hanishi. That smell reminds me of my mother. I miss her cooking something terrible." He tried to look hungry as he said this.

She laughed. "When we're done, I'll let you sample my fish stew."

"Fish stew?" Tora, smacked his lips and dashed back outside.

When all the supplies had been brought in and put away, Hanishi found a bowl and ladled stew into it. She gestured at the earthenware ovens that heated two rice cookers. "Sorry, the rice isn't done. Ran out of wood after making this fire."

Tora tasted the stew. It was good. He did not have to pretend pleasure, and started gobbling it. "Who needs rice with something like this," he said with a full mouth. "Oh, that brings back memories. You're a wonderful cook, Hanishi."

She preened herself a little. "Well, I like to feed hungry men like you. Do you have a wife, Tora?"

She gave him a very considering look, and Tora thought of lying, but in the end he said, "Oh, yes. A wife and a son. I'm a family man." He gave her another grin, hoping he had not discouraged her altogether. "But my wife's been raised here. She doesn't know how to make fish stew like this."

"Oh," she said, a little deflated. "I suppose I could tell her easily enough. Another bowl?"

He made her a bow. "You're a generous woman in addition to being the best cook in town. But let me go out first and bring you some wood to fire up the rice cookers. Where do you keep it?"

She positively glowed with good will again, showing him the huge wood pile behind the kitchen. Tora worked hard, and when he had carried in enough kindling and logs, he helped her lay the fire. Then he sat down with a sigh of relief; he had done more work for Masaie's household this morning than he normally did at home.

"So," he asked her when she brought him his second bowl of stew, "do you like it here? Do you have a good master and mistress? They say this Lord Maseie is a very wealthy man."

"He is that. He's got three wives, but they're meek as mice, no trouble at all. Now his daughter, she was something! The spirit of that girl." She heaved a sigh. "Poor thing. I loved her, no matter what they say now."

This was going better than Tora had expected. He raised his brows. "Oh? There's a story there. Why do you call her a poor thing?" He got up to help her carry a pail of water to the rice pot.

"Thanks. Lady Masako's dead. She was her father's favorite and entered the palace last year. Her father really doted on her. It's funny the way the meanest men turn soft as goose down when it comes to little girls. She was always beautiful. A little princess even then." Cook stopped what she was doing to look dreamily into the distance. "She'd come running to me for sweet dumplings and oranges all the time. Oh, she was something. And beautiful! She grew tall, but slender and quick. The master taught her how to ride and use bow and arrow, and he took her hunting. She was much better at those things than the young lord. He'd come home in a mighty temper, that boy." She laughed at the memory.

Tora smiled. "Can't blame him. But I wish I'd had a sister."

"What's your family like?"

Tora preferred no distractions from the flood of reminiscences and said, "There's no one now. They all died." It was true enough.

"Oh, I'm sorry, Tora. Well, the lady Masako died this past winter. She killed herself, except we're not to talk about it. They say she brought shame on the family." She turned away, overcome with emotion. "It's hard to stop loving her." Her voice broke, and she sniffled. "I have no children. I was very fond of her."

"You're a soft-hearted woman. What happened?"

"A man, what else?" she said bitterly. "And it wasn't His Majesty. The young emperor didn't want her, poor child. She came home in despair to tell them. Her father raged because His Majesty hadn't bedded her yet. Every time she came for a visit—you know His Majesty's ladies have to leave the palace when it's their time of the month—his lordship would talk to her. She cried and cried. It wasn't her fault." Hanishi heaved a deep sigh. "I wish my lord hadn't been so hard on her. Or that her mother had taken her side. My young lady was so unhappy. Well, she went back to the palace and met another man. If you ask me, His Majesty should've taken better care of her."

Tora listened with rapt attention. "You don't say?" he breathed. "What a love story! I thought men weren't allowed near His Majesty's ladies."

"That's what you think," Cook said darkly. "Turns out it's a very good place to meet men. All those parties every day." She paused, suddenly nervous. "But don't you go talking about it. I shouldn't have mentioned it." She sat down abruptly on an upturned basket and started weeping softly. "Her father and her brother, they both say terrible things, call her a slut, and worse."

"Don't cry," said Tora, jumping up and putting an arm around her shoulder. "I won't say a word, but I'm thinking it must be a terrible thing when a father won't help his child. And she was just a girl."

Cook wiped her face with a sleeve and nodded. "A terrible thing. He drove her to kill herself, that's what her father did. And when they told him, did he care? Oh, no! Him and the young lord went hunting as if nothing had happened."

To make sure he had his facts straight, Tora said, "I suppose it took a long time for the news of her death to get to Sagami."

"We were here then. Had been for months. The master was waiting for the good news from the palace." She said bitterly, "Some good news!"

At that moment, the kitchen door flew open and in stalked a burly soldier in half armor, his boots shining with polish, and his long sword swinging from his sash. He stopped when he saw Tora. "What the devil's this? What's he doing here? He didn't come in through the front gate."

The little round Hanishi jumped about two feet and started gabbling about deliveries and fire wood.

Tora interrupted her. "I'm Tora. I've come on a visit from her family back east," he told the soldier, making him a bow. "Hanishi's people asked me stop by and see how she's doing." He stared back at the man.

For a moment, nobody said anything. The soldier's gaze faltered. He turned to the cook and asked, "Is that true?"

Tora frowned. "Are you calling me a liar?"

Hanishi cried, "No trouble, please, Tora and Tomogoro-san. The master wouldn't like it. Yes, it's true. He comes from my home."

The armed man relented. He gave Tora a sour look. "I see she's been feeding you," he grumbled. "That's more than she's doing for us. Where's our grub, woman?"

It was a good thing that Lord Masaie's retainer had restrained his appetite until now. It would have been even better, had he waited until after Tora's departure. "I see you don't show women much respect here," he remarked. "Or maybe it's only the custom in Sagami. Hanishi needs help. You should show some appreciation for a fine cook like her. I found her trying to carry heavy baskets and barrels, and she had no wood for the fire to cook your rice. Does your master know she's not getting any help from you?"

The man reddened. "We have out duties, and carrying wood isn't one of them."

"Well, just remember, without a fire or supplies, there isn't going to be any food."

They glowered at each other for a moment, then the warrior said to the cook, "I'll mention it to my sergeant."

"Thanks, Tomogoro-san. The rice'll be ready in an hour. Do you want some stew now?"

He nodded. "Just a bowl. I'll tell the others their food is coming later."

As she filled his bowl, Tora said, "Well, Hanishi, I must be going. It's a long journey back. I'll give them your messages and tell them not to worry. And I hope they'll be treating you as well as you deserve."

He gave the soldier a meaningful glance. The man took his stew and said nothing.

Hanishi walked him to the back gate. "Thank you, Tora," she said. "That was smart thinking. He can be a nasty one. And thank you for your help."

"Think nothing of it. Thanks for that delicious stew. I'd like to check back to make sure all's well with you. I didn't like the way he treated you."

Her eyes moistened. "Better not. They might want to know how come you didn't go back home." She grinned, then reached up and patted his cheek before closing the gate behind him.

Tora smiled, too. He had got what he came for.

13

Good and Bad News

After his chores, Genba set out to give Ohiro the good news that his master had promised his help. His heart overflowed with gratitude as he walked through the warm dusk. Had Akitada been in mortal danger at that moment, Genba would have thrown himself in the way of the fatal spear, arrow, or sword. He thought himself blessed by such goodness when he was worthless himself. Or if not worthless, then not clever and brave like Tora, and not nearly as useful as Saburo with his secretarial skills. He, Genba, could not keep the master's accounts or wield the brush with skill. As for Saburo's stranger talents, he felt nervous just thinking about them. He had almost been relieved when Saburo had met someone better than himself.

But then, that attack also meant the loss of the contracts. Genba had sworn to himself he would pay his master back for buying out Ohiro.

In spite of such drawbacks, Genba reached Ohiro's tenement with a spring in his step.

He had heard the music and laughter from some distance away and wondered at it. When he turned the corner, he saw a crowd in festive clothes, singing and dancing among paper lanterns as if this were a fair at one of the great temples celebrating a holiday. The colored lanterns competed with the fading rosy light in the sky, and men and women wore costumes almost as colorful as the lanterns. There was much laughter and perhaps happy drunkenness.

It could not be a holiday. No, he would not have missed that. So why have a fair here among the tenements of the poor?

Vaguely uneasy, he sped up a little. Most of the lanterns and people were in front of Ohiro's place. Someone was playing a flute, and a woman's voice was raised in song. Raucous laughter and shouts accompanied it.

A dirty ditty. Sung by one of the girls from the Sasaya.

Genba was a good deal more straight-laced than Tora and frowned at the blunt language. Still, this was where many of the prostitutes kept rooms, and such things must be expected. But it shamed him again to bring a woman from this life into his master's house. He had seen the expression of distaste on Akitada's face, heard the hesitation before he had assured Genba that Ohiro would be welcome.

Ohiro was not like these women who flaunted themselves in gaudy costumes before men they would not accept as customers because they were too poor but who often kept them as lovers when they were not working.

That was really all he was: Ohiro's man.

Shame washed over him. He pushed through the merrymakers without looking at them and made for Ohiro's door. He had almost reached it when he heard a woman shout his name. He did not turn, but she caught him just as he laid his hand on the latch.

Shokichi.

Red-faced with drink and smiling broadly.

"Genba, have you heard? The most wonderful thing has happened. Ohiro was dancing with happiness. And so was I. Look!" Shokichi wheeled about, tattered silk gown and sleeves all aflutter and her hands waving in the air.

Genba looked at her, dazed. What wonderful thing? She must mean Tokuzo's death. It was not proper to celebrate a man's death even if he had mistreated them. Maybe the new owner would be a better man. "What wonderful thing?" he asked.

"Oh, go in. Let Ohiro tell you herself." She gave him a push, laughing.

Ohiro must have heard, because she opened the door. Her face broke into a wide smile when she saw Genba, and then she flung herself at him, babbling with joy.

He held her and lifted her over the threshold, closing the door firmly behind them.

"Oh, Genba," she breathed, still clutching him.

Her embrace stirred his lust. "So eager?" he asked with a smile, setting her down.

"I got the contract! It's mine. Someone returned all the contracts of Tokuzo's girls. See!" She swept up a crumpled sheet with writing on it and waved it happily in the air.

The news dumfounded Genba. He snatched the paper from her hand and smoothed it out. Frowning with concentration, he deciphered the writing, the signatures, Ohiro's name, the money owed.

She giggled. "I danced on it when I saw what it was."

The document looked authentic. It must be part of the haul taken from Saburo last night. But stealing the contracts to return them to the women who had worked for Tokuzo made no sense. The contracts were valuable. Did such a document become illegal if acquired by theft?

On the other hand, who could prove the contracts hadn't been sold legitimately? Or that the women had not bought themselves out? Improbable though that was.

Genba sat down abruptly and looked at Ohiro. She'd never been prettier, he thought. Her happiness made her face glow. He swore to himself he would try to put that look on her face as often as he could. "How did you get this?" he asked, half afraid.

"Shokichi got it, along with her own, from one of the begging monks. He told her it was a gift from the Buddha and to thank him. Isn't it wonderful? Isn't it a miracle?" She came to kneel beside him and hugged him. "Oh, Genba, you look worried. Say you're happy, too. Say you'll marry me now. Say we can finally be happy together."

"A begging monk?" Had Saburo's attacker returned the papers to the women? And what did it mean for Ohiro and himself?

He put one arm around her, held her, and said, "I love you, Ohiro. I'll marry you with or without this contract. We will be happy together somehow and sometime, but I don't know if this is legal. The contract was stolen. All of them were stolen. What if Tokuzo's heirs claim you back because they were stolen?"

"Stolen? How could that be? Maybe Tokuzo made a will. That's why a monk brought them back. Maybe he was trying to make up for his bad life. Or his heirs are trying to make up for his sins. Can they really force me to work for them again?"

"Ohiro, there's no will. At least not one leaving the contracts to you and the others. The heirs own your contract, and they'll either keep you or sell you to someone else."

Tears rose to her eyes. "How do you know they were stolen? The others outside are celebrating with the silver they'd saved up to buy themselves out. I gave them some of our money for my share." She wailed, "Oh, Genba, you must be wrong."

"Never mind, Love. You did right to pay your share."

They sat close together, arms around each other's waists, and grieved the unreliability of good fortune.

After a while, Genba said, "I forgot. I came to tell you that the master will help us. So you see, all will be well after all." He smiled down at her.

"How very good he is! But Genba, if only we didn't need to borrow the money from him. Do you know that most of the girls are going to sell themselves again? To a better master, they think. They want the money. And they like the life. They say while they're young and pretty and men will pay to lie with them, they'll make as much money as they can. They think there's time enough to settle down with a husband when they're no longer young. By then they'll have a good dowry, and a husband will be found easily, even if they're no longer pretty."

Genba frowned. "That's foolishness." He paused, then asked, "That's not what you would do, is it?"

Ohiro's eyes grew round. "Of course not. I love you. I could never do such a thing."

He held her close and kissed her, but he thought he might not be able to pay back what he owed. It was such a very large amount of money. And he also worried about bringing Ohiro into the Sugawara house. Even if the master and mistress made her welcome, the others would surely remind her where she had come from. He pictured her tears to himself and sighed deeply.

"Oh, stop it." Ohiro jumped up and stamped her foot. She waved the contract in front of his face. "I don't care what you say, Genba. We don't need your master's money. I'm free. See?" And before his eyes, she tore the document into a lot of small pieces.

"You shouldn't have done that," he said weakly.

She fetched the oil lamp and fed the pieces, one by one into the flame until nothing but ashes remained. "Now who is going to prove Tokuzo owned me?" she demanded triumphantly.

Genba just shook his head. But he could see she had a point. The contract was gone. His spirits lifted. Surely it was fair she should be free. She had paid for her freedom many times over and been beaten black and blue for her efforts. A smile broke out on his face.

Outside, the festive noise subsided. He listened a moment, then got to his feet and went to the door. Opening it, he peered out and saw that Ohiro's neighbors had gathered at the street corner.

Ohiro came to join him. "What happened?"

"I have no idea. Should we go take a look?"

They stepped outside just in time to see Shokichi detaching herself from the group to run toward them.

"Police," she gasped when she was close enough. "They're coming for you. You'd better run."

"Police?" Genba stared at her. "Is this still about Tokuzo?"

"Yes. They want both you and Ohiro. Oh, those cursed contracts!"

Ohiro giggled. "All gone," she cried. "No proof! You'd better go right now and burn yours, Shokichi."

Genba saw the crowd was breaking apart and red coats appeared. The red coats marched toward them.

Shokichi shook a fist at them. "Too late. Somebody told them where to find you."

Ohiro looked up at Genba. "Can they arrest us?"

"I don't know."

"Oh, Genba." Her face crumpled. The bruises showed clearly even in the fading light.

Genba waited with his arm around Ohiro. Shokichi disappeared.

The redcoat in front was the senior policeman, a sergeant to judge by his head dress. He grinned and waved his constables, five of them, armed with cudgels and chains, forward. "You're the one they call Genba?"

"I am." The constables surrounded Genba and Ohiro. For a fleeting moment, Genba considered fighting them. Six altogether, but he was much bigger and those little cudgels wouldn't help them. But he rejected the idea. There was Ohiro to be considered.

"And she's the prostitute Ohiro?"

"She is my *wife* Ohiro."

The sergeant barked a laugh. "Wife? You must be joking."

The constables sniggered.

"Ohiro is my wife. How can we help you?"

The sergeant grinned at his men. "He's a cool one, isn't he?" He mimicked, 'How can we help you?'"

They laughed.

"And he's taken the harlot for his wife."

Genba clenched his fists and started forward, but Ohiro snatched his arm. "No, Genba. Please, no! You'll make things worse."

She was right.

"Mind your tongue," he growled at the sergeant. "What do you want?"

They still sniggered. The sergeant fished a piece of official-looking paper from his sleeve. "You, Genba, and you, Ohiro, are both under arrest for the murder of the businessman Tokuzo and the theft of his gold and his contracts with the women belonging to his house." He folded it and returned it to his sleeve. "Chain them!" he ordered his men.

Genba pulled Ohiro closer and stepped back. "There's some mistake. That matter's been cleared up."

It did no good. The constables wrapped them in chains in a moment.

Genba did not fight them. He pleaded with the sergeant, "I didn't kill him. And Ohiro wasn't anywhere near Tokuzo's place."

"Ah! But we just got new evidence!" The sergeant grinned and pointed a thumb over his shoulder at the celebrants, who were watching anxiously from the distance. "Seems like you two stole the contracts and handed them around to the other girls."

"That's not true."

The sergeant ignored this. "Search her place," he commanded. Two of his men went into Ohiro's room. Genba thanked the Buddha Ohiro had burned the contract. Of course, the other women probably had not. Who had pointed the finger at them?

Ohiro voiced her own suspicion. "Who told you such lies about us?" she demanded.

"We'll soon find out if they were lies," the sergeant told her. "We've got ways of dealing with scum like you."

The constable emerged empty-handed. "Not there."

"Search them!"

What followed was humiliating and painful. The five constables conducted a body search of Genba and Ohiro that was both thorough and rough. In the case of Ohiro, it was also sadistic. They stripped off most of her clothes and groped her, squeezing and joking about a woman's secret places. Genba writhed helplessly in his chains, turning his wrists and ankles bloody. Ohiro bore it silently, but she wept.

They marched them away, past the crowd of silent watchers. Ohiro still half-naked, and Genba bloody and glowering. As they passed the others, the sergeant said, "We'll come back for you thieving hussies later."

14

Saburo Dismissed

Tora sat across from his master and grinned.

"So Minamoto Masaie was in the capital when his daughter died. Good work, Tora."

"Thanks, sir. It was nothing. His cook makes the best fish soup I've ever tasted." He added with a chuckle, "I'm afraid she had plans for me. I had to tell her I was married and a father. That seemed to discourage her a bit, but I'm not sure she'll keep her hands off me next time."

Akitada cast up his eyes. "No doubt you'll manage," he said dryly. "I think we may need to consult her again. Her fondness for the young woman makes her likely to be helpful. I wish we could tell her of our suspicions. What did you think of her attitude toward the father?"

"Well, being fond of the daughter, she hasn't much good to say of the father. She blames him for what's happened. And she really dislikes the brother. Says both were hateful and talked cruelly about Lady Masako after the scandal. Calling her names."

"Really? I assume the cook thinks her death was suicide."

"Yes. Says the father's to blame. Berating his daughter for failing with the emperor is what caused her to jump off the cliff."

Akitada grimaced. "She has a very loose tongue for a servant."

"She loved the girl and is very angry."

"Didn't she know about the affair?"

"She knew, but she thinks her lady's unhappiness made her a prey for the prince. She thinks His Majesty and Lord Masaie both are to blame. They didn't protect her against overeager young men, it seems." Tora smirked a little.

"The prince is my age," Akitada said dryly. "Hardly an eager young man any longer." Sitting here in his study and looking around at his father's books and his own, and at the few scroll paintings he had gathered on his many journeys, he felt that most of his life was already over. Yes, he had once been eager. But also foolish, he reminded himself. The prince, it appeared had never grown up.

"Let's call him a man in the prime of his life then."
Tora grinned at his master.

That got a chuckle and a headshake, but Akitada
sobered quickly. "The woman isn't far wrong, though.
Lady Masako became a victim when she left her father's
house and entered the imperial apartments. There's
enough blame to go around. The prince is a notorious
womanizer, as I know from a past incident. He probably forced his attentions on her. The father, on the
other hand, played politics with his daughter. And His
Majesty was openly uninterested in her. He is, of
course, still very young and cannot be expected to handle such situations diplomatically. And where was the
young woman's mother? Why wasn't she more supportive under the circumstances?"

"According to the cook, she's a timid mouse. Come
to think of it, it's surprising that a man like Lord
Masaie, who seems to keep his womenfolk in fear,
should have spoiled his daughter with so much love and
attention."

Akitada snorted. "Love?"

"Oh, Cook says he doted on her. Preferred her to
his son, taught her to ride and shoot like a man, then
offered her to the emperor. I bet when he found out
about her and the prince, he snapped like the string on
a bow."

"Well, I wouldn't call that love, but you're quite
right about the probable reaction. But would he have
killed his own child?"

Tora made a face. "Maybe. Yes, I think he might
have. Thinking she's dishonored his name or some-

thing. Or maybe he had her killed. Yes. What do you think?"

"I don't know, Tora. I'd like to meet the man. It seems inconceivable that a father could do such a thing." He thought of his own little girl and shook his head. He definitely did not want her to go to the palace when she grew up. Never. But then he was not Masaie. "But killing her didn't really prevent the scandal." He frowned, then added, "It's very interesting that he has returned to the capital, bringing only soldiers and a cook."

"Why?"

"I'm not sure. It looks as though he was in a hurry and expected trouble. But it may mean nothing. Much as your cook blames her master, it's too early to call anyone a killer."

They did not miss Genba. Everyone assumed he was celebrating by spending the night with Ohiro.

Akitada was discussing the day's chores with Saburo when he discovered that Genba had not spent the night in his room. Saburo thought he had probably celebrated by staying with Ohiro. Akitada was shaking his head at this when Tora showed in Superintendent Kobe.

Akitada saw at a glance that something unpleasant had occurred but thought of Kosehira. He told Saburo he could leave, but Kobe stopped him.

"It concerns Genba," he said in a tight voice. "He's in more trouble, and this time I frankly don't know if we can extricate him. Saburo may be helpful."

"Please sit down." Akitada looked from one to the other. "I take it this concerns the murder of the brothel keeper?"

"Tokuzo. Yes. It appears someone stole the women's contracts from his house the night after the murder. The thief may also have taken a great deal of gold. Today these contracts were returned to the women, who promptly started a street celebration that alerted the constables. When the police arrived and learned about the reason for the party, they looked for Genba and found him with the young woman he intends to marry. Given the fact that Genba had threatened the man the night before the murder for beating his girl-friend, the theft of the contracts is being laid at his door also. Genba clearly had a better motive than anyone else."

Akitada noticed that Saburo had paled. The scars on his face stood out sharply. He met Akitada's eyes and nodded his head slightly.

In view of Saburo's involvement, Akitada was at a loss for a moment. He could hardly tell the superintendent about this. It would simply suggest that Genba was the instigator.

Kobe noted both his hesitation and Saburo's guilty reaction. "I see," he said heavily. "I had hoped you two would clear Genba and the girl."

Akitada said quickly, "We have information that someone else visited the brothel last night. In fact, Saburo was attacked by this person. I think it must have been the thief."

"Really?" Kobe looked pained. "Surely you can do better than that. What were you doing there, Saburo?"

"I went to have another look at the place, sir. I thought I might be able to find out what happened." He paused and gave Kobe one of his horrible grimaces that passed for a smile. "We're a household of men curious about murders."

Kobe scowled at him. "Don't make stupid jokes. Why would you do such a thing in the middle of the night?"

Saburo wiped the smile off his face. "Nighttime is the best time for thinking about a problem, I find. And I think best by looking at a place. At night there are no distractions." He glanced at Akitada. "Perhaps I should have mentioned something I saw before I was attacked."

Kobe was clearly getting angry. "What?"

"Two people came out of the brothel. A man and an old woman. They had a key and locked up after themselves."

"If they had a key, they weren't thieves."

"Perhaps or perhaps not. I thought it interesting that the man carried a large bag. It looked heavy and clinked. Sounded like coins to me."

Kobe looked at him. "It sounds like Tokuzo's brother and mother," he said slowly. "Both claim that the thief who stole the contracts also took Tokuzo's gold."

Saburo shook his head. "Sadly, people will tell lies. If they say the gold has been stolen, they'll escape the tax collector."

Kobe stood up abruptly. "There's nothing to be gained here," he growled. "I suggest you leave Genba's case to the courts. Now you will excuse me. If I stay any longer, I might find myself arresting your entire household." He turned and made for the door.

Akitada tried to catch up. "Wait, Kobe," he called out. "There must be something that can be done."

But Kobe merely grunted and walked faster. Akitada followed him to the veranda where he stopped and looked after the superintendent as he strode toward the gate. His figure was rigid, and his every step looked angry.

Thoroughly shaken by the scene, Akitada returned to his room. Saburo fell to his knees and knocked his head on the floor. "I'm sorry, sir," he muttered. "Please forgive me. I should've told you."

"Sit up," snapped Akitada. "Seimei never behaved in that groveling fashion."

Saburo sat up. He looked ashen but said nothing.

"I take it *you* stole those contracts?"

Saburo hesitated. "Yes, but I didn't take the gold. That was taken away by Tokuzo's brother."

"It makes no difference. I will not have a common thief in my household."

Saburo's face worked horribly. He started knocking his head on the floor again.

Akitada roared, "Stop that. What in all the devils' names, possessed you to steal those contracts?"

"I tried to help Genba and Ohiro, sir. Genba is a good man. He was kind to me. And those women had a terrible life. That monster raped and beat them."

Akitada felt reproved for his anger. Saburo, who had found so little kindness in his life, had felt gratitude for Genba's kindness. Perversely, the notion that he could have been too harsh made him lash out again.

"It's not a question of motive," he snapped. "It's a question of breaking the law. When you serve in the household of someone who represents it, such behavior cannot be tolerated. You heard the superintendent just now. He was my friend and trusted me until this happened. Now he thinks me implicated in your lawbreaking."

Saburo bowed his head. "Yes. I didn't think of that. I'm truly sorry. I'll leave if you wish."

A brief silence fell.

Akitada sighed deeply. "I regret this, Saburo, but it's clear that your background simply makes you unfit for my service. Your nightly excursions will get you into some other trouble sooner or later. So perhaps it will be best for all of us if you found employment elsewhere."

Saburo bowed. "Please convey my gratitude to your lady, sir. I shall always remember you and your family for the goodness you have shown me." He rose and walked out quietly.

Akitada sat still for a long time, feeling nauseated and ashamed of what he had done. There were times when he wished his work did not lay such burdens on him.

It had been doubly hard to dismiss a cripple. Saburo's disfigurement still caused him inward shudders, and he could never quite relax around the man.

What would happen to him now? Perhaps it was his disfigurement that caused Saburo to break the law. He must feel resentment for what people had done to him and for the disgust he saw in their faces and the rejections he received when he asked for work. Akitada had felt it his duty to help this unfortunate man, but though he had tried to, he had not overcome his discomfort in Saburo's presence. He was ashamed of it, and yet his decision was just. Saburo had admitted to stealing the contracts.

Needing to unburden himself, he went to his wife's chamber.

Tamako was brushing their daughter's hair. Instantly his heart warmed to both of the women in his life. Yasuko was in her seventh year and a very pretty, fairy-like creature. Her fragility was deceptive. It hid an enormous firmness of purpose that usually got her what she wanted from her doting father. He admitted it freely. Yasuko had ensnared his heart. This reminded him of Lady Masako, the favored daughter of Masaie.

Oh, how variable had been that man's heart!

He sat down heavily to watch his wife and daughter. His wife's room pleased him as much as his study did, yet it was very different. Tamako had colorful painted screens, while he had landscape scrolls painted in ink. And here there were pretty feminine boxes and knick-knacks. A large silver mirror caught the light as Yasuko shifted it to eye her hair. Was she vain already? He put the thought from his mind as frivolous in view of his interview with Saburo.

Tamako saw his expression and stopped brushing. "What's wrong?"

"Nothing. Or rather, I'm worried that I may have done a cruel thing."

Yasuko fixed him with bright, inquisitive eyes. "What did you do, honored father?"

Tamako said quickly, "It may not be any of your business, Yasuko. Run along. I'm done with your hair."

Yasuko got up, but she was curious and not at all afraid of her father. She said, "I want to know what my honored father did. If he was cruel, then I hope I never do such a thing. But my father would never do a cruel thing, so I don't understand." She gave her father a melting smile. "Please allow me to stay and learn."

Tamako cried, "Yasuko!" She looked shocked, as if her child were some sort of changeling.

Yasuko gnawed her lip, gave her father a teary look, then bowed, and turned to go.

"No, wait," Akitada said, secretly amused by the act. "You're quite right, Yasuko, though Master Kung Fu would be shocked at your manner. He did not consider women and children capable of understanding and disapproved of their voicing such opinions."

Tamako flushed. "The old sages had some very old-fashioned notions about women," she said tartly.

Akitada suppressed a smile. He had known his comment would break the impasse between Tamako's disapproval and Yasuko's curiosity. But he was not at all sure that a seven-year-old would understand his dilemma.

"I've had to dismiss Saburo for theft," he said bluntly and waited for reactions.

Tamako cried, "For theft? Are you sure?"

Yasuko asked, "What did he take?"

Akitada explained.   He directed his account to Tamako, but Yasuko listened avidly.

Tamako, dismayed, just shook her head.

Yasuko protested. "He was helping Genba. That's a good thing, isn't it? Don't you want us to help others?"

"Yes, but we mustn't do it by breaking the law." Akitada knew that would puzzle his daughter.   She would think of it as breaking a rule, while the law was a complex and profound concept. To the child, Genba was part of their family. He added lamely, "We mustn't do so by hurting someone else. And stealing hurts someone else."

Yasuko looked stubborn. "But the man he stole from was a bad man. You said so yourself. He beat Genba's girlfriend. That's breaking the law, isn't it? Shouldn't we stop bad men from beating women?"

Akitada sighed and looked at his wife. "Yes, Yasuko. But that is why we have laws, and we must let the police take care of such matters and not have everybody make their own rules."

His daughter pondered this with a frown, then nodded. Brightening, she ran to the door. "I'll talk to Saburo and explain it," she cried and was gone.

Akitada chuckled weakly.

Tamako was still frowning. "You'll have to see what you can do for him."

He stiffened. "I cannot recommend a thief."

She looked at him. "You'll find a way."

Akitada stared at his wife blankly, then got up to leave. "I don't know how, but I'll think about it," he muttered, a little resentfully.

He went in search of Saburo, though he had no idea how to soften the dismissal. Maybe something would come to him. When he got to the room Saburo and Genba shared in the stables, he found it empty. The neat blue robe and black sash Saburo had worn in his service lay neatly folded on his bedding roll.

As he walked back to the house, he met Tora, who held Yasuko's hand. Tora's normally smiling face looked grim.

"You dismissed Saburo, sir?" he asked, anxious eyes searching his master's face..

"Yes. He stole the contracts. I cannot employ a thief."

Yasuko cried, "I explained it to Tora, Father, but he doesn't understand."

Tora said bitterly, "All he did was try to help Genba and his girl. And you know damned well how Tokuzo's been treating her and the others."

Shocked by this attack and Tora's language, Akitada glanced at his daughter. She looked back at him, unsmiling. With some difficulty, he controlled his anger.

"Tora, I will not have you use that tone or language. Especially not in front of my daughter!"

Tora flushed. "Sorry." He bent to Yasuko. "Leave it to me, sweetheart," he said. "Don't you worry, Tora will take care of Saburo. All right?"

She nodded. But she gave her father a look so filled with doubt that he was struck to the core. His own child had turned against him.

Tora was unaware of the bitter resentment that was building in Akitada's heart. "Saburo didn't steal the contracts," he said in a calmer voice. "Someone else took them from Saburo after attacking him. There's your thief."

That might be true, but Saburo had been the first thief. Akitada said nothing and stepped past Tora to head for his study.

Tora followed uninvited. They sat down, and Akitada glowered at Tora. Apparently he was still unaware of how deeply he had offended. They had all turned against him. What ill fortune had marked this day for his entire family to oppose him as if he were an ogre? Controlling his anger with difficulty, he said, "Kobe was here. He accused me of covering up for a murderer. You know I'm engaged in a very important case concerning Lord Kosehira and the prince. I relied on Kobe's help in that matter. The last thing I needed was for my people to get into trouble over conditions in a brothel."

Tora raised his chin. "Genba's important, too. And so is Saburo. What will he do now? He has no work or money. Nobody will hire him."

"I've paid him his wages. How can he not have any money?"

"He gave his savings to Genba to buy out Ohiro."

Akitada chewed his lip. They were all set on proving him in the wrong. Even Tamako had not been supportive. "What am I to tell Kobe?" he demanded.

"It seems to me," said Tora, "that you ought to find the bastard who attacked Saburo. I bet it's the same man Genba ran into in that alley outside Tokuzo's place. There's your killer. That's the man Kobe wants."

Akitada stared at him. "Someone tangled with Genba before the murder? Why didn't anyone tell me about this?"

"Because you make snide remarks when we mention the Willow Quarter."

"Tell me now."

Tora recounted the tale of the polite stranger who had dropped an assassin's needle Saburo was very eager to own, and that was taken from him the very next night along with the contracts.

Akitada followed the tale with frowning concentration. "Great heavens! Spies and assassins seem to roam the streets of the capital these days. What have we come to?" After a moment, he got up. "I'll speak to Kobe again and look in on Genba. You go back to the quarter and start asking questions about that mysterious stranger. But be careful."

Tora grinned with relief. "I'm on my way, sir."

15

Genba Takes the Blame

kitada was turned away at Kobe's headquarters. The word was that the superintendent was not there. Since it was the middle of the day, and Akitada knew Kobe to be assiduous in his duties, he had the uncomfortable feeling it was a lie. Kobe probably had decided he wanted no further dealings with Akitada.

Only once before had Akitada been forced to humiliate himself in order to conciliate the superintendent. He had been much younger then. Now such a step was utterly unpalatable.

In a gloomy mood, he went on to the jail and asked to see Genba. Here at least the news of his offense had not arrived yet. Kiyonobu, the supervisor, knew him as

Kobe's friend and a frequent visitor in the past. Besides, he had been expecting him.

The man bowed deeply. "My Lord, I regret very much this unpleasantness. Genba and the young woman have been given every consideration. Surely you'll have them released in no time. Perhaps even now?"

"Thank you, Kiyonobu. No, I don't have any good news yet, and I'm very concerned about the charges. Genba is innocent, and so is the young woman, but until we find the real killer and thief, I'm afraid I must leave them in your care."

"They'll be looked after like my own kin, sir."

Knowing that nothing in this world is free, and especially not in a jail, Akitada passed the man two pieces of silver. "This is for any costs you may have. Thank you. Your care is much appreciated."

He found Genba housed in a relatively clean cell, provided with water, and only chained by one leg so he could move around a little.

The big man greeted him with abject shame. "I have troubled you, sir," he said, getting up from the straw he was sitting on and making a very deep bow. "Oh, please forgive me for involving you in this business. I don't deserve this visit."

"Never mind, Genba. I gather it wasn't your fault. The real problem is Saburo's meddling."

Genba looked even more worried. "Saburo's only been trying to help us, sir. It was kind and generous of him, but it really was me who brought us here and caused you such embarrassment."

Akitada frowned. "No, Genba. It was Saburo who engaged in this theft. You would not have done so."

Genba's eyes grew round. "Is he in trouble?"

"I've not told Superintendent Kobe what he has done, but I've had to dismiss him."

Genba closed his eyes. For a moment he looked as if he would faint. "Oh," he muttered, clenching and unclenching his big fists. "Oh, no! Oh, what have I done?" He covered his face with his big hands.

"Calm down. He'll be fine. He managed very well before coming to us and will do so again." Privately, Akitada had some doubts on that score, but thinking about it made him feel guilty. He said more briskly, "Tora and I will try to find the mysterious man you ran into near the brothel. We think he may be the same man as Saburo's attacker. If he is, he stole the contracts, and that also makes him a suspect for the murder."

Genba nodded dully. "I feel bad," he muttered. "About Saburo. It isn't right he should suffer for me."

Becoming irritated, Akitada said, "He isn't suffering for you but for himself. He's responsible for what happened. Besides, he won't be suffering. He's not the one in jail, and he's a very clever fellow. Too clever for our staid household."

Genba hung his head. "Maybe so, but if he isn't good enough, then neither am I, sir. Besides, there's Ohiro now. I have to look after her. Maybe we'll go to the country where no one knows about her past. Yes, that's what we'll do."

"Did I hear you correctly?" Akitada stared at the big wrestler, who had grown gray and fat in his service. "You cannot be threatening to leave my service?"

Genba looked up and flushed. "Not threatening, sir. Just going away so I won't cause more trouble to you and your lady. And the little ones." Tears rose to his eyes and spilled over. "I shall miss them." He heaved a sigh. "And you, sir."

Akitada was speechless.

And angry.

Very angry.

And hurt.

So much for loyalty and friendship. They had been together for more than thirteen years, and Genba was throwing all of it away. For what? For a woman from a brothel and a former spy who had been with them a comparatively short while.

He turned on his heel and stormed out of Genba's cell.

Akitada regretted his anger at Genba almost immediately. It was really all Saburo's fault. Why had he taken the man on when he had known his background? Honesty reminded him he had also taken on Tora and Genba, and their past offenses had been more serious than Saburo's. Having proven himself wrong did nothing for his temper, but it did send him to the amusement quarter in the vague hope he might learn something there that would free Genba and his "bride" from jail. He would deal with the Saburo situation later.

By asking questions, he found Tokuzo's brothel quite easily. The exterior looked neither impressive nor clean. It was clearly just a low dive. He saw the building consisted of two parts, a lower floor that dispensed wine, and an upper floor where the harlots plied their trade, having a ready access to drunken men from below.

He grimaced. Genba's woman had worked there.

When he walked into the large room, groups of men sat around, laborers or those who worked in the markets and businesses of the capital. They were drinking and talking, when they should have been at work. A slatternly female with a flat face and small eyes approached him, staring with surprise at his formal robe and cap.

"May I be of service?" she asked, bowing deeply.

Young but not particularly attractive, thought Akitada. And certainly not clean. Still, she probably was tempting enough to the men in this room.

"I want to speak to the owner." Akitada glanced around. It had become silent, and he saw stares. "In another room."

The waitress looked confused, then bowed again. "This way, Your Honor." Swinging ample hips, she led him through the room of drinkers, down a dark hall and into a small backroom. "His Honor wishes to speak to you, Mistress," she announced, and left, closing the door behind her.

Akitada looked down at an old woman who was bent over a big ledger. Her white hair was getting thin on top. She raised her head, her mouth opening with surprise. When she began to struggle to her feet, he snapped, "Don't trouble, woman. Are you the mother of the late Tokuzo?"

She bowed several times. "Yes, Your Honor. This miserable old woman has lost the best son in the world. Oh, what will become of me?" She dabbed at her eyes with her sleeve, peering expectantly up at him.

Akitada hated officials who bullied the common people, but in this case he decided to put some fear into this woman. She was engaged in a dirty business, her son had abused the women who worked for him, and she had helped pin the murder and theft on Genba. Neither her appearance—she had sharp little eyes like black beads and a nose like beak—nor her sly manner impressed him favorably. He put on his most ferocious face.

"I'm Lord Sugawara," he informed her. "How dare you accuse my retainer of stealing?"

He saw the fear in her eyes. She collapsed to her knees and knocked her head on the desk before her. "This humble widow did not do so, your Honor."

"You lie. The police say you blamed him."

"We only told them what happened. The truth. Only the truth."

"Lies! You claimed he stole your gold, but there are witnesses who saw you and your son carrying the money away in a bag."

Her voice quavered. "Only a few coins."

"I don't believe you. As for the contracts, Genba had no reason to steal them. He had the money to buy the girl out."

She raised her head at this, bobbing another bow. "Oh. That's quite another matter then. If he wishes to buy her out, we can come to an agreement. And we'll let the police know we made a mistake." With an ingratiating smile, she added, "There. That should solve the problem. I'm so happy to be of service to your lordship."

Akitada kept his frown in place. "It doesn't excuse the false charges. As for buying the girl out, you claim you no longer have the contract."

Her expression changed to a look of cunning. "The thief took the contracts, but I can easily look up the information," she said. "We could draw up a new contract this moment." One claw like hand opened and closed in anticipation of the pay-out.

It was indeed possible, since such information was kept on file in the city offices, but Akitada balked. "You would need to prove you are your son's heir."

She blinked. "I'm his mother. He left the business to me and my other son. My other son isn't interested in the business, so I'm taking care of things."

"Hmm." Akitada looked about and frowned. "You and your son may have had good reason to wish Tokuzo dead."

She paled visibly. "Oh never! He was my son. And Kotaro loved his brother. We're grieving his death." She sobbed. "A terrible thing! Aiih."

Akitada said nothing.

Controlling her grief quickly, she returned to business. "Ohiro's a valuable girl. She's very attractive to customers. That's why Tokuzo paid fifty pieces of sil-

ver for her. And she did a fine business, so there's that
to be considered, too."

Akitada glared at her. "I hear he beat the girl black
and blue. How valuable does that make her?"

She bristled. "Ohiro stole his money, that's why.
The girls will keep back earnings they're supposed to
turn in. It's stealing, that's what it is."

"Such beatings apparently were a frequent occur-
rence."

"Not really, but some girls are greedy. There's a
great temptation to do business on the side and tuck the
money away or give it to a lover. Tokuzo was a businessman. You can't blame him for looking after his
money."

"Someone clearly blamed him. It seems to me you
should be trying to find your son's murderer quickly. If
you decide to enforce the girls' contracts, you may well
be next."

She gulped. "The police—"

Akitada snapped, "They think they've found their
man and will do nothing. Perhaps you'd better think
who else may have had a reason to hate your son."

She looked frightened now. "He was a good man,"
she protested. "A good son and a hard worker. This is
a hard business. The girls lie and cheat, and the customers get drunk and break the dishes and furnishings.
One set fire to a room. Another threw a girl from a
window. My son had to pay for the doctor. He paid
every time one of the girls got a bruise or a bloody nose.
He took good care of them. They ought to be grateful."

"Spare me. We know he beat them. This murder was violent enough to suggest a man is the killer. Who might have wanted your son dead?"

"The girls have boyfriends, and a couple are married, though it's against the rules. They may have lied about the way they were treated."

Akitada glared at her. "Names."

"You said your man couldn't have done it. Ohiro's one who might have told stories."

"Leave her out of it. She had nothing to do with this. Others?"

Eventually, she recited a fairly long list of names. Akitada told her to write them down. She did not write well, but he could make out the names and nodded.

"I didn't put down two names. They're dead," she offered. "Miyagi and Ozuru."

The fact she mentioned them last made Akitada suspicious. "Add them. How did they die?"

"Ozuru's the one the customer threw out the window, and Miyagi had a miscarriage and bled to death." She was matter-of-fact about these deaths. In her business, such events were apparently commonplace and considered part of the liability.

Disgusted, Akitada took the list and turned to leave.

"Wait, your lordship," she cried. "What about Ohiro's contract? When can we settle it?"

"I'll let you know." Akitada hoped he could avoid paying this woman a single copper coin for Ohiro's freedom.

16

Out of Work

The remnants of Saburo's savings were almost gone after he bought himself some decent clothes to replace those he had left behind. He spent most of his money on a plain gray robe of good ramie, adding an inexpensive pair of narrow cotton trousers and a black sash. It seemed like a foolish expenditure for a man without income, but he hoped it would help him find employment as a scribe.

The four years he had spent in the Sugawara household had changed him. He no longer tolerated the free and easy vagrant's life he had led before, picking up a few coppers here and there, tossed by people who averted their eyes in disgust and pity. He also no longer could face sleeping in dirty alleyways or rubbing shoulders with robbers in hopes they might offer a share in their loot for information.

He had told the literal truth when he assured Akitada he was no thief. He had never stolen anything, but he had helped those who did steal and had sometimes shared in their success. But he did not want to return to those days.

What he had done to help Genba had been another matter, though he understood his master's anger and accepted his dismissal as fair. But he would do it again. He would do it for friendship, as one friend for another—because to a man like Saburo having a friend was more precious than all the gold in the world.

Unfortunately, he had made things worse for his friend, and he must try to fix that.

He walked to one of the southern wards of the capital where he knew of several cheap hostels for travelers, but his first objective was a small, ramshackle house that took in lodgers.

The widow who owned the house was an acquaintance. She had seen worse things in her long life than Saburo's disfigured face. As one of the women paid by the authorities to clean abandoned corpses before burial or cremation, she had dealt with the bodies of newborn babies, diseased beggars, abused women, and tortured youths. Almost all of them had died by one form of violence or another. Saburo's face did not shock her.

She was too old and too fat now for such work and eked out her existence by renting out two rooms to poor laborers. She only rented to men, having found women more trouble than help. Women brought drunken men home with them, and those were likely to beat the woman and destroy a room in a rage over inadequate service or stolen money.

Saburo had helped her once when a couple of young hoodlums had taunted her. One look at Saburo's face had sent the youths running. She had thanked him. They had chatted briefly, exchanging interesting facts about their past lives.

Now he knocked at her door with his bundles under his arm. She opened, blinked, then gave him a toothless smile. "Oh, is it you, Saburo? You startled me. You look well." She peered more closely after she said this. "Maybe just a little peeked."

Saburo's heart warmed to her, and he smiled his crooked smile. In truth, he had been feeling low—very low— but the reason for that was his dismissal. He had been almost happy until then.

"Thank you, Mrs. Komiya. I'm quite healthy. I wondered if you might have a room for me."

"You need a room?" She hesitated just a moment, then nodded. "For you, yes."

"How much?"

"Ten coppers a week, but you got to keep it clean and you got to lend a hand sometimes. I'm getting old and can't climb ladders anymore or lift heavy things. My lodgers always help me."

He bowed. "A pleasure, dear lady."

That made her smile again. "Well, come in then and take a look."

The room was a mere cubby hole, just large enough for him to stretch out at night if he put his head on his bundle of possessions, but it was clean and had a separate door that led to a small vegetable patch in back of the poor little house.

Saburo deposited his bundle and shook out his new robe and trousers, draping them over an exposed rafter to smooth out the wrinkles.

"Oh my," his landlady said. "How very fine you are! Are you sure this room is good enough?"

Saburo counted out ten coppers and passed them to her. "I'm very poor. These clothes will help me find work as a scribe. If you'll have me, I'm content."

"A scribe?" She tucked away the money and made him a little bow. "I'm honored, Master Saburo."

And so it was a bargain.

Saburo asked if she needed help with anything. This pleased her. She gave him two wooden buckets and directions to a well where he could get water.

Saburo found the well, but he frightened several women and children away with his face. This brought back his depression.

Fetching water was women's work, but Saburo was long past being proud, and hauled up the water, filled his buckets and carried them back.

Having satisfied his bargain for the time being, he changed into his new clothes, retied his topknot, and set out for the city offices. There he applied for work as a scribe. His clothes got him into the office of one of the senior scribes, but there he was turned away. The man saw his face and shook his head. "Can't have you frightening the public away," he said. "And can't have you working in the back because everyone will come to stare at you. Sorry, but we serve the people and must make allowances."

Saburo did not remind him that he, too, was people. He nodded and left. During the rest of the day, he visited several other public offices with no better results. Eventually, exhaustion drove him back to Mrs. Komiya's to sleep.

The next morning, he started the process all over again. Again he was turned away. His money was almost gone, and he skipped both his morning and midday meals. He was beginning to feel quite faint when it was getting dark and turned toward the merchant quarter, thinking to buy a cheap bowl of noodles in the market before returning to his new home.

When he took a shortcut down an alley between two streets of merchants' houses, he passed the back of a rice dealer's business. Loud curses and a crash reached his ears, and he stopped, stepped on a barrel, and peered over the wall. He could see across a courtyard piled high with equipment, past open shutters into a room lit by an oil lamp. A middle-aged man was hopping about holding his foot and damning all the devils of hell. Saburo grinned. Apparently he had kicked his desk out the open doors.

He guessed the man must be the owner of the business. No employee would dare treat his master's furniture in this fashion. The merchant was portly and well dressed, and he had probably been working at the desk that now lay broken outside. Papers, a large account book, writing utensils, and an abacus also lay strewn about. Saburo took a chance.

"What seems to be your problem, friend?" he asked.

The man stopped hopping and peered into the darkness. With a scowl he asked, "What's it to you?"

"I was passing on my way to the market and heard you. If it's bookkeeping that makes you angry, I'm a bookkeeper. Maybe I can help."

The man squinted, and Saburo realized he had weak eyes. "My advice is free, if you don't mind my face," he added.

"Why should I care what you look like?" the merchant said ungraciously. "There's a gate at the corner. Mind you, I'm not paying you."

"I said it's free." The gate was low and only latched from the inside. Anyone with a long enough arm could get in. Saburo's arms were quite long enough. He crossed the yard and stopped to pick up the desk and the broken leg.

In the room, the merchant gaped at him. "Dear heaven," he gasped. "You weren't kidding about your face. What happened to you?"

Saburo gave him one of the abbreviated versions. In this one, he had been tortured by a group of robbers who had hoped to find the hiding place of his master's gold."

"Did you tell them?"

"No. I sent them off to another place. I knew the constables would catch them there."

"You escaped? You must've been barely alive." Fascinated, the merchant studied the disfiguring scars.

"Yes." Saburo set down the desk and propped up the edge missing the leg with a couple of ledgers. "Let me have a look at your accounts. What was wrong with them?"

"I caught my clerk, the young demon, in bed with my daughter and threw him out. Now I can't make heads or tails of my books."

Saburo nodded and picked up the account book. Gathering the writing utensils and placing everything on the desk, he said, "Could you bring some water, please?"

The merchant padded off.

Saburo frowned over the scribbling of his predecessor. When the merchant came back with the water, Saburo mixed fresh ink and said, "Your clerk's been stealing more from you than your daughter."

The fat merchant's jaw dropped. "How?"

Saburo showed him in entries. "Here and here." He reached for the abacus and started adding sums. "My guess is he took about twenty pieces of silver last month."

The merchant gasped. "I'll kill him."

Saburo grunted. "Where are the new figures?"

The man gathered some of the fallen papers and sorted them. He had to dictate the figures to Saburo, who entered the new information neatly, added, subtracted, and showed the result. "I might take the job," he said.

The merchant looked at the neat handwriting and nodded. Then he looked at Saburo's face and nodded again. "Why not," he said. "My daughter won't give you a second glance, and if you work out, I'll pay you a silver piece every other week."

It wasn't much, but Saburo agreed. "I'll be here tomorrow to record the new transactions."

"That will take only a few hours' work," the merchant protested.

"Take it or leave it," Saburo said, getting to his feet. "And I expect to eat here."

The man hesitated. "We can try it," he finally said grudgingly.

"Good. I'm Saburo, and you?"

"Sosuke. You'll be back tomorrow?"

Saburo nodded and left quickly by the alley gate.

Greatly cheered at having thus settled the problem of his lodging and income, Saburo continued to the market where he splurged on a meal of fried sea bream and vegetables accompanied by wine. Even the fact that the waiter seated him in a dark corner did not affect his contentment.

As he ate and drank, slowly and with enjoyment, he considered his options. The shock of being dismissed so quickly and bluntly after four years of service had not lasted long. He had been afraid it would happen. In fact, it might have happened much earlier. Saburo had always known that Sugawara Akitada, for all his generous and fair demeanor, had an absolutely rigid interpretation of the law. He had accepted it as part of his lordship's profession—much in the way in which breaking into people's homes and spying on them was part of his.

What had hurt was the fact that Saburo had tried to help Genba, and his erstwhile master had not acknowledged that. If he was to serve a man like Lord Sugawara, he should be able to use the skills that were available to him to protect the members of his family.

But here he was, and Genba and his girlfriend were still in jail. And Lord Sugawara was still at odds with Superintendent Kobe of the police. These problems must be corrected.

Saburo swallowed his last bite of fish (it had been a most delicious sea bream) and finished the last of the rice, moistened with the rest of the wine, then smacked his lips. He would not be able to live like this again for a long time. What the merchant paid him would just cover his rent and a few meals bought from noodle sellers and dumpling bakers. He needed his spare time to look for the mysterious man who had attacked him and taken the contracts.

This stranger was someone like himself, though much more dangerous. The long needle he had carried meant he was not just a spy. Saburo had never been asked to kill anyone, but he and the stranger had probably received similar training. The fact that this man had dropped the needle when he had tangled with Genba in the alley near Tokuzo's brothel suggested he was there because someone had hired him to kill Tokuzo. He had carried out his assignment but, having lost the needle, he had used cruder methods. A needle inserted through a man's ear or nostril into his brain would have caused an undetectable wound or something like a nosebleed. The death would have been blamed on an accident or some mysterious illness. Instead, the assassin had provoked a murder investigation by the police.

Why, then, had he returned to the scene of his crime to get the contracts? It made no sense.

Saburo paid the waiter, who was barely civil, conveying the message that he was not welcome in the future. Saburo refrained from giving the man a tip, and left, hearing "Hope you rot, you ugly devil!" behind his back.

It was night, but he felt strengthened by his meal and thought the time right for a visit to the beggars' guild. He returned to his lodging where he took off his new clothes, hanging them again carefully over an exposed rafter. Then he undid his bundle and took out his black pants and shirt. He missed the old brown jacket he had left outside the brothel that night, but there was no point in going back for it. Someone had long since picked it up.

That he had returned the contracts had caused Saburo to adjust his opinion of the assassin. That had been an unselfish act. Men who are hired to kill someone don't go to the trouble this man had gone to. The assassin could have sold his haul. What made him so considerate of whores?

Perhaps the contracts had been his primary objective. In that case, he had been hired either by the women themselves or by a man close to one of them.

Someone like Genba.

Saburo dismissed the thought. Genba and Ohiro did not have enough money to hire an assassin. The women who worked for Tokuzo could have pooled their savings, though. He was not happy with this idea either. Whores had rarely the foresight to save.

Who then? And why?

The attack on himself he explained by the fact that the assassin had seen him enter the brothel by the side door, and had then lain in wait and knocked him out. When he had searched him, he had found the contracts and his needle.

It was embarrassing.

Never mind. He would find the slippery bastard and have it out with him. With interest for the head-bashing.

By the time Saburo reached the abandoned temple, it was quiet and dark. The sky was overcast, and a smell of rain was in the air. Saburo slipped along the ruined galleries like a ghost. In the open areas of the big temple courtyard, two fires burned and dark shadows sat around them or moved about. A faint glimmer of oil lamps came from some of the huts and lean-tos. The beggars had come home from their labors.

The man he wanted was the giant. That was why he circled around to the ruined wing of the hall where he had regained consciousness. He thought everyone probably had their assigned space, and the giant would be in the same place as last time.

He was, or near enough. He and three old men were shooting dice for coppers by the light of two lanterns with oil lights. Saburo thought he recognized two of the players as the old men he had nearly vomited on, but he could not be sure in the murk.

"Greetings, Jinsai" he said, joining them. "I thought I'd come to thank you."

They jumped a little, then relaxed. The giant frowned. "So it's you again. Someone's been looking for you."

Saburo's heart missed a beat. Surely not the assassin. But who else would look for him here? "Really? Who? What did he want?"

"You. And when he didn't get any help from me, he asked for Bashan or Kenko. What did you tell him?"

"What did he look like?"

"Good looking. Nice clean clothes. Lots of teeth."

Tora.

Saburo's heart warmed a little until it occurred to him that Tora's errand might not have been friendly in nature. The beggars stared at him with undisguised displeasure. He said, "He's a friend who took me in. I had to tell him what happened. He doesn't mean you any harm. He likes beggars."

Jinsai growled, "You'd better be careful what you say. There are people here who get very nervous about being found."

"Sorry. I didn't know he'd come. It won't happen again."

There was a brief silence, then one of the old men asked, "Join us in a game?"

Saburo couldn't refuse. "Just for a little while."

They watched him counting out twenty coppers. "I'm a poor man," he said in explanation of the meager offering.

One of the old men guffawed. "You're thief. You'll just steal more when that runs out."

"How would *you* know what I do for a living?" Saburo demanded, affronted.

They all grinned knowingly.

"Bashan knows about these things," Jinsai announced. "He told us."

Saburo thought of protesting some more but saw it wouldn't help his case. They believed whatever Bashan told them. Bashan's service to their community had given him at least as much standing here as the priest Kenko. So he laughed it off as a joke and concentrated on the game. He was rewarded with a couple of wins and relaxed a little.

"So, Jinsai," he asked, as the dice passed to another player, "I recall you told me someone was walking away from me just before you found me. I've been thinking about that. I think he must be the one that attacked me. He stole something from me, and I'd like to get it back. So I'm hoping you'll help me find him. It was a man, was it?"

Jinsai stared at him. Then he shook his head. "I saw nothing."

"You said you saw a man."

"I saw nothing."

One of the old men snapped, "Play or go elsewhere if you just want to chat."

The friendly atmosphere had changed. He was no longer welcome. Saburo stayed a little longer, losing all of his stake, and then returned to Mrs. Komiya's.

17

The Grand Lady

Akitada had planned to speak to Kobe again, taking with him the list of suspects Tokuzo's mother had given him. Surely Kobe must agree to release Genba and his girlfriend while the police investigated the murder further.

But then Kosehira arrived in a carriage to take him to his cousin, the prince's wife.

Akitada was torn. Tora had accused him of helping his friend Kosehira before his own retainers. There was the implied charge that he, Akitada, would always prefer his own kind over a common man, even if he was part of his family. And a nobleman's retainers considered themselves part of his family, bound to him by their service and loyalty. To forget this was, in Tora's eyes, shameful.

He admitted to himself that Tora was right. He had responsibilities to those who served him. Both Tora and Genba had risked their lives fighting for him, and Tora had saved Akitada's life several times in the past. But Akitada also had obligations to Kosehira. Besides, Genba had got himself involved in the unsavory murder of a brothel owner through his own questionable pursuits.

In the end, Akitada donned his best silk robe and court hat and climbed into Kosehira's carriage. He felt guilty, but he looked forward with much greater interest to meeting Lady Kishi than to another unpleasant encounter with Superintendent Kobe.

The imperial guard was still posted at the prince's gates but they recognized Kosehira's carriage and let it pass into the entrance courtyard. When Kosehira explained his visit was to his cousin, they had no objections. A servant was dispatched and returned after a short while with the prince's majordomo, an older man with a stiff manner, wearing a very formal dark silk robe and hat.

With a bow, he announced in a high voice, "Her highness is pleased to receive you, my lord."

The carriage was backed up to the gallery of the main house. Kosehira and Akitada stepped out of its back and followed the majordomo through several halls and along some galleries to the north pavilion, the traditional living quarters of the owner's senior wife. There he threw open the carved double doors, revealing a large and well-lit room where a number of women bustled about, setting up screens and removing small children. It was a domestic scene, but one so elegant it might as well have played out in the emperor's palace.

The room's appointments were extremely rich. The screens had been painted lavishly with flowers and grasses, birds and small animals; the grass mats of double thickness had a purple silk trim; wide bands of silk brocade trimmed the green reed curtains; and all the furnishings and utensils had been chosen for their beauty and rarity.

Prince Atsuhira's ranking wife sat behind hastily assembled screens, surrounded by her gowns in fold upon fold of lustrous silk in shades ranging from deepest forest green to a pale rose. She hid her face behind a costly fan, but Akitada saw the almond-shaped eyes rested on him longer than on her cousin.

Kosehira was not impressed by pomp and circumstance. "Hello, Kishi," he greeted the grand lady unceremoniously. "I've brought Akitada. Thought you'd be curious to meet him after all the years of my bragging about him." He kicked two cushions into place and said, "Sit down, Akitada, before her eyes bore a hole through you."

"Always the same, Kosehira," said Lady Kishi in a soft voice. "Rude and unmannerly. Lord Sugawara, you must ignore my cousin. He has had no upbringing at all. Please be seated. Will you take refreshments?"

Akitada bowed, sat, and murmured a polite refusal.

Kosehira rubbed his hands. "Never mind him. Of course we want some of that good wine your husband got from Kyushu. And maybe a few of those little fried things your cook makes so well."

The lady gestured to two of her attendants who ran to carry out her command. "What brings you?" she asked. "You visit me so seldom I must assume it has something to do with the trouble you and my husband are in."

When she had turned her head to her attendants, Akitada could see her profile for a moment. All of the chancellor's daughters were considered exquisite beauties, but he saw nothing beyond a conventional appearance. Heavily made up with white paste, coal-black mascara, and painted brows, she seemed merely round-faced, though her hair was very thick and glossy.

Kosehira chuckled. "Good for you, Kishi. Get right to the point. Yes, I thought we'd better get your husband out of the muddle he's in. You seemed the obvious ally."

She raised her fan and laughed, a gentle, tinkling sound like clear water splashing over small rocks. "You know I can do nothing. I'm a mere woman. It is men who do things in this world. Women merely wait and bear the consequences."

Akitada suppressed a snort. The lady had a reputation for meddling in affairs of state. Her entire marriage had been marked by repeated efforts of putting her husband on the throne.

Kosehira would have none of it either. "You'd better rethink your position, Cousin. As your husband goes, so go you and your children. Given the fact that Atsuhira is a favorite among the people, the present charges will go away if you speak to your father and un-cles. They cannot want to damage the family's reputation further by persecuting the one potential heir who has popular support."

A clever argument. Akitada looked at Kosehira with new eyes. Even if Kishi's ambitions to become empress had been foiled, there were still her children. Prince Atsuhira had fathered two sons and a daughter with his first lady. The sons would expect court ranks, and the daughter was in line to become an empress someday.

"My husband gives little thought to his children," she pointed out with a glance at Akitada. "He spends his time mourning someone who has no claim on him instead of defending himself against these ridiculous charges."

"Precisely. With your help Akitada and I hope to wake him to his responsibilities."

Lady Kishi was silent for a long while. Then she asked, "What do you think I can do?"

Akitada decided to speak. "Your ladyship has access to the imperial apartments. Can you arrange a meeting between me and someone who was close to the Lady Masako before she left the palace?"

Lady Kishi glanced at him. Her fan moved more rapidly. "Why should I do such an extraordinary thing?"

"I believe the Lady Masako may have been murdered by the prince's enemies. If so, her friends may have useful information." Akitada had no proof of this, but it was a possibility, and the only one he could think of that might weigh with Lady Kishi."

She hissed her surprise. "Murder? How do you hope to prove such a thing? The police say she took her own life."

"The police consider the death suspicious." Akitada hoped she knew of his past collaboration with Kobe and would believe him.

There was another silence, then she said, "What you ask is impossible. No lady in the imperial service would agree to meet a man secretly, let alone discuss palace matters."

Kosehira laughed out loud. "Oh, come, Kishi. You know that's ridiculous. For one thing, Lady Masako herself managed quite well to meet with your husband."

She bristled. "What can you expect from such a person?"

"Must it be secret?" asked Akitada. "Is there not a way in which a lady might speak to me without damaging her reputation? What about Lady Masako's attendants? I assure you, I've never caused any scandals of the sort you fear."

Kosehira added, "Akitada is the most boring fellow I know. He dotes on his wife."

Lady Kishi eyed Akitada over her fan. "You have only one wife?" she asked.

Not sure if she would hold the fact against him, Akitada admitted it.

"But you have mistresses."

"No mistresses."

Kosehira cast up his eyes and shook his head.

"You see?" said Lady Kishi, turning to her cousin. "Not all men are like my husband." She paused. "That is, if your friend tells the truth."

"Oh, it's the truth, Cousin." Kosehira grinned. "He leads a very dull life. He works all day and plays with his children at night."

Somehow this little exchange, though embarrassing to Akitada, broke the impasse. Lady Kishi turned back to him and said, "Very well. I'll see what I can find out. But it will not be easy."

Kosehira clapped his hands. "I knew you had a clear head, Kishi. And, by the heavens, we're glad to have you for an ally." He rose.

Akitada also got to his feet.

Lady Kishi looked up at them. "Please understand I do this for my children and no one else."

Kosehira positively bounced with delight. He seemed to think all their troubles would now disappear in no time at all. Akitada was not so optimistic. Lady Kishi could be very helpful, but he still had no clue how or why Lady Masako had died. And until her murder was solved, he doubted Prince Atsuhira could be cleared of the charge of treason.

They parted on Nijo Avenue, Kosehira to return home, and Akitada to his office in the Ministry of Justice. He had been missing too much time from his work, and even a tolerant superior like Fujiwara Kaneie might lose patience.

He spent the next hours working feverishly through paperwork that had stacked up, dictating letters and

comments to his clerk, sending junior clerks on search-
es for documents and precedents, and reporting to
Kaneie about the disposition of a tax case..

But in the back of his mind hovered a dark cloud.
Genba was in jail and wanted to leave his service.
Saburo was homeless and would soon go hungry. His
family was shrinking, and those closest to him had lost
faith in him. What troubled Akitada most was that both
Genba and Saburo had put their trust in him, and he
had disappointed them.

When it was getting dark enough to light the oil
lamps, Akitada's patience and his back rebelled. He
got up and stretched. Then he gave his clerk instructions for the next day and left for the jail, hoping to reassure Genba of his support.

He was not allowed to see him. The supervisor
looked apologetic but said he had orders not to allow
visitors in the future.

This sent Akitada to Kobe's office. The superintendent was in, but Akitada spent some time waiting in
the corridor. The experience humiliated him and
proved their changed relationship. Kobe no longer
treated him as a trusted friend but rather as a suspicious
character whose rank did not require any courtesies.
But Genba's fate was more important than his pride,
and Akitada said nothing about the delay when he finally found himself face to face with Kobe. Kobe had also
been working late and looked irritable.

Not a good beginning.

Akitada said somewhat stiffly, "Forgive the interruption, but I have some new information about the murder of the brothel keeper Tokuzo."

Kobe stared back, unsmiling. "Yes?"

"I have spoken with his mother. She admits now there was no theft of gold. Only the contracts were taken. She also supplied a list of names of several women who worked for her son and had been mistreated. These women and their male friends or husbands had good reason to want Tokuzo dead." He pulled out the list and handed it to Kobe. "I think the police should investigate these people. The killer might be among them."

Kobe frowned at the scratches Tokuzo's mother had produced. "In that business, you always find people with grudges," he said, dropping the paper on his desk.

Akitada bristled. "You mean you'll do nothing to solve the case?"

"Not at all. We have two suspects, and we aren't finished interrogating them."

Akitada gasped audibly at this. "You are torturing Genba to get a confession?"

Kobe glared. "I don't like your choice of words, Lord Sugawara. We do not use torture."

"You used to. Why should I think you won't do so again?" Akitada clenched his fists and took a step forward. "This is not some thief or robber you've arrested. This is Genba. You know Genba isn't violent, and Genba doesn't lie. He will not confess to a crime he didn't commit. If you keep beating him to get a confession, you will be torturing an innocent man."

Kobe turned away. "We have nothing more to discuss, and I'm very busy."

"I want to see Genba. They turned me away at the jail. Your orders?"

"For the time being. Good night, sir."

18

A New Ally

Akitada was too depressed to spend the night with Tamako. He did not want to talk about the way he felt, and he would have to do that if he told her about his visit to Kobe. Therefore he pretended to have brought work home with him, sat late in his room, and eventually spread some bedding there for the night.

He slept poorly and was up again at dawn, pacing the floor and turning over in his mind all sorts of impractical schemes for rescuing Genba. He was impatient to speak to Tora, to see if he had been able to find Saburo.

Eventually, he could not wait any longer and went to look for him. To his surprise and irritation, Tora and Yuki, his son, were kicking a football back and forth as if they didn't have a care in the world. He did not think it was proper to discuss Saburo or Genba before the child, so he glowered and said pointedly, "Good Morning."

Tora dropped the ball, which made Yuki claim victory.

"I didn't know you were up already." Tora looked apologetic.

Good.

Yuki, flushed with triumph and in the knowledge that Akitada was quite fond of him, cried, "Sir, will you play? It's no fun with just two players. Oh, and can Yasuko come and play?"

Akitada prided himself on his skill at *kemari*, but football was a man's game. Why would his dainty little daughter be expected to play? "Yasuko surely doesn't know how to play," he said.

"Oh, but she does," cried Yuki. "She's almost as good as I am."

Akitada smiled and was about to explain that boys and girls played different games, when Tora said with a laugh, "She's better. She beat you soundly the other day, Yuki."

Akitada looked at them blankly, "I had no idea." Suddenly he was aware of how little time he spent with his children. He saw the eager face of the boy and said, "Well, let me go see if she's up."

She was. Squealing with delight, she took off her skirt and, dressed only in shirt and trousers, ran off to join Tora and Yuki.

Tamako sat before her mirror and smiled. Akitada said, "I didn't know she played *kemari*. Do you approve?"

"Why not? They are children. Children should run and play as much as possible."

"But she's a girl."

Tamako raised her brows. "I don't think kicking a ball is beyond her capabilities."

"Perhaps not, but is it . . . seemly?" He thought of Lady Masako, who had been taught a man's skills by her father and lost her chance at becoming an empress.

Tamako said firmly, "Of course. They're at home and not in the street outside."

Akitada left, shaking his head. To his amazement, Yasuko proved an agile and skillful player.

But the game with Tora and the children depressed him further. He had not had any vigorous exercise for some time and was quickly out of breath, dropping the ball several times. The thought crossed his mind that he and Tora should practice with the fighting staffs again.

But of course more serious matters lingered in the back of his mind.

Eventually, they left the children to their own play and went to Akitada's study, where Akitada asked, "Any news of Saburo?"

"No, sir. I've searched the markets and even went to the beggars' lair. I thought he might have gone back there because they took him in."

"Yes. Good point. And?"

"Nothing, sir. They clammed up and told me I was unwelcome. Some crazy old man in women's clothes sent you a message, though."

"Really? Did you talk about me?"

"No. Didn't mention you at all. That's what's so crazy."

"What's the message?"

"Those who wait get what others leave behind."

"Is that good or bad? What do you think he meant by it?"

Tora grinned. "No idea. As I said, he had on women's clothing. Lost his mind, I'd say. One thing about those beggars, they've got all sorts of respect for old people. You should've seen how they bowed to the old geezer, bringing him food and drink and asking him how he was feeling."

"Yes, there's good in all people." Then Akitada thought of the police lashing Genba to get a confession. "Well, most people," he corrected himself. "So you got nothing?"

Tora shook his head. "I'll go back, if you like, but they didn't want anything to do with me. It was almost like they were protecting Saburo."

"Maybe," said Akitada. "He may be among them, and they think he's in trouble. Remember, Saburo stole those contracts."

"That wasn't stealing," Tora said. "He was returning something that belonged to Ohiro and the other women. Tokuzo owed them, what with all the beatings and rapes."

"In the eye of the law, it was stealing. For that matter, the killer may have acted for the women also. Does that make the murder acceptable?"

Tora frowned. "Maybe."

"Well, he may cost Genba and Ohiro their lives."

Tora nodded glumly. "We've got to find him."

"If Saburo is right that he is a hired assassin, finding him won't be easy or safe. I suggest we start at the other end and find out who hired him." Akitada told Tora about the list of names Tokuzo's mother had given him, and that was now in Kobe's hands. "Kobe may or may not investigate those women. I have no reason to think he'll do anything I ask him to do."

"I'm sorry, sir. I know he was your friend."

"Never mind. I think you'd better go back to the women who worked for Tokuzo. Talk to them. Find out who was mistreated, and if they have male family members or lovers who might have taken revenge."

"My sort of work," Tora said approvingly. "I'm on my way."

Akitada sighed.

Having made a start on Genba's problem, he returned to his duties at the ministry with a lighter conscience. Tora would get the information, and they could interview the women. Even if the "assassin" was not the killer, surely enough information about Tokuzo would emerge to find another suspect. Akitada had no sympathy for the victim or his relatives, but he could not allow Genba to be convicted for something he had not done.

In Kosehira's case, getting the assistance of Lady Kishi would set things in motion there. He was convinced that Lady Masako's death was connected with the events preceding her death.

By the end of the day, some of his hopes were dashed. A messenger had arrived with a letter. It was from Kosehira, and it was bad news. He had been ordered back to his province. Kosehira said nothing else beyond the usual closure of good wishes for Akitada and his family. It was ominous and suggestive. The fact that he gave no explanations meant he expected his letters to be scrutinized. It was a warning to Akitada that their interest in the prince and Lady Masako had become known in the highest places, and action was being taken to stop them.

Had Lady Kishi betrayed them?

The more Akitada thought about this, the less likely it seemed. Her fortune was tied too closely to the prince's for her to cut those ties and join his enemies. Yes, he had provoked her anger with his many affairs, but Kishi was a practical woman.

Obviously someone objected to the questions he and Kosehira had been asking, and ordered Kosehira back to his post. Would they approach him next? Very probably. And he did not have Kosehira's connections and had a reputation for meddling.

With a sigh, Akitada went to see his wife to inform her of developments.

Tamako listened calmly. "Well, we knew it might come to this," she said. "How will you proceed?"

Akitada's heart warmed to her. How brave she was! And how lucky he was that she supported him in his decisions.

"I think I'll go on without Kosehira," he said.

"Yes. But what will you do? Without Kosehira, you may not have access to the people who are involved."

"Lady Kishi has promised to help."

"Really? That's good, very good." Tamako looked thoughtful. "I wonder who knew about the prince's affair. She evidently did. Was his whole household aware? The other wives?"

Akitada had considered this, but the prince's lack of cooperation had closed the door to asking questions of his household. And Lady Kishi was not likely to approve of such investigations either. If the guilty party was to be found within the prince's family, she would suppress the fact at all cost.

"I don't know," he said. "And I have no way of finding out."

"Why not ask Akiko? She knows Kishi."

"My sister? Dear gods! You can't be serious." Akitada was shocked at the idea. He had not spoken to Akiko in several months. Mostly she irritated him. Of his two sisters, Akiko, the older, had inherited her mother's social-climbing ways. She had spent most of her time promoting her husband Toshikage, a harmless and friendly brother-in-law who was besotted with his wife, in his rise in the government. Toshikage had had several rank promotions and now served in the imperial guards as a captain. There was nothing in the least martial about him, but such positions tended to be purely honorary while carrying very tangible salaries.

Tamako smiled. "Yes, your sister. She'll jump at the idea. Akiko is a natural-born snoop. Her curiosity about other people's activities never sleeps, and the more highly placed the person, the more interested she'll be."

Akitada frowned. "That may be true, but I cannot risk having Akiko meddle in this dangerous affair. Akiko doesn't have the sense to protect herself or anyone else."

"I think you're wrong." Tamako reached for her writing box. "I'll send her a note, asking her to come. It's time you saw your sister again anyway."

"I wish you wouldn't."

"We'll talk to her together."

It was a pity that of Akitada's two stepsisters it should be Akiko who lived near them. Tamako saw her frequently because their children played together, and because Tamako tolerated Akiko's temperament a great deal better than Akitada, who bristled every time some remark by Akiko reminded him of his stepmother.

His other sister, Yoshiko, was married to a commoner. Her husband Kojiro had been a suspect in a murder case, and Yoshiko, a gentle and loving young woman and Akitada's favorite, had scandalized her brother by carrying on a secret love affair with him. Now they lived in Nagoya in distant Owara province, where Kojiro had become a large landowner and local dignitary, thereby proving that status could be flexible when a man was inspired to prove his worth to the woman he loved.

But it was Akiko who showed up later that day, having received Tamako's message. She was accompanied by her maid and her little daughter, looked excited, and breezed by Akitada with a rustle of rich silks, a flash of a smile, and a "Greetings, big brother!" as she headed for Tamako's quarters.

Akitada followed more slowly. Unquestionably, Akiko was a handsome woman, though some of that was due to her attire which must cost Toshikage a small fortune. He much preferred Tamako's unpretentious beauty, or even Yoshiko's gentle face and small, quick figure.

A bustle and chatter over the children, Akiko's clothes, and Tamako's new screen ensued while Akitada stood by impatiently. Eventually, the children left to play outside, and the adults sat down.

"So," said Akiko briskly, "I hear you need my help, Akitada?"

"Well . . .." Akitada shot his wife a look, wondering what she had written in her note. "I wondered if you could ask a few harmless questions. It's easier for a woman to do this. And the information would be helpful in a case I'm engaged on."

"Dear heavens! My stiff and superior brother asks *me* to help in one of investigations? How can such a thing be? You've never given me credit for my good sense before."

Akitada blushed. "Not at all, Akiko. You exaggerate."

The two women laughed. Tamako said, "You've mentioned knowing Lady Kishi quite well. It occurred to me that you might be able to find out some things from her."

Akiko's brows shot up. "Lady Kishi? Of course. Dear me, Akitada, you *are* playing with tigers these days. Don't tell me you're trying to save Atsuhira again."

"Not exactly. Kosehira got himself involved, and they want to drag him down also. The prince is probably innocent, but he won't lift a finger to save himself. He mourns the death of a lover."

Akiko's eyes shone. "Ah, the emperor's woman! I never believed that silly tale about her death from some sudden illness while she was visiting her old nurse. It just made people believe she was giving birth and things went badly."

Tamako nodded. "I thought the same thing. I wondered if it might have been the emperor's child."

"Never!" Akiko was emphatic. "His Majesty thought her too ugly to have near him. He demanded that she was to be seated in the background on all occasions they attended together."

"How cruel! Did she know?" Tamako looked shocked.

"How could she not know?"

Akitada had followed this exchange with wrinkled brow. Was nothing secret these days? Apparently the most private palace matters were common gossip among women.

Akiko turned to him. "So, was it murder? Was she given poison?"

He said, "No. She was found at the bottom of a cliff. Please don't ask for details. At least not yet. What does Lady Kishi have to say about the death?"

His sister pouted.

"Come, Akiko," her brother pleaded. "All that is required is that you visit Lady Kishi and chat about her recent troubles. When I saw her, the room was full of women and children. They withdrew when we arrived, but no doubt they'll stay for you. That household knows more than we do. Please try to find out something. Anything."

"If you're trying to pin the girl's murder on Kishi, you can forget it," she said, chin in the air. "She's absolutely innocent and my friend. I'll not help you make her life even more hellish."

"Hellish? Come, that's surely an exaggeration."

"She's desperately unhappy. Her husband doesn't care for her, merely doing his duty now and then, and he has stopped that also. Meanwhile, he carries on affairs with totally unsuitable women, and makes no effort to look after the future of his children."

Akitada was scandalized again by the intimate gossip that seemed to pass between women. He glanced at Tamako, saw her mouth twitch with amusement, and turned back to Akiko. "I thought she was the one who created most of their difficulties. For example, why does she have to keep agitating to make her husband a crown prince when he's not interested?"

Akiko said, "Because she's a mother, silly."

"Nonsense. Her children are guaranteed the highest positions."

"Not if he divorces her."

Akitada was dumfounded. "Divorce her? Why would he do a thing like that? She's the chancellor's daughter and has given him sons."

"Don't ask me why. Who knows why men do stupid things?"

Tamako broke in, "Please don't quarrel. There's work to be done."

They fell silent and looked away from each other. Akitada wondered if Akiko could be right. Would Atsuhira have divorced Kishi to make Lady Masako his senior consort? He had claimed to have loved her passionately, and there would have been a child. Since Atsuhira had no wish to ascend the throne someday, he might well have rid himself of a wife who had made his life difficult with her ambitions.

And that would give Kishi an excellent motive for murder.

19

Tora Investigates

Never one to hold a grudge for long, Tora walked into town in a very forgiving mood toward his master. He had sent him on an errand of the kind Tora particularly relished and had done so without the usual biting remark about Tora's past weakness for pretty women. Perhaps he was trying to make amends for having dismissed Saburo and relegated Genba and Ohiro to the ranks of outcasts.

Saburo was still lost, but he was a resourceful character and would manage. Their paths were bound to cross sooner or later. Tora ached to learn some of Saburo's more dubious skills. His sleuthing and spying talents, in his opinion, were wasted on secretarial duties. Breaking into houses to spy on suspects, on the other hand, was a skill worth cultivating if one was engaged in tracking murderers.

But Genba's case was worrisome. Tora had no illusions about the miseries of being jailed. It had happened to him. The floggings could get very nasty. And the falling-out between his master and Superintendent Kobe meant that Genba could not expect any protection from that quarter. His master's anger had been reasonable in that regard.

He reached the Willow Quarter feeling cheerfully optimistic. Tokuzo's brothel was already open for business. Tora had decided that it would be a great deal easier to get the list of names replaced by Tokuzo's mother than to search for the women on his own. Besides, he wanted to find out what she was like..

Since it was still well before the midday rice, the downstairs room of the Sasaya was nearly empty. A very young and pretty girl came to ask what she could bring him. He eyed her appreciatively and asked, "How old are you, little charmer?"

She blushed, not a common reaction among the women employed in the quarter. "Thirteen, sir." She paused, then blushed even more furiously. "I'm not allowed to work yet."

"Well, aren't you a waitress?"

"Yes, but . . ." She cast a glance toward the ceiling. "The mistress says I need more training."

Tora nodded. "Like going to school, right?"

She giggled.

"Well, tell your mistress I'd like to speak to her. It's about Ohiro."

She ran off, light-footed like a child, but already with that seductive little motion of her slender hips. Tora shook his head.

She reappeared quickly and took him to a backroom where a thin old woman was working over a ledger. Tora looked Tokuzo's mother over and decided he did not like her. This did not prevent his greeting her with his friendliest smile and most affable manner.

"Ah. The lady of the house looks as charming as her girls."

She eyed him with a frown. "The girl said you've come about Ohiro."

Tora sat down across from her, giving her the full benefit if his brilliant smile. "I'm Tora, Lord Sugawara's assistant. He sent me to tell you he's working out an arrangement."

The frown disappeared and she positively beamed. "Fifty pieces of silver, your master said. And cheap at that. Do we still have an agreement?"

"I expect so." Tora glanced around the room and at the account books and writing utensils. "I bet you have a lot of trouble running this business. Didn't Tokuzo have a brother?"

She sighed. "It's a lot of work, and I'm an old woman," she shot him a glance, "no matter what pretty lies you tell me, young Tora."

"Never say that! There are men who appreciate a mature female. A good woman is above the price of pearls. But you shouldn't have to slave away over dusty books and deal with rowdy drunks. I would have expected Tokuzo's brother to look after the Sasaya. It must be a good business."

"My other son is an official. He likes the money well enough, but he doesn't want to dirty his hands." She managed to sound both resentful and proud.

"Then I bet you're better at the business than he is."

She chuckled at that. "Maybe. So what's on your mind, Tora?"

This was moving too fast in the wrong direction. Tora said, "Here's the problem: before we can do the business with Ohiro, we'll have to get her and Genba out of jail. My master's passed the names you gave him to the police, but I thought we might speed up things if I went and asked those girls a few questions myself."

She looked a little disappointed but nodded. "Be my guest. I'd like to know who my enemies are. I've been thinking, and the most likely are Ona and Hanishi." Her smile was gone, and she looked almost witchlike. "Ona's the one Tokuzo caught passing her earnings to a boyfriend. And Hanishi was always causing trouble with the customers. I wouldn't put it past them to be behind my poor Tokuzo's death." She waved a finger at Tora. "Get whoever did it, Tora, and you'll do a good deed."

Having obtained detailed directions to the girls' lodgings, Tora decided to see Shokichi first. He caught her just as she returned from washing clothes in a nearby canal. She had shared quarters with Ohiro and was her friend, so he expected to get help from her.

Shokichi was a tall girl and would have been hand-some except for her pockmarked face and crooked teeth. Life in the brothel had hardened her, and she eyed Tora with suspicion. His big smile and flirtatious manner got no response. He decided to plunge right into the reason for his visit.

"You must be Shokichi, Ohiro's friend," he said. "And I'm Tora, Genba's friend. Let's see if we cannot put our heads together and help them."

Shokichi relaxed, invited him into the poor lodging, and poured him some cheap wine. He drank, smacked his lips, and said, "We need to find the guy who did away with that Tokuzo scum. Any ideas?"

She shook her head. "That bastard. He had more people hating him than there are flies on a dead dog."

Tora grinned. "Good. How about his girls?"

Her face closed. "No. They wouldn't have dared."

"Maybe not, but can you be sure? Did he beat you?"

"Of course, but I can take it." She squared her shoulders and lifted her chin. "The scum didn't make *me* cry and plead."

"Good for you. But others weren't that strong. What about Ona and Hanishi, for example?"

"No. They're like me. Used to it." She turned away. "But not all the girls are like that. The animal nearly killed a couple. And one he did kill."

Tora asked quickly, "Which one?"

"What does it matter?" Then she turned back to him, her eyes wide. "I think Miyagi came back as a ghost."

The spirit world held many terrors for Tora. He knew the souls of people who had died violently or been wronged in their lives could not find rest after death and sought out the living who were responsible. But Tokuzo's wounds had not been left by a ghost. Still, the killer could have been sent by the dead woman's ghost. "Really? What happened to Miyagi?"

"It was terrible. Miyagi was still very young. Only fifteen, and she got pregnant. Maybe she wasn't careful. But Tokuzo had just bought her and paid a lot, and now she wasn't going to make any money for him. So he made her drink medicine. But all that happened was that she got real sick. And soon the men could see she was pregnant and left her alone. One night Tokuzo took her back to his room. I don't know what he did, but she started bleeding. Only she didn't stop, and the next morning she was dead."

Tora shuddered. It was surely enough to make Miyagi become an angry ghost. "She have any family?"

"Her grandparents came to bury her. Tokuzo paid for the funeral, and they thanked him."

Well, most likely then they would not have hired a killer. They must be poor. And that would be true of the rest of the women. Tora was becoming discouraged. "Did anyone else die?"

"Only Ozuru. One of the customers threw her over the railing. She broke her back."

That could not be laid directly at Tokuzo's door. "Listen, Shokichi, could the women have pooled their savings and hired an assassin?"

Shokichi laughed bitterly. "No. Ohiro and I, we were always talking to the others about ways of getting out of our contracts. They liked the idea but we didn't know anyone who would do it."

"I expect some of the women have lovers or husbands. Or brothers. Could one of the men have killed Tokuzo? The way he was mistreating them, surely someone got angry enough."

Shokichi looked away. "The men are cowards, and the girls don't tell their families. They're too ashamed."

Nothing.

With a sigh, Tora got up. "The girl Ozuru?" he said. "Where was she from?"

"Yasaka village. I went to her funeral. Tokuzo allowed some of us to go. I think he wanted us to think that it wasn't his fault."

"Why didn't one of you tell the police? Or at least the warden of the quarter?"

"The police?" Shokichi snorted. "You forgot what happened to Ohiro?"

Tora said nothing.

"The warden knew. You've got to report deaths. But who's to prove it was Tokuzo's fault?"

Tora nodded. She got up, a tall, slender girl. Not pretty, but he saw character in her face. "Are things better now?"

"A little. The bastard's mother is just interested in the money. She doesn't beat us. I swear he got his kicks out of hurting women."

Tora nodded. "Well, I'll go talk to Miyagi's people."

"She grew up here. I'm not sure where. She was a timid thing. Real quiet. You'd have thought she was a nun the way she kept her eyes down and wore nothing but dingy clothes. Tokuzo beat Ozuru, too, but it was a customer who threw her over the railing. He said she was stealing his money. I never believed that. If he'd said she was a dead fish in bed, it would've been different."

Something about Shokichi's description made Tora pause. "Who would know about them? Tokuzo's mother?"

She nodded. "Or the warden. We're all registered there."

"Right. I forgot. Thanks, Shokichi."

She came to the door with him. "Good luck, Tora."

The warden of the quarter was a new man. He eyed Tora coldly but eventually provided an address for Miyagi, along with the information that her death had been listed as the result of illness, and Ozuru's as an accident. "The owner said she was drunk and fell down the stairs."

Tora grimaced, muttered, "Why doesn't that surprise me?" and left.

Miyagi used to live in a very staid neighborhood of small neat houses, built close together to conserve space. A fire trap, thought Tora, but there were signs that the people who lived here were aware of the danger. He saw buckets at every door and water barrels at every corner. Clearly, they were looking out for each other. He eyed the house the dead woman had lived in. Somehow it did not look like the family was desperate enough to sell their daughters as sex workers. He walked through the small gate and knocked.

A young woman with a baby on her hip stuck her head out of the door.

Tora bowed. "Please forgive the trouble. I'm looking for the family of a young woman called Miyagi."

She smiled at him. Tora almost always got smiles from women. "Miyagi? No. Never heard of her. You could try the next street."

But Tora knew he had the right place. "Have you been here long?"

She shook her head. "My father-in-law bought the place from some people called Satake. About a year ago. But they were just two old people."

Tora thanked her and asked for the warden's house. It was two blocks away, and the warden was on his roof, repairing some wooden boards held down by large stones.

"Satake?" he asked, peering down at Tora. "Yes. The old people sold the house. They left and I heard they've both died. Him first, then the old lady a little while ago. Very sad. Why do you want to know?"

"Just checking the tax register," Tora lied and gave the man a wave.

This trail had ended, and his next call required a horse. He would have to ride all the way to Yasaka village in the foothills to find out if Ozuru had any living relative who might have taken revenge for her death. He wasn't very hopeful, and returned home.

20

An Answer of Sorts

Saburo returned to the beggars the following night. He found the priest Kenko in a corner of the temple ruins that served as the beggars' place of worship. The reason he found it was that Kenko had lit a number of candles and was dusting the altar. He had evidently salvaged odd pieces of statuary and religious objects from the rubble and set them up on a broken table covered with pieces of silk and brocade. The effect was at once flamboyant and sad, but the flickering lights lent the arrangement a certain eerie sparkle.

Saburo bowed deeply several times, first to the chipped Buddha presiding in the center of the arrangement, and then to the priest.

"Forgive me, Reverence," he murmured.

"Ah, Saburo," said the old man, turning. He wore a multi-colored surplice over the red silk gown and a green trouser skirt. Like his altar, he was a colorful sight, though all the garments were sadly wrinkled, stained, and even torn in places. "You've come back to us. Will you stay?"

"Sorry, no, Reverence. I have found work and a place to live. But I need some help."

"All of us need help," said Kenko, frowning. "It sounds as though you manage better than most of us. How then can I help you?"

"The man who attacked me committed a murder. My friend and his wife are now in jail because the police think they did it. I must find the real killer. Jinsai saw him, but he won't tell me about it."

Kenko said nothing. He stood quite still and looked away into the night, cocking his head as if he were listening. Saburo heard nothing and thought the old man might be hard of hearing or had somehow drifted off into some meditation. He said a little louder, "Reverence? Did you hear me?"

"Buddha hears all, but not all requests are answered."

Saburo was getting angry. "That isn't just. You must tell Jinsai to help me. Buddha cannot let the innocent suffer for the guilty. What sort of faith is that?"

Kenko looked at him. "You were a monk once; you tell me."

Saburo hissed in frustration and flung out of the makeshift Buddha hall.

As he headed toward the street, he almost collided with Bashan. The blind masseur was entering the ruined temple compound with his medicine case strapped

across his broad chest. His shaved head gleaming faintly in the light of the distant fires.

They stopped simultaneously. Then both bowed,
smiled, and passed each other, Bashan tapping his way
with his staff.

As Saburo headed for his lodging, he wondered if
he should have thanked the man. But Bashan had
seemed in a great deal of hurry. Perhaps he had been
called to someone who was sick.

Back at Mrs. Komiya's, he lay down on his bedding
and fell deeply asleep.

The next morning, he woke to a realization. His
failure to elicit information from the beggars and their
priest could only mean one thing: they were protecting
one of their own. He felt angry about this. The assassin had taken advantage of him, left him with a sore
head, and was responsible for the trouble his friend
Genba was in.

But he could not think of any way to get the beggars
to talk.

He got up and did Mrs. Komiya's chores. He carried in wood, fetched more water, swept outside her
front door. Then he peeled some vegetables. As a re-
ward, she gave him a bowl of gruel.

He put his good clothes back on and set out across
the city to the Sugawara residence. The gate was closed,
and all was quiet within. They must be strapped for
servants by now. He prepared to wait for Tora. Someone—and he hoped very much it would be Tora—must
soon appear to do the day's shopping.

I. J. Parker

He was proved right. After a short time, the small gate set into the large one did indeed open, and Tora stepped out. He did not have the cook's basket, however, and set off at a determined pace. Saburo hurried after him.

When Tora heard running steps, he swung about, an arm half raised against an attack. But seeing Saburo, he dropped it and instead flung both arms about him for a powerful hug. "Where have you been, you slippery bastard?" he scolded, grinning widely. "You've given me no end of trouble, brother."

Saburo gasped for breath but smiled. Being called "brother" warmed his heart, but he asked coolly, "Oh? What did you want?"

"Don't be so cursed proud. I wanted to make sure you were all right. The master's already sorry he sent you away." Tora stepped back and eyed Saburo through narrowed eyes. "You look very fine for being out-of-work and homeless. I looked for you among the beggars."

"I heard." Saburo sniffed. "So that's what you think of me? No good for anything but begging in the streets? I'll have you know I already have another job and a place to live. No, it's not among the beggars." In truth, Mrs., Komiya's backroom was not a great deal better, and his job paid barely enough to keep himself alive.

Tora's face fell. "You've found another place already? You don't want to come home?" he asked.

Home?

Saburo relented. "We-ell," he admitted, "I might be open to other offers."

In the silence that followed, Tora eyed him suspiciously. "You're putting me on," he accused. "I would've thought you'd want to help us get Genba out."

"I do. How is he? I've been trying to find the man he ran into outside the brothel. I think he's the one who killed Tokuzo and knocked me out. The beggars told me you were asking about me."

"They told me nothing. What did *you* find out?"

Saburo shook his head. "Same here. And that means they know who he is. He's one of them, and they're protecting him."

Tora whistled. "So that's it. We'll make them talk."

"I don't think we can. I wish we could talk to Genba again. I don't remember anything about my own run-in with the fellow."

Tora brightened. "I want to see Genba, too. Come on, let's see if we can get in. I know a guard who might swing it for us. This sort of thing used to be easier when the master and Kobe were still friends."

Saburo muttered, "That's my fault."

"No, nobody's fault. It's just the way things are sometimes. It's happened before. The master and Kobe, they're both as stiff-necked as they come." He chuckled. "If it wasn't for low-lives like us, nothing would ever get done. In this world, you've got to bend with the storm, or you break."

"That's true enough, but you can't build houses from bamboo. I deserved what I got."

"Never mind arguing about it now. Let's see what we can do at the jail."

At the jail's main gate, Tora asked for Gonjuro and was pointed in the direction of the jail's kitchen. Gonjuro, a short man with a round belly, was slurping down a bowl of soup. When he saw Tora, he held up the bowl. "Hey, Tora. Get you fellows some soup? It's had a bream dipped into it and is pretty tasty."

Tora laughed. "No, thanks, Gonjuro. Too early for the midday meal, and you look like you should skip a few."

Gonjuro finished his soup and patted his belly. Then he caught a better look at Saburo, and his jaw dropped. "Great heaven," he gasped. "What did you do to your brother?"

Both Tora and Gonjuro thought this hilarious and bent over in paroxysms of laughter. Saburo glowered.

"He's my friend Saburo," Tora managed after a moment. "As smart a fellow as you'd want to meet even if he isn't pretty. We both work for the Sugawara family. We came to see Genba. How's he doing?"

"Fine. I guess it's all right for you to see him. Lord Kobe won't let your master in any longer."

Saburo looked stricken and muttered again, "It's all my fault."

The guard looked interested but Tora said quickly, "We're just buddies. You know how it is. I'd be much obliged." He passed the guard a coin and added, "Drink to our health tonight and that things will turn out well for us."

The guard grinned, tucked the money away, dropped his empty bowl in a basket of other dirty utensils, and led the way. Inside the jail building, he took a key from a hook, told the guard, "Visitors," and proceeded down a long row of cell doors. He stopped halfway to a chorus of shouts from other cells and let them in. "I'll be just outside," he assured them and locked them in.

Genba staggered to his feet, his face breaking into a slow smile. "Tora, Saburo! How good to see you. I thought the whole world had forgotten me. How's everything? How's the master? And the little ones?"

"All well," said Tora. "And you and your lady love?"

Genba's face fell. "I haven't heard about Ohiro. It worries me. What if they're beating her? Can you find out something, Tora? Can you help her? She's such a little thing. She can't take it." Tears began to roll down his face. He sniffed, wiped at them, and turned away, ashamed.

Tora muttered a curse under his breath. "They won't let the master in. He tried. I'll have a talk with one of the guards. Don't worry. Ohiro's stronger than you think." They all knew the beatings well enough. Tora had tasted the bamboo himself.

Saburo shrank into himself. "It's all my fault," he said again. "Forgive me, Genba."

Genba turned and embraced him. The chain rattled softly as he moved; they had allowed him enough length to take the few steps. "No, no," he said patting Saburo's back. You tried to help and lost your place. And that's my fault, not yours. You have to forgive me."

Tora snapped, "Stop it. It's nobody's fault, but maybe Kobe's for not trusting any of us after all those years. What good is a man who has no faith in his friends?"

They all stood silent for a few moments, pondering events and shaking their heads.

"Let's sit," said Tora.

They sat on the dirt floor, Saburo carefully lifting his robe first.

"We've been looking for the killer," Tora informed Genba. "Separately. Saburo thinks he belongs to the beggars' guild. Trouble is, the bastard knocked Saburo out before he could see him. We think the man you ran into in the alley across from the brothel was the same man. What did he look like?"

Genba looked from one to the other. "You're very kind," he said, "but what will the master say if you waste time on me?"

Tora cut him off. "The master told me to find the killer. He wants you and your girl released. And Kobe won't listen unless we give him another suspect."

"And you, too," Genba said to Saburo. "When you should hate me. I lost you your place."

"Don't start that again." Tora was getting impatient. "Genba, what do you remember?"

"Oh. I'm sorry. It was night and very dark in that alley. I couldn't see his face. I think he'd tucked his chin into his collar. I saw his eyes once or twice, just sort of gleaming. He had a cloth tied around his head, like a laborer. But then he attacked me and I wrapped my arms around him and squeezed." He paused to explain, "It's a wrestling move. Takes the opponent's breath away, and without breath he loses his strength. Anyway, at that point I didn't look at him. He was shorter than me. And skinny, though he put up a good fight. Not an old man. Young and strong, but not very tall or big. No idea what his clothes looked like, except they must've been dark. Sorry. It isn't much use."

It was not much use. Saburo and Tora looked at each other and sighed.

Genba said anxiously, "The only other thing . . . he had a smell."

"A smell? What sort of smell," Tora asked quickly.

"I don't know. I've been trying to think. It reminded me of something."

"A bad smell?" asked Saburo? "Or a food smell?"

"No. Not bad at all, and not like food."

"How about sake?" asked Tora hopefully. He had once found a killer because he worked with an ingredient used in brewing rice wine.

"No, but I'd recognize it again."

Tora and Saburo did not find this helpful and sighed again.

Silence fell.

Well," said Tora getting to his feet. "We'd better be on our way. I'm supposed to go Yasaka village. That's where the girl Ozuru that died is from."

Genba frowned. "Yes, terrible story, but what has she got to do with anything?"

"Maybe revenge. Maybe nothing. The master and I thought if we could find someone who really hated Tokuzo, we could tell Kobe about it."

"The master is very kind, seeing he has his own troubles."

"You're family, Genba."

Genba hung his head and muttered something.

"What? You did what?"

Genba sighed.

"You told the master you're leaving him? You can't be serious. You can never leave him. You've sworn to protect him and his family."

"I'm no good anymore," said Genba, his voice breaking.

Tora shook his head. He looked from Saburo to Genba. "So. Both of you have turned your backs on him. For shame!" He strode to the cell door and pounded on it. "We're going," he shouted.

Saburo got up. "He told *me* to leave."

Tora just gave him a look.

The door creaked open. Behind them, Genba had gotten to his feet. "I think, "he said, "he smelled like he'd just come from the bath house."

21

The Mountain Villa

Having to wait for whatever Lady Kishi or his sister Akiko might report frustrated Akitada, who normally handled such errands himself. Since the ministries observed their two days of rest per week, he decided he would take a look at the place where Lady Masako had died. Thus, the day following Akiko's visit, he got on his horse early in the morning and set out.

It was springtime in the countryside. He had almost forgotten about that in the capital. Or rather, he had been too preoccupied with his various troubles. Now he and his horse enjoyed the gallop through rice fields still under water and ready for their first seedlings. The sun was very bright and reflected blindingly from the watery surfaces.

Akitada's spirits lifted. The sight of farmers planting their fields, ensuring rice harvests that would feed the nation, filled him with pride. It was hard and humble work, performed by poor, uneducated men and women, but it gave his country its strength. The gods watched over the rice culture, and the emperor himself worshipped them, bowing deeply to these *kami*, and praying for a good harvest every year. Surely, before such blessings, his own troubles counted for little.

When he reached the foothills, woods closed in on the narrow road, and the scent of pine and cryptomeria hung in the moist air. Bright green ferns uncurled from cushions of darker green moss, and small star-shaped flowers bloomed among them. Then the road turned rough and stony as it climbed ever more steeply into the mountains. Soon the trip became arduous for rider and horse.

Akitada's thoughts turned to Lady Masako's death and brought a feeling of danger that became more palpable the closer he came to the top of the mountain. He looked over his shoulder from time to time, but saw no one on this path. Even so, he shivered with a strange foreboding.

At a turn in the path was a small clearing, and here stood a simple hut that must be the caretaker's. On its wooden stoop an old man sat in the sun, dozing. Apparently he had not heard Akitada's approach even though his horse made a good deal of noise on the loose rocks.

"Good Morning, Uncle!" Akitada called out. It was a common form of address for elderly men. But this old man seemed ancient, and he might have used "grandfather." This time, he turned his head slightly and grunted a reply. Something about his unfocused glance told Akitada that he must be partially blind. It did not promise well for finding out who had visited the prince's villa last winter.

His horse was tired, and Akitada dismounted to let it graze beside the path. Walking up to the old man, he asked, "Are you Prince Atsuhira's servant?"

The old man blinked, cleared his throat, and asked in a cracked voice, "Who are you?"

"Lord Sugawara. A friend of your master's."

The old man reached beside him and brought forth an old kettle and a stick of wood that might have been part of a broom or rake once. With the stick, he beat on the kettle, producing high, reverberating sounds that sliced the air and sent a number of birds into flight and Akitada's horse into the woods.

Akitada covered his ears. Was the man demented? "Stop that!" he shouted.

The man put the kettle and stick down and gave him a toothless smile. Then he leaned back against the door jamb, closed his eyes, and went back to sleep.

It was hopeless. Akitada turned away. He could see the roof of the villa among the trees on the crest. How could such an old, blind, and demented man take care of anything, let alone a building easily half a mile and a steep climb away?

He shook his head and caught his horse.

He had just swung himself back into the saddle when he heard someone coming up the path and turned. An old woman was climbing toward him, bent double under a huge pile of brushwood tied to her back.

He watched her reach the hut, then stop and release the rope tying the load to her back. She straightened and looked at the dozing old man.

"What d'you want, old man?" she shouted.

He opened his eyes and pointed to Akitada.

So the banging on the kettle had brought the old woman, most likely the man's wife. Akitada smiled. They had their own ways of communicating.

The old woman had turned and now regarded him with slack-jawed surprise.

Akitada dismounted again. "I'm Lord Sugawara," he told her. "I've come to talk to you and your husband about what happened last winter and to have a look at the villa."

She said, "I didn't hear you coming up the road. Sorry, sir. My hearing's not good anymore." She glanced at her husband and chuckled. "But my eyes are still good. Between us, we manage. Nobody's been here since then. His highness and the police were here then, and a gentleman who's a friend of the master's. His highness was in such a state. How is he now?"

"Still not very well. That's why I'm here. Sometimes three pairs of eyes and ears are better than two. I suppose the police officer asked you if anyone went up to the villa the night Lady Masako died."

She nodded. "Nobody came but the pretty lady and his highness, sir. That's what I told them. It was a terrible thing, such a pretty young lady killing herself like that! And his highness never knowing what she was about."

"You expected both of them that day?"

She looked down and twisted her hands in her mended robe. "They'd come when they could. They were in love," she murmured. "You could tell. They were so much in love, so happy." She sighed and wiped her eyes.

"These visits had happened before, and you had seen them together?"

She looked up briefly, then glanced in the direction of the villa. "Four times. The first two times they came together. His highness stopped and asked us to make a fire and heat some wine he'd had brought along. Then they sent us home. The other times, they didn't come together. His highness told us to keep things ready for them, and they didn't stop but went straight up. Him on his black horse with the white patch, and her on her gray one. Both looking so handsome. Like something in a fairy tale." She dabbed at her eyes again.

She was clearly a romantic soul, but Akitada stuck to the important facts. "And the last time, the fifth time?"

"The last time was the fourth time, sir."

Well, that was very precise; she seemed to have an excellent memory. Akitada glanced at her husband, who was awake now and was watching them with a smile. "Does your husband remember it the same way?"

The old man said, "It's a busy day. Coming and go-ing." He chuckled.

"He's not himself most of the time, so you can't tell what he remembers. We're getting old. Don't know what's to become of us now."

There were more victims in this case than Lady Masako and her imperial lover. Akitada said, "I'll try to remind the prince. Perhaps he'll let you move back to the city and get someone younger to stay here."

This did not make her happy. She looked at the lit-tle hut, her garden, the trees enclosing it all, and shook her head sadly. "Needs must, I guess. Thank you, sir."

"I won't trouble you now, if the villa is open."

"If you don't mind going on ahead. The shutters in back aren't latched," she said with a glance at the pile of brush she had gathered.

Akitada got back on his horse and completed the climb to the top of the mountain. The villa was astonishingly rough and rustic.

Why would a member of the imperial family use such a modest wooden house in this desolate and inac-cessible wilderness? The Prince Atsuhira he had known, while pleasant and amusing in company, had certainly not appeared the sort of man who relished solitude and an ascetic lifestyle.

He swung himself out of the saddle and tied his horse to post. There were several of these here; clearly the prince and his visitors had all come on horseback. No carriages, wagons, or even palanquins had ascended the steep track. Over to one side of the clearing stood

an open shed. There a horse or two might have sheltered on the days when he and Lady Masako used to
meet here. Otherwise, the mountaintop was un-
touched. Birds flew through the branches of tall
cryptomerias and pines, a fox appeared from nowhere,
stared and melted into the brush again, and overhead
some squirrels chattered at Akitada's intrusion of their
territory.

It should have been remote, safe, and very private,
yet a murderer had known about the secret meetings
and lain in wait.

For the first time, Akitada considered whether the
prince might have been the real target, and that Lady
Masako, arriving early, had caught the assassin waiting.
He might have been forced to kill her because she
would have warned the prince. But why had he not
waited for his real prey afterward?

Atsuhira had been very late. Perhaps, the murderer,
shaken by what he had just done, had been too terrified
to face a night in the place where he had killed the
young woman. Most people believed an angry ghost
could not only haunt but kill the person who had been
guilty of their death.

Yes, it could have happened that way, but this did
not make his job easier. It complicated it further.

He inspected the villa first. The main door was secured with a lock. He walked around the building to
the back. Here the land dropped off, and a broad veranda jutted out. He climbed the steps and turned to
take in a vast view of hills and mountains, blue and
misty, all the way to the distant capital, which beckoned

like a golden jewel far below. No doubt, this prospect was why the villa was here, that and its inaccessibility. Had the prince brought his other women here also?

Akitada turned to the shuttered doors that ran along the back of the house. These, he found, opened easily. He flung all the shutters back to get light into the interior and entered.

The space had been subdivided with partial walls to make four rooms. The largest of these contained thick grass mats, two lacquered trunks, a few silk cushions, and a small lacquer desk evidently used to eat from, for it still held some clean bowls and ivory chopsticks. He saw also a lantern, two oil lamps, and two candle sticks with candles. A large brazier stood near the fire pit. Yes, this humble wooden house had a fire pit like any small farm house. It would have kept the room comfortable for romantic meetings in the middle of winter. The fire pit still contained charred timbers.

A thin layer of dust covered everything.

There were no painted screens here, but on two of the walls hung scroll paintings depicting deer and a family of foxes.

Akitada went to the trunks and opened them. Both contained bedding of luxurious silks and thick padding. He did not see any clothes. Apparently, the lovers rarely spent more than a few hours here.

Except for that last night when the prince had been detained.

What must have gone through Lady Masako's mind? Had she worried about being found out if she spent the night here? But perhaps it had no longer mattered. Her pregnancy could not have been hidden much longer.

Whatever Kosehira's role had been in the delay, the prince was the more to blame. He could surely have left at the usual time, had he really wanted to. This again spoke to Atsuhira's irresponsible behavior toward women he claimed to love.

Apart from the dust and a lot of faint footsteps, the room was quite tidy, except that the cushions were not stacked neatly. Instead they lay oddly scattered, as if someone had kicked them about. Perhaps Kosehira and Kobe had done this when they searched the villa. He would have to ask.

Next, he looked at the other three rooms. One must have served as a rarely used kitchen. It held supplies of lamp oil and some wood to make a fire. A barrel contained water, but dust and scum had settled on the surface. The other two rooms were uninhabited, their wooden floors bare and very dusty. Here there were also scuffed tracks. Again, perhaps Kosehira and Kobe had left these, or the caretakers, though there was not much evidence of caretaking. In one of the rooms, various wooden staffs called *bo* were stored. They were of differing lengths and had perhaps been used by the prince and his male guests for practice bouts. He was about to turn away when he saw a tiny bit of something blue moving against the white-washed plaster wall. He went closer and found a few threads of blue silk attached to a nail protruding from a support beam. A draft of air from outside had made them move. It seemed strange that someone should have walked just there where there was no door.

And then he saw a slightly darker spot on the dark wood floor a few feet away from the wall and the blue threads. He licked a finger and bent to rub at it. It came away faintly reddish brown and smelled of blood. There was very little, just a few drops and a faint smear. If he had not seen the movement of the blue silk threads, he would not have noticed them. Now he squatted beside them and glanced from them up to the threads. He wished he knew what Lady Masako had worn that night, because the image in his mind was of the young woman cowering against the wall, trying in vain to escape her attacker.

Eventually, he stood and looked once more around the room. He could not rid himself of the feeling that a violent encounter had taken place here. Perhaps it had started in the main room, where the cushions had been kicked aside. Whoever had come in had found the young woman and frightened her. She had fled, hotly pursued, and she had been cornered just here.

But, of course, it might have been altogether different. There was nothing to show when or how the blood had got there and the blue thread could have come from anything.

He left the house and walked the steep path to the promontory. It was not far and a very pretty walk among trees and boulders. He could hear the waterfall before he reached it. The rocky site gave him an excellent view of the cascade which originated in a cleft to his left and plunged down in a series of steps, each misty with white spray, until it reached a small, shallow pool at the bottom. From there the water made its way down the mountain as a burbling stream.

An ugly memory intruded, as he looked down. His pursuit of Morito, the killer of the lovely lady Kesa, had brought him to a waterfall like this one, a famous place for suicides. He had expected Morito to have killed himself in remorse and had climbed down to look for the body. Morito, too, had been involved in an ill-advised romance. Only in his case, the man had killed the woman he loved.

Could the prince have killed Lady Masako? Had she become adamant about marriage, and had he fore-seen the fury of Lady Kishi and the subsequent loss of protection he had enjoyed from the family of the re-gent? The more Akitada thought about it, the more feasible this scenario became. The caretaker couple had seen the prince arrive after Lady Masako. Perhaps there had been a quarrel, and he had lashed out. She had fallen and, thinking her dead, he had taken her to the promontory to suggest a suicide. Yes, it might have happened like that. He wished he could ask Kosehira what they had talked about before the prince had left for his tryst.

Thinking glumly about the situation, Akitada re-turned to the villa. He wandered around the house and stood looking out at the view. The solid ground con-tinued for twenty feet or so and then descended abrupt-ly.

He was not quite sure why he went to look over the side. Perhaps he wondered that the young woman had not been tossed over here, rather than from the more distant promontory. He saw right away it would not have suited the killer. It was not a precipitous drop as on the promontory, but rather a steeply stepped descent of rocky outcroppings to a depth far greater than that of the waterfall pool. Here and there, stunted shrubs and trees clung to the rock and rubble. Any of these could have caught a body heaved over the side. On this rough mountainside, the chances of the young woman's clothing becoming entangled were very high.

Besides, the idea had been to suggest suicide.

As he stood looking down at the rocky surface of the mountain, he saw a slender, polished *bo* caught in a struggling bush. It was an odd thing to find clinging to the mountainside. Even from the distance, it looked like one of the fighting sticks in the empty room.

He took off his hunting coat and started to climb down.

He reached the *bo* without too much trouble and saw it was a sword-length practice staff. Remembering the traces of blood in the villa, he leaned forward to examine it. The polish was badly chipped, showing paler wood beneath. And there on the underside, he saw what looked like a small stain as well as two or three long hairs. If it was proof that Lady Masako had been attacked with this weapon, the killer likely had rid himself of it by tossing it down the mountain.

He leaned forward and stretched out a hand to grasp it when he heard a noise above him. He looked up, saw a dark shape outlined against the sky. Then a large object hurtled down and struck his head before he could jerk away. Shocked and blinded by pain, he twisted. The rocks under his feet gave way, he slipped, arms flailing, and started to tumble down the mountain. Dirt and rocks shifted, sharp objects tore at him, and then he lost consciousness.

22

Panic

Saburo returned to his work for the rice merchant and his lodging with Mrs. Komiya. Tora went home, kissed his wife and son, and saddled a horse for the trip to Yasaka village. Genba stoically faced another interrogation. All three were in better spirits after their meeting in the jail.

Tora's journey, while pleasant enough in the springtime weather, produced little in terms of results. Yasaka village turned out to be no more than a hamlet of rustic farmhouses gathered among pine trees on a slight hill. All around them stretched rice fields, most already flooded so that the village looked like a small island in a broad sea. The road to it led along a narrow dam between fields and was almost like crossing a lake on an extremely long bridge. The notion amused him, and he felt once again the pull of the simple peasant life. How good it would be to live in such a place, peacefully, close to the land, sheltered by the gods.

Reality was otherwise: Ozuru's family was large and very poor. Theirs was the smallest of the houses and was in poor repair. The thatched roof had rotted in places and collapsed inward so that the rain had gotten in and driven the family into one corner where the wooden floor was still sound and where they lived together behind ragged straw mats suspended from ropes stretched between roof supports.

The oldest male was the grandfather. He was too old to do any work. Three boys were still young, but there were seven or eight females of all ages. They apparently did most of the work. Tora guessed the children's father had died, leaving his elderly parents and his wife to cope as best they could. It explained why Ozuru had been sold to Tokuzo. Poverty forced people to sell their daughters into prostitution and their sons into the army. He came from the same background and understood.

His questions about Ozuru met with surprise. Yes, their poor Iku—Ozuru had been her professional name—had died. It had been her karma. She had died because she had done something bad in a previous life. A great pity, for the girl had done well for herself in this one. She'd come for a visit, dressed in fine clothes, and brought them money. Those had been good days, but it had pleased the gods and Ozuru's *karma* to make her fall and break her neck. A great pity.

Tora left them some money and turned homeward. The trip had been a waste of time. Ozuru's people clearly held no grudge. Rather the reverse. Somehow, Tokuzo, Ozuru, and their own wishful thinking had left them with the impression their daughter had lived a life of pleasure and plenty. They had quickly sold two more girls, but that money was gone already, and the two girls had not come back with gifts.

Feeling glum, Tora hoped his master had thought of other possibilities. There must be something he could do. Somewhere there was a man who had hated Tokuzo enough to kill him.

To his disappointment, the master had not yet returned from a visit to the prince's villa. As it was well past sunset and quite dark outside, this was a little unusual. Tora turned his tired horse over to the boy he had hired to fill in in Genba's absence. The kid was slow and spoke with a stutter, but he knew enough to feed and water the horses and clean the stable.

Then he went to see Lady Tamako. She seemed calm enough about the master's absence. Tora assumed the trip to the villa must have been more interesting than his own. He settled down to a good meal with his family and an enjoyable bedtime with Hanae.

Early the next morning, he stepped out into the yard to a glorious blue sky and birdsong and washed at the well. When he turned, he noticed something white lying among some weeds near the outer wall. He would have to speak to the boy about keeping the place clean. It was a large stone with some paper attached to it. He went to inspect it and found the paper was folded and had been tied to the rock with twisted hemp twine.

Someone must have tossed the rock over the wall. Since he had returned after dark the day before, it was not at all clear when the missive had arrived. He hesitated a moment, then untied the paper to read it. The message was brief so he could make out its meaning quite well.

Those who meddle in the affairs of His Majesty will die.

He saw neither signature nor superscription, but assumed it was meant for the master and took it into the main house. His master, however, was not in his study. The room was dark and empty.

Frowning, Tora went next to her ladyship's quarters where her maid was just throwing open the shutters.

"Hope you slept well, Sumiko," Tora called out. "Is the master inside?"

"No. Did you look in his room?"

"He's not there. Didn't he come home last night?"

They stared at each other in dismay, then the maid turned and ran inside. A moment later, her ladyship appeared, pulling her robe hastily about her.

"What is it, Tora? Has my husband not returned?"

"I don't think so, my lady. Did you expect him last evening?"

"Yes. Something is wrong, I think. He would have sent a message." She frowned.

Tora hid the message behind his back and gulped down his fear. "I think I'd better saddle the horse and go looking for him," he said.

She clutched the robe to her. "Yes, you'd better, though it's probably nothing. Perhaps the horse went lame." She paused, then added, "Take a sword, Tora."

Tora's eyes widened as he digested that.

She saw his surprise. "He may have made enemies trying to clear the prince. Perhaps he ran into someone like that."

That sealed it.

Tora brought forth the paper and extended it to her. "I'm sorry, my lady. I just found this inside the wall. Tied to a stone."

She read the message, bit her lip, and said, "If someone left this overnight, it may not have anything to do with his being late. Most likely it's just an empty threat."

Neither believed this.

Tora said, "They may have left it before last night. I wasn't here yesterday and got home after dark. And it was hidden behind some weeds."

"I see." She thought a moment. "I think I must go call on Superintendent Kobe. But you'd better be on your way. And be careful. Do you know where the villa is?"

"I think, so." Tora bowed and left for the stable at a run.

Tamako returned to her room and dressed swiftly, while Sumiko sent the boy for a palanquin. Taking some money from Akitada's chest, she got into the palanquin, telling the bearers to take her to police headquarters.

Her arrival there attracted a curious crowd. High-born ladies were not expected to have business there. She stayed inside the palanquin and sent a message to Kobe.

Kobe emerged moments later, looking shocked. He bent to peer into the palanquin. "Lady Sugawara? I didn't believe it when they told me. Has something happened?"

"Yes, Superintendent. Forgive this unceremonious visit, but I didn't know what else to do. Akitada has disappeared, and I'm afraid something may have happened to him. I've sent Tora after him and that meant I had to come here myself. We are a household of women and children now." She added the last rather pointedly.

He was not pleased. "What exactly do you mean, he has disappeared?" he demanded.

His tone shocked her, though she should have expected it. Suddenly she felt both helpless and angry. Tears rose to her eyes and spilled over. She brushed them away and explained. "Akitada left yesterday early in the day to visit the prince's villa in the mountains. He expected to return the same day. But he hasn't come home, and Tora found this in our courtyard." She passed the crumpled note out of the palanquin with trembling fingers.

Kobe, whose face had turned red with embarrassment at her tears, read it. He said, "I see. I'll send some of my men up there. The old couple may know something. Don't worry. It's probably nothing. He may have extended his excursion. Or perhaps his horse has gone lame. It's a rough track."

"He would never delay his return without telling me," she said thickly, wiping more tears away with her hands, and hating the fact she could not control them.

Kobe beckoned over an older policeman. "See to it that Lady Sugawara has an escort home and then station five men at her house for protection." He turned back to Tamako. "Please calm yourself. I'll do everything I can to bring your husband back." He cleared his throat and tried to look stern. "Really, he ought not to put you to such worries. What is he thinking of?"

She managed to say in a firmer voice, "You were his friend once and should know Akitada will always take risks to right an injustice. He told me about this case because he knew it might be politically dangerous. I support him in whatever he decides to do."

Kobe looked away. "Yes, ahem. Well, you'd better go home now. We'll see to it." He gave a signal to her bearers who picked up the palanquin and trotted off.

Tora pushed his poor horse unmercifully. No more leisurely trotting like on the way to Yasaka village. No more pleasurable viewing of the countryside. He had nearly worn out the beast when the road began to climb into the mountain and he had to slow down because of loose rocks on the path. He worried he might have taken a wrong turn. This poor track seemed unlike anything an imperial prince would travel, let alone one of the emperor's women. Eventually he dismounted and led the horse. He had not seen a soul for miles and should have asked direction from the last peasant he had passed a long time ago.

When he reached a hut where an old man was sunning himself on the front steps, he was relieved. He walked over, calling out, "Greetings, grandfather. Is this the way to Prince Atsuhira's villa?"

The old man smiled and bowed his head in greeting.

Or maybe he had nodded. One could not be sure. In any case, he was still smiling and blinking against the sun.

"I'm on the right path then?"

No answer.

Tora looked around. Perhaps there was someone else he could talk to. He tied his horse to a post and started around the hut. The old man took his stick, got up, and followed him. He moved slowly, swaying from side to side.

It was terrible getting old. Tora slowed to let him catch up. "Are you alone here, grandfather?" he asked, raising his voice in case the old-timer was deaf.

The old man, still smiling, shook his head. "Nope. Birds," he croaked. "Deer. Badgers. Foxes."

"But no people?"

"People?" said the old man dubiously. "A few."

"What about the prince? Have you met him?"

This time he got what was clearly a nod. After a moment, it was followed by a shake of the head. Tora sighed. It was better to die young than to end up like this, old, weak, and crazy.

Then he heard the woman's call.

The old man turned and started back. "The wife," he said.

Thank heaven, thought Tora, unless she proves even more decrepit.

They found her standing beside Tora's horse. When she saw him, she asked sharply, "Are you looking for someone?"

"As it happens, yes. My master, Lord Sugawara. He came up here yesterday, and hasn't come home."

"Amida!" She clutched his arm. "Come. Maybe you can do something. If it isn't too late." She pointed to his horse and started up the path, huffing and puffing as she hurried.

Tora, his heart heavy, untied his horse and caught up with her. "Where is he?"

"Fallen over the cliff," she gasped and kept going.

Tora cursed, got on his horse and drove it uphill.

Those who meddle in the affairs of His Majesty will die.

The first thing he saw when he reached the plateau where the villa stood, was his master's horse, still tied to its post.

He was consumed by a furious anger at those in power or wrangling to gain power. They thought nothing of getting rid of anyone who stood in their way. He swore he would make unending war on them, if they had harmed his master.

The old woman caught up and disappeared around the corner of the building. Tora left his horse and scrambled after her. Behind the villa, the mountain dropped off into space. Below lay the green and golden plain where many hundreds of roofs and pagodas spread all the way to rivers and the edge of the northern mountain range. He took in none of this. His eyes were on the edge, where the old woman stood looking down into nothingness.

She shouted, "Ho, down there? Can you hear me? Someone's come for you."

If matters had not been so desperate, Tora might have laughed that he was being announced like a messenger. As it was, he went and looked down. He saw nothing, just a steep decline of rocks and twisted pines and a few patches of grass.

"How far down is he?" he asked, despair gnawing at his belly.

"Don't know. He could've fallen again during the night."

Oh, gods!

"How do you know he's down there?" Tora tested the edge and noticed a freshly broken section.

"I thought he'd left. I heard his horse on the path. Later I went up to see if he'd closed the shutters. He hadn't. And there was his horse, so he couldn't have left. I didn't know what to do. Then I thought I heard someone calling. From just about there." She pointed toward an outcropping that hid what was below. "I shouted down, but there was no answer. I left after a while. I thought I'd imagined it."

All night!

He'd fallen and shouted for help and no one had come. And the old woman had done nothing.

Tora felt vomit rising in his throat and swallowed.

"He could've fallen again," she suggested.

Tora wished her to the devil. The damned ghoul had been useless. He gauged the way down to the outcropping and saw some places where he might get enough hand- and foot-hold to climb down a ways. Starting downward gingerly, he let his feet seek for support as his hands grasped at likely shrubs and protruding rocks. It had rained overnight, and the rocks felt greasy with moisture.

The old woman watched him. "You'll fall down the mountain, too. Better get back here." She sounded anxious.

She was not nearly as nervous as Tora, whose boots kept slipping on the wet ground. Nevertheless, he moved slowly downward. A small crippled pine was strong enough to hold on to, and he mastered another long step. Soon he would be at the edge of the outcropping and able to see past it. But the next stretch was tricky. The more he felt around with his free foot, peering down, the shakier he felt and the more tenuous the next step became. It might just be feasible if he could reach that old root protruding from a crack, but he would have to let go with his other hand and trust the root would hold his weight. If it did not, then both he and the master were lost.

The old woman had fallen silent. Tora did not bother to see if she was still there. He thought of Hanae and Yuki. They deserved better than to have him die today by falling off a mountain. And the master might already be past saving. He reflected sadly that they had always deserved better than a husband and father who was forever looking for danger and excitement.

He let go and flung himself downward, catching the root which cracked ominously but held long enough to let him take another quick step to a small ledge.

Catching his breath, he looked down and gasped.

The master lay some twenty feet below him, prone on another ledge, one so narrow that his arm and one leg hung over the side. He was not moving. Tora was afraid to call out, because he might startle him into make a sudden move and tumble over the side. Below was a straight drop no man could survive.

But the continued stillness of the figure below might mean that rescue was already too late.

Tora looked back up and realized for the first time that he had no way of bringing up his master's body. In fact, he did not know if he could climb back up to the top himself.

23

Akiko Investigates

Tamako was pacing. She was far more upset than at any time since the terrible illness had taken their son Yori. There were similarities, she thought. Both times she had had a premonition, a very strong conviction that disaster loomed, and that she must act to avert it. Only she did not know how any more now than she had then.

This time it was Akitada who might be taken from her. Perhaps he had already been taken. The possibility of having lost him was unbearable. For all that he had frequently irritated her in the past with his stubbornness, Tamako knew him to be a gentle and caring man who loved her. To her, he was everything, perhaps even more than the children, though the thought shamed her. If his duties and interests took him away too much and occupied his mind to the exclusion of his wife and family, then that was a man's privilege. A woman lived for her husband and children. Oh, what would become of all of them?

Into her terrified imaginings burst her sister-in-law.

"Wait until I tell you," she cried, eyes sparkling with excitement and her movements those of a young girl. "Where's Akitada? Send for him. He must hear this!"

When Tamako made no move, her eyes sharpened. "You've been crying," she said accusingly. "You look terrible. What's the matter with you?"

The reprimand did nothing to steady Tamako. "Akitada's not come home," she wailed. "Something's happened to him. Oh, Akiko, what shall I do?"

"What? Don't be silly. Nothing's happened to him. Nothing ever happens to Akitada, you know that. He gets into a bit of trouble and immediately gets back out. What do you mean, he hasn't come home?"

Tamako explained with a shaking voice.

"Oh, is that all? You know very well that his horse may have gone lame and he decided to spend the night somewhere. Just hope he doesn't have a girlfriend someplace."

That was so ridiculous it made Tamako smile. "Not Akitada," she said loyally.

"He's a man," Akiko said darkly.

Tamako shook her head. "No. I have this feeling. Something's wrong. And he's been working on this cursed case. He knew it was dangerous and asked me about it, but I told him he should go on with it." Tears started flowing again.

Akiko went to the door and called for the maid.

Sumiko appeared, saw her weeping mistress, and cried, "What's happened to the master?"

"Not you, too," snapped Akiko. "Go make your mistress some soothing tea. And if you put honey and a little juice from an orange in it, you can bring enough for two."

The maid disappeared, and Akiko made Tamako sit down and tell her where Akitada had gone and why. "Surely," she said, "there's nothing to be found after all those months and when the police have already investigated."

"Perhaps not, but your brother was restless. So many things have gone badly lately. I thought he should have something to occupy him."

Akiko was amused. "I see you manage your husband much the way I manage mine."

They exchanged a smile. Tamako asked, "What was the great news you were bringing when you came in?"

"Oh, I've had such fun, Tamako. No wonder my brother gets involved in every murder he comes across. You should have seen me. I asked questions, put my nose into matters that shouldn't have concerned me, told such fibs, and flattered so grossly that Akitada would have been proud of me. And I got results. I wish he were here. You know, I sometimes get the feeling he hasn't a great deal of respect for me."

Tamako blinked. "Oh, I'm sure you're wrong. It's just that his mind is always on other things."

"Yes, that's true. The man cannot pay attention. I have a notion I may be much better at this than he is." Akiko grinned. "I do wish women could get about more. Perhaps I could specialize in crimes committed in the women's quarters. I think I'd be very good at that."

Sumiko came with the tea, and the ladies sipped. Tamako found that she had relaxed and regarded her sister-in-law fondly. "Thank you for coming," she said simply. "I needed your visit."

Akiko waved that away. "You and I always got along. I give Akitada credit for choosing the right wife. Even Mother agreed. Now let me tell you what I found out."

"Yes, of course."

"Well, I visited Lady Kishi yesterday. She seemed in good spirits, and we talked a bit about children. I said I worried every day about securing the futures of mine. She made suggestions for the boys, and we drifted quite naturally to the fate of girls, then to marriage and husbands who have outside interests." Akiko paused to giggle. "You and I don't have that problem, but I pretended I was familiar with her predicament."

"Akiko! How can you speak that way of your husband who is the best of men?"

Her sister-in-law preened herself a little. "I make sure he stays interested. But to go on, her main worry is also for her children. She says she's decided to ignore the prince's escapades and wait for the day when a son of hers will gain enough power to provide his mother with the status she desires. So, I don't think she would have bothered with having the emperor's woman killed. It doesn't make sense. Kishi knows what's good for her."

"Her name is Lady Masako," Tamako corrected. "She never was in His Majesty's bed. And you cannot believe everything people tell you."

"How do you know she's not shared his bed?" Akiko raised her brows quizzically.

"Well . . ."

"She was a woman. And as you pointed out, you can't believe everything. Women don't tell their lovers the truth. It's entirely possible the child she carried was the emperor's."

"Oh, Akiko. How horrible! Surely she wouldn't have gone to the prince while expecting His Majesty's child."

Akiko smiled and shook her head. "His Majesty's still a boy. He's not nearly as dashing as Prince Atsuhira, a mature male with the most extraordinary good looks."

"You have seen the prince?"

"Certainly. His looks are common gossip among women. I saw him years ago when I was peeking out of a carriage at some festival. And I've seen him since when calling on his wife."

Tamako pursed her lips as the pondered this. "But what motive would her killer have had in that case? Punishing her for her infidelity?"

"No. The succession, of course."

"Akiko, this is becoming more dangerous by the minute. And now Akitada has gone missing. I think we must stop."

"Nonsense. Akitada will be back soon, and I love a good story. Anyway, I didn't say anything about my suspicions to Lady Kishi. Instead I asked her help to find out more about Masako. She told me that Masako had an attendant assigned to her in the palace. She is Nagasune Hiroko. A good family but without influence. And the girl is plain. The two were supposedly close. I shall try to pay her a visit next."

"In the palace? Oh, I don't know, Akiko. I think perhaps you should wait. I have an awful feeling about all of this."

"Silly, she's not in the palace any longer. She's gone home to her family. She lives with her uncle Kintada. He's a colleague of my husband's brother in the Bureau of Palace storehouses. I think that's how he got her assigned as an attendant. You can imagine the man's disappointment when his niece ended up serving Masako who'd been rejected by His Majesty. Still palace service is palace service. It pays well, and there's always a chance that His Majesty may take notice or else some nobleman might take her to wife. It's a chance to meet people when the rest of the young women are hiding in their homes. I shall certainly try to send both of my girls to court."

Tamako smiled a little at the skill and expertise with which Akiko analyzed people's motives. Perhaps Akitada's father had passed on certain talents not only to his son and heir but also to at least one of his daughters. For better or worse, Akiko embodied traits of both her parents. "You will be careful?"

"Oh, of course. Now here is what I was thinking: if Masako and this Hiroko were really close, Hiroko will know all about the affair. And that's the sort of thing Akitada's interested in." She paused a moment. Then, her eyes shining, she added, "For all you know, I may be able to solve his murder case for him."

Tamako began to suspect that Akiko's resentment of her brother was due to envy rather than ill humor. Akiko wanted to be like Akitada.

"Akiko," she said hesitantly, "I think you're very proud of your brother, but he is a man. He can go places where no woman is allowed to be. Let him solve the crimes."

"I can go places where he cannot go," Akiko cried. "Men are just as limited as women are. In fact, if you made an effort to be more sociable with the right people, you'd be a big help to him."

So much for kinder feelings toward Akiko. Tamako flushed with embarrassment and hurt. "He hasn't complained," she said coolly.

"No, of course not. Men like obedient wives who stay home with their children. I like an obedient husband. But I must be on my way. We are to have guests tonight. Be sure to send someone the moment Akitada returns."

Tamako did not mention that she had no one to send. She thanked her sister-in-law and saw her to her palanquin.

24

The Hungry Mountain

Tora clung to the side of the mountain. He had looked carefully at the wall of rocks and loose debris above him without finding the foot- and hand-holds he had used on his precipitate trip down. Everything looked different from this angle. He did not know how to climb up again.

But there was also no way down. Or at least none he could see beyond one more move. This he accomplished with the greatest care. It put him below the outcropping that had hidden his master's lifeless figure on the ledge below. It brought him a little closer, but now he was cut off from a view of the top and from help.

The voice of the old woman came to him faintly, "Don't move!" she shouted. "The mountain is hungry. It's already swallowed two people."

Tora shouted back, "Get help. I see my master, but he's unconscious, and I can't reach him."

She shouted back, but he could not make out her words. Then all became silent. How and where she might find help, he did not know, seeing that she had been unable to so far.

He clung to the rock and peered down. From this position, he could see blood under his master's head. It might well be from a fatal injury. He'd seen corpses that had lain in such a pool of blood which had poured from their ears, noses, and mouths as they expired. He bit his lips and tried to think positive thoughts. After what seemed a long time, he risked calling out softly, "Sir? Please don't move. Help is on the way. Just lie still."

Nothing happened.

He thought it could not hurt to continue the conversation. It gave him something to do and might have a soothing effect on Akitada if he were even a little bit aware. So he talked about meeting Saburo and their visit to see Genba. He interspersed his narrative with repeated warnings to lie very still, followed by assurances that help was coming.

He did not have much faith in the old woman but, being by nature hopeful, he made his chatter as cheerful as he could under the circumstances.

Circumstances deteriorated. It started to rain. This time of year and in this place, rain meant a drastic drop in temperatures and a chill wind. Tora was soon shivering.

Wet and increasingly desperate, he made up his mind that he must climb back to the top to get help. This undertaking had become much more dangerous in the rain. All the surfaces of the mountain had become slippery.

He told the still figure below him, "I'll climb back up now for a little while, sir. Will you promise to lie very still while I'm gone?" And as he peered down through the rain, he thought he saw one of Akitada's fingers twitch. Maybe it had been his imagination or the effect of the rain and the moistness in his eyes, but Tora preferred a happier interpretation. His heart sang for a moment at the thought that his master was not dead after all. He repeated his warning and began the dangerous climb to the top.

It soon became hopeless. His fingers slid off surfaces that felt as if they had been covered with oil. Under his feet, rocks shifted, leaving him breathless with panic. He had managed to get past the overhang, when he heard a shout from above.

"Ho!"

A man's voice. Tora peered upward, blinking against the rain. An irregular line of round boulders rimmed the top of the rock wall. One of them must surely be a head. He blinked again and decided that there were more heads up there, looking down at him.

"Don't do that," shouted the first head. "We have ropes."

Tora said a quick prayer to the god of the mountain and two more to Buddha.

"Hurry up. I'm getting wet," he shouted back.

A snort of laughter, and some rude comments about peeing your pants floated back. But then the rope appeared, dangling and whipping about in the wind. Tora caught it and almost slipped again. Being more careful, he tied it around his chest, tested the knot, and began his ascent once more.

He was greeted by a group of wet policemen who were grinning in spite of the weather. More banter ensued and was interrupted by Superintendent Kobe, who strode into the group with a sharp, "Order!" and asked Tora, "Did you find him?"

Tora noted the anxiety in the question and nodded. "He's just below the outcropping." He pointed down. "I couldn't reach him. He wasn't moving, or maybe just a bit. A couple of fingers. But I couldn't be sure. There's blood."

The lump in his stomach was back, and he swallowed.

Kobe looked over the side and shouted commands about more ropes. Tora watched the constables scramble about, then said, "I'm going back down."

"No," snapped Kobe. "This is work for experts. And you're tired and wet."

"I'm going back down."

Akitada became aware of voices gradually. He had drifted in and out of silence for a long time. Once he had heard Tora's voice and taken it for a dream. Tora seemed to be strangely agitated. He had felt a sense of danger. And discomfort. But now he also heard other voices. He drifted off again.

"Don't move!"

Easily done, he thought fuzzily. He lay relaxed and was very sleepy. But he was cold, and something was wrong with his head. Never mind. He would check later. He had time.

Later came sooner than he cared for.

Someone shouted near his ear, "He's alive!"

Hands touched him, and pain shot through his body. Two people spoke. Tora and a stranger.

"Sir? Sir, can you hear me? Where are you hurt?"

That was Tora. Where was he hurt? He tried to shake his head and groaned. More hands on his body, feeling his legs and arms, poking his back. More agony.

"We'll get you up to the top, sir. Don't you worry."

That was Tora again. The hands stopped touching him. Akitada sighed and relaxed. He was not worried. Tora was taking care of the situation.

But what followed rattled him into greater and far more painful awareness that something was very wrong. He was pulled about and man-handled as someone tied him up. He tried to shout but got no answer. Then the hands pushed and pulled him off his bed, and he felt ropes bite into this chest and hips as he was suddenly raised. The hands were back, guiding, but he bumped his way upwards until there was no longer any point in dozing off, and he opened his eyes.

What he saw was disconcerting, part of a nightmare. But this time he was wide awake. Below him was the face of a stranger, of a young man with his wet hair plastered against a face red with effort, and beyond that the world dropped off into an abyss, into a gray cauldron of swirling rain and mist. He closed his eyes again, and tried to comprehend.

A sharp crack against his head and a shout from Tora, brought him back. More shouts to be careful. More pushing and tugging. More pain. More strain on the ropes that bound him. And then finally he understood.

Akitada cursed.

"Well, he sounds all right."

That had been Kobe. Akitada was surprised at his presence. He had reached the top by then and could feel solid ground under him again. Someone dragged him a little ways, and then they untied the ropes. He muttered against the jarring pain, and looked up into the faces of Kobe and Tora.

"I slipped," he said.

"You mean it was an accident? Nobody pushed you over?" Kobe sounded disappointed.

Akitada did not answer. He was concentrating on various parts of his body. There was still some pain, but it was not unbearable, and he could move both legs, though his left arm would not obey. And his head hurt. He raised his right hand to check. He was wet, but there also seemed to be a cut and a swelling. He tried to sit up, but a jarring agony in his left shoulder stopped him. He groaned and fell back.

"A litter," said Kobe. "He can't ride in this condition. I wish he wouldn't go off on these wild excursions by himself. It makes work for everyone."

"Sorry," muttered Akitada. "You shouldn't have bothered. Tora and I could've managed.

Kobe snorted his derision and walked away.

Akitada bit his lip. Kobe had, after all, come to his rescue. No doubt the excursion had caused untold trouble to a lot of people. He wondered if he should apologize, but there was the matter of Genba. And besides he had not been on a wild excursion.

That reminded him. Someone had tried to kill him.

"Tora?" His voice was thick and he seemed to have no strength to raise it.

But faithful Tora was beside him. "Yes, sir?"

"There's a *bo*. It was used on Lady Masako." He took a breath and tried again. "A little ways down the mountain. Caught on a small pine."

Tora frowned. "A *bo*?"

"Yes. A short fighting stick. There's some blood and hair on it."

"Not in this rain," Tora remarked, but he went to look. Then he went to speak to Kobe. Together they walked to the edge and looked over. In the end, a constable was lowered with one of the ropes. He brought up the *bo*.

Akitada almost smiled. It had not been in vain.

Kobe came over, carrying the *bo*. "What makes you think that's what killed Lady Masako? She fell to her death quite a distance from the house."

"The killer hit her. Inside the villa. Then he carried her to the promontory." It was a big effort to say this much.

Kobe shook his head. "That doesn't make sense. Besides, the *bo* is clean. It could have been tossed over at any time."

Akitada closed his eyes.

The descent from the mountain was excruciatingly painful. Two sturdy constables bore the litter and kept up a stumbling trot downhill. This caused a constant bouncing of Akitada's head and shoulder. They had bandaged his head after a fashion, but even with the added padding, Akitada made efforts to raise it. His neck muscles eventually hurt as badly as his head. Neither pain was as awful as that of his injured shoulder.

They had inspected it and caused him to shout at them not to touch him. Tora had muttered something to Kobe and both looked worried. They ignored his protests long enough to strap his left arm to his body. Akitada assumed his upper arm or the shoulder joint were broken.

When he was not groaning or drifting in and out of consciousness, he called himself every kind of fool imaginable. He was not about to mention his attacker to Kobe.

25

Bashan Returns

Ever considerate, Superintendent Kobe sent one of his men ahead to tell Tamako that her husband was alive and on his way home. The constable had orders not to frighten the lady with gruesome details of the rescue and Akitada's condition.

Tamako thanked the young man and sent Sumiko to the kitchen to tell cook to have something warm and filling ready for Kobe's men.

Only then did she ask the constable, "Have you seen my husband?"

The youngster said proudly, "Yes, I have, my lady. And I helped bring him up, too."

"That was very good of you. I take it he had taken a fall?"

"Oh, yes. Horribly far down it was. And the cliff was very steep and slippery in the rain."

"You must be a very good climber."

The constable said modestly, "We had ropes, my lady. Too bad his lordship didn't. He must've been on that ledge all night and part of the morning. We had a terrible time bringing him back up when he could do nothing for himself."

"I see. My compliments and thanks for performing such a difficult rescue. Are the others far behind you?"

"Oh, yes. It's impossible to hurry with a litter on steep mountain roads, and the bearers have to take turns. Besides, his lordship cannot take any shaking."

"Well, thank you. Now go to the kitchen for some wine and food."

When the youngster had left, Tamako tried to suppress another panic. The news, while reassuring as to Akitada being alive, was not at all hopeful about his condition. The fall had clearly been a bad one, and he was helpless and severely injured. She set about spreading his bedding and sorting through her medicines with shaking hands. Then she sent Sumiko for their physician. And finally, she wrote a note to Akiko and had the boy deliver it.

Then came the waiting.

Doctor Kumada arrived first. He was a frail and kindly elderly man, much given to treating his patients with ingenious concoctions of herbal teas and pulverized roots. In this he reminded Tamako and Akitada of Seimei, particularly since he also had another characteristic of their old faithful retainer. He liked to insert the odd bit of ancient wisdom in his conversations.

Now he greeted Tamako with a bow and a smile. "Where's the patient, dear lady?"

"He's on his way," she said, glancing past him toward the gate. "I'm so glad you're here. I don't know how bad it is, but he's seriously injured, and I think he's unconscious."

The doctor raised his thick white brows. "How then can he be said to be on his way?"

"Oh." Tamako brushed her hair back with a distracted hand. "I'm sorry. Sumiko didn't make herself clear. My husband has taken a fall in the mountains. They're bringing him by litter."

The white eyebrows contracted. "Good heavens. I'm very sorry to hear it. Shall we go inside and make preparations?"

"Yes, of course. I did that, but you'd better see for yourself."

Doctor Kumada approved, but he also ordered water to be heated in the kitchen and then bent over his basket of medicines to lay out some likely herbs for infusion. As he was doing this, the patient finally arrived.

When they finally brought Akitada into his room after a horribly painful and long journey, he found Tamako waiting, her face pale with worry. She exclaimed at his appearance. He tried to reassure her, but when they set his litter down, the jolt to his arm caused him to cry out. He had rarely been this miserable. His clothes were soaking wet and he shivered uncontrollably.

Tora and Kobe had come in with him, their faces drawn.

The constables next lifted Akitada from the litter onto the bedding, a process that caused him to utter several long moans.

"What happened, Tora?" Tamako asked, wringing her hands.

"He must've fallen yesterday, my lady. The old woman caretaker went looking for him. She heard cries for help but couldn't see him. She's too old and infirm to be much use, so he was on the mountain all night. By the time I got to him, he was unconscious."

Their doctor came to bend over Akitada. "He has a bad cut on his scalp," he announced. It must've bled a good deal. That could explain why he was unconscious, but the wound isn't serious."

Dazed with the pain of the journey, Akitada bore the doctor's probing of his head patiently. But when he started moving his limbs and got to the left arm, he snarled, "Don't!"

Doctor Kumada paused and asked for a sharp knife to cut the sleeve of Akitada's robe away from his shoulder. He was gentle, but even this was exquisitely painful. When the sodden layers of robe, shirt, and undershirt were peeled back, Akitada risked a look. His shoulder joint was grossly swollen and angry red and purple in color. Besides, something was badly wrong with its shape.

"Is it broken?" Tamako asked with a gasp.

The doctor probed and shook his head. "Not at all. As they say, if you know the disease, the cure is near.

Your husband has pulled his arm out of its proper place. I expect it's very painful, but I don't think there's any lasting damage. The injury has caused the swelling and bruising. I won't touch it myself, but I know some-one who is said to be very good at this. He's one of the blind masseurs. Send for him, while I check the rest of the patient."

As Akitada absorbed this, Kobe said in a hearty voice, "Well, that's good news. My men and I will be on our way. There's work to be done. Glad we got your husband back in one piece, dear lady."

Tamako bowed very deeply. "You have saved him. We are deeply in your debt."

Akitada bit his lip. Ashamed of having cried out with pain, he almost wished the injury had been worse. "Yes, it was very good of you, Kobe. Sorry to have been such a nuisance."

"All in a day's work," Kobe said and left.

Akitada detested the notion of being indebted to Kobe after all that had passed between them. "Tora could've handled it," he said sourly.

"Don't be ungrateful," his wife said.

Tora cleared his throat. "Did you say a blind mas-seur, Doctor?" he asked. "Isn't there one who treats the beggars? He's called Bashan."

Doctor Kumada nodded. "That's him. He does a lot of free work for the poor. He wears plain clothing but has a heart of brocade, as they say. Bashan's very good at manipulating limbs, also with needles and moxa treatments, I hear. You'll probably find him in the Jade Arbor, a bathhouse in the sixth ward."

"I'm on my way."

"No, Tora," said Tamako. "Send the boy. You need to get out of your wet clothes and have something to eat."

"If you say so, my lady." On his way out, Tora added with a grin, "Patience, sir. You'll soon be as good as new."

The doctor nodded. "Patience is the remedy for every misfortune."

Akitada was neither patient nor did he have much faith in blind masseurs. In fact, his misery was still so great that he had only listened with half an ear to the chatter. He resented the fact that they were all so cheerful. Even Tamako smiled. The pain in his shoulder was too great for such good humor. He gathered something was wrong with the shoulder, but the pain radiated down his entire arm to his very fingertips. He could not move any of them. It also extended up to his neck and spread from there to his back and chest. He had to avoid breathing too deeply.

And what were they planning to do about his injuries? They were turning him over to a blind masseur. Were they mad? How much pain did they wish him to suffer? His own family was set on torturing him. He glared at Tamako, who knelt beside him, stroking his head.

The maid came in with hot water, and Doctor Kumada began the ritual of mixing one of his concoctions, murmuring explanations as he selected the ingredients. "This will serve to dispel the heat in your shoulder," he said. "It will cleanse the poisons from the flesh and reduce the swellings. It's the old eight-herb formula, but with some of my own substitutions." He held them up, one by one. "Here you have mint, and here bellflower, and cassia, gardenia, and vitex. To those I add ginseng for the fever and ginger and cinnamon to reduce pain." He stirred these ingredients together in a large earthenware bowl, then added steaming hot water to them. An acrid smell filled the room.

"Must I?" grumbled Akitada, wrinkling his nose. "I think a cup of hot spiced wine would be a good deal better. I'm still as wet as a drowned rat."

"Do you want us to take off your clothes?" asked Tamako, jumping up. "You didn't want anyone to touch you."

"No, no. Don't. I'm getting quite warm."

The large cup, reeking of heaven knew what, approached his clenched lips while Tamako propped up his head. The first sip burned his lips and he jerked away. This jarred his shoulder and convinced him of their cruelty.

"It's too hot," murmured Tamako. This set the doctor to blowing on the brew. In time the evil cup approached again. Akitada sipped and gagged. "It tastes like cat's urine. I'm not drinking this."

The doctor looked stern. "The illness of those who are too proud to heed reason is absolutely incurable."

"You will drink it, Akitada," his wife said, "because if you don't, you may die of a fever after spending the night in the rain on a mountain. That's right, Doctor, isn't it."

"Very true, my lady, but I'm afraid good advice is as painful to the ears as good medicine is bitter to the tongue."

They both chuckled. What did they care? Akitada gnashed his teeth but submitted to the nasty brew.

After that, he had a period of peace. Kumada prepared several packets of herbs for additional doses of the nasty brew, collected his pay, and departed.

"Try to rest," Tamako said and sat down beside him. He nodded and dozed. "I wish you'd let me get those wet clothes off you.," she said after a while.

"Maybe later."

He must have slept a little, because when he opened his eyes again, a monk was leaning over him, his eyes half closed and his fingers moving lightly across his chest. Had he died? The fingers next felt his head, brushing across the bandage, and returned to his neck. From there, they crept toward his shoulder.

"Don't," Akitada growled.

The monk stopped and smiled. "Ah, you're awake. Now pay attention. I will pull on your arm until it finds its way home."

Akitada's eyes popped open. "NO!"

The monk smiled more widely. "You may, of course, wish to continue in your present discomfort. In that case, I will wish you patience and depart."

Akitada glared back. He realized that he was not dealing with a monk but with the blind masseur. "What do you know about such injuries?" he demanded.

"I would call them fortunate accidents. They are common and easily treated, except in cases where the victims have an unreasonable dislike of even a small moment's pain."

Akitada hated the man. How dare he speak to him this way? How dare he suggest that he could take no pain? How dare he insult him in this manner? He looked past the shaven head to Tamako, who stood by expectantly and with a smile on her face. Feeling resentful, his eyes returned to the smooth face of the monk. "A moment's pain? A fortunate accident? Is nothing broken or torn?"

"I don't think there is any damage. And yes, it will hurt quite a lot for a moment, but after that you'll feel much better, and soon you'll not remember the pain at all."

"Must you pull my arm?"

"Yes."

Akitada closed his eyes. "Do it then," he said ungraciously and prepared himself to bear the procedure without making a sound. He'd show them.

The masseur felt around the joint one more time, then reached for Akitada's wrist and gave his arm a single powerful jerk and a twist.

White-hot agony sliced through Akitada's shoulder. The effort not to cry out caused him to become absolutely rigid from the soles of his feet to his head. He dimly heard his bones come together with an odd, slippery sound and felt an immediate relief.

"There," said the masseur. "That should do it. Keep your arm still for a day. I'm told your doctor left some medicine for pain. I'll only rub on a little ointment. It won't hurt."

Akitada opened his eyes slowly. The pain was almost gone, and the relief was overwhelming. The ointment felt pleasantly hot on his skin. He said, "Thank you. Please forgive me for doubting your skill."

A small smile twitched the masseur's lips. "It was nothing. As I said, a fortunate accident. I'll take my leave. Not all my patients are as easy to cure."

Feeling the implied reprimand, Akitada flushed. "I believe payment is in order," he said to establish a more proper relationship.

"A piece of silver will do."

He was not cheap. Akitada eyed the slender figure with the shaven head. The man belonged to the lower classes, perhaps even to the untouchables, but his speech was educated. Though his manner had hardly been proper, he had done his job well and must be paid. "Tamako, please get the money."

As Tamako paid the masseur, putting the money in his hand and adding her thanks, Tora came back in. He eyed the masseur with interest. "You must be the one who treated a friend of mine. He was attacked and got a bad head wound. You took care of him at the beggars' temple. His name's Saburo."

The masseur cocked his head in Tora's direction. "It may be so. A friend of yours, you say?"

Akitada said, "Saburo worked for me. If you have treated him, it's only right that I should pay his debt also."

The masseur hesitated. "Thank you. But it was nothing. I treat the poor without taking pay."

"Then I'm sure you can use the money," Tamako said. "It was a kindness, and we're grateful." Tamako pressed another piece of silver into Bashan's hand.

Bashan bowed, then felt around for his staff. Tora handed it to him, and led him out.

"What an odd character," muttered Akitada. "I think I'll change now." Assisted by Tamako, he struggled out of his wet, torn, and filthy clothes and put on dry ones. His left arm was still fairly useless and somewhat painful, but he found he could tuck it inside his robe where it was adequately supported. He was beginning to feel almost human again and decided to sit down behind his desk. Tamako watched him, smiling to see him so greatly improved.

Suddenly he felt a rush of happiness and gratitude. He had almost died on the mountain. Certainly his attacker had intended him to die. Tears came to his eyes. He was ashamed that he had behaved like a spoiled child.

"I've been foolish and careless, and I've given you a very hard time," he told his wife. "Please forgive me."

Tamako laughed softly. "You were in great pain and protested. It's what people do when they're hurt. Oh, Akitada, I'm so happy you're back."

The door opened and Tora was back. "Good man, that Bashan. I don't think I could've done as well as you, sir. All that rough handling to pull you up the mountainside, and then the awful shaking on the litter."

"You saved my life, Tora. You might have fallen yourself." Akitada paused, frowning. "I thought I heard you talking to me, but I must have been dreaming."

"It was me. Telling you not to move. You were lying on this very narrow ledge."

"Good heaven." Akitada grimaced. In his carelessness, he had risked not only his own life, but also those of Tora and the brave constables. And he had gained little or nothing from his trip. He wondered if he should tell them about the attack and decided against it. No sense in frightening Tamako now that he was safe.

He said, "I'm afraid I haven't made any progress. There were a few scuffed footprints in one of the rooms, and a thread or two of blue silk and some drops of blood. I'm convinced she was struck with that *bo* and then dropped off the promontory."

Tora shuddered. "Who would do such a thing? What if she was still alive when he pushed her over?"

Tamako had turned white. "Oh, how terrible!"

"Yes," Akitada said heavily. "The killer was very cruel."

Tamako shook her head, and he extended his good hand to her.

Tora cleared his throat. "Well, I've some chores to do," he muttered and left quickly.

Akitada pulled Tamako down beside him, put his good arm around her, and kissed her hungrily. He was incredibly happy to be alive.

But the door flew open again, and Akiko rushed in. "There you are, Brother. Thank heaven you're all right." She took in the scene. "You can do that later. I think I've solved your case. Just wait till you hear."

26

The Novice

Akitada released his wife. He was touched. His sister had never shown much fondness for him in the past. "Thank you, Akiko. I'm quite well on the whole. Just a little bruised from the fall."

"There, you see, Tamako? He's taken a tumble, that's all."

Tamako shook her head. "He might have died," she said. "Or been more badly injured. He fell quite far. They had to transport him on a litter."

Akiko stared at her brother. "You mean someone really tried to kill you?"

"Nothing so dramatic. I slipped and fell, that's all."

"Clumsy of you," his sister remarked.

Akitada smiled and nodded.

Tamako made an impatient gesture. "Well, there was that warning. I really wish Akitada hadn't got himself involved in Prince Atsuhira's problems again. It's dangerous and has already caused nothing but trouble."

"What warning?" Akitada asked.

Tamako explained about the note tied to the rock. "And you hadn't come home. You really must be more careful in the future."

Akiko would have none of it. "Oh, come on! You make it sound as if there were assassins lurking around every corner. As you see, Akitada's quite capable of falling down mountains on his own. Anyway, I've found Lady Masako's companion, Akitada. I sent her a note and got an answer. What do you think of that?"

The news about the threat troubled Akitada, but now he brightened. "You did? Good work, sister. What does she say?"

"She's a Lady Hiroko, and she'll meet me tomorrow. We must put our heads together to see what questions I should ask her."

Akitada smiled and shook his head. "Thanks, but I think I'd better handle that."

His sister stiffened and raised her chin. "Oh, no, you don't. Not after all the work I did."

Akitada exchanged a glance with his wife. "Akiko," he said reasonably, "It is my case. Besides, it isn't at all suitable for such matters to be handled by women."

"What? And this from my own brother?" Akiko glowered and even Tamako looked at him with raised brows.

"Well, the subject of such a scandalous affair is hardly something that should be discussed by ladies."

They both burst out laughing.

Akiko said, "You have very little notion of what women talk about, brother. And that means you're not qualified to conduct your investigations in women's pavilions."

"She is right, Akitada," Tamako said. "Besides, it isn't quite proper for you to speak to a lady you are not related to."

Akitada frowned. "I've done so before and will do so again. Lady Kishi received me, and she surely outranks this Hiroko."

Akiko said, "You were with her cousin. Besides Lady Kishi is a married woman and of such rank that no one questions her behavior."

Akitada's head started throbbing again. "No," he said. "I can't risk it. Perhaps we can pay the visit together?"

The women looked at each other. Akiko said, "Very well. But I want to know what will be discussed and I want to ask my own questions." She got up. "Now I must run. Guests, remember?" And with a nod to Akitada and a touch to Tamako's shoulder, she was gone.

"You have created a monster," Akitada said accusingly.

"Not I. Your sister is a great deal like you. And now she has found a way to prove herself. You should really give her credit sometimes. She feels you don't approve of her."

Akitada had the grace to flush. "Akiko irritates me with her selfish ways and her pursuit of rank and fortune."

"Yes, though that is a woman's role once she is married and has children to care about. Her own aspirations no longer exist, and she becomes a mother."

Akitada thought about this for a moment, then changed the subject. "I could eat something."

After another dose of Doctor Kumada bitter medicine and a rather large meal—after all, he had not eaten for more than a day—he became so sleepy that he allowed Tamako to spread out his bedding again. There he fell into a deep sleep from which he did not awake until longer after dark.

When he opened his eyes, they fell on Tora, who sat at his desk, frowning over a book by the light of a candle.

"What's the matter?" Akitada asked. "Don't you like the story?"

Tora's smile flashed. "You're awake! How do you feel?"

Akitada thought about it. "Quite well. Have I slept until night?" He sat up. "How are you? Did you have your evening rice?"

"Yes. That and my midday rice also. Shall I go to the kitchen for something for you? The fires are still on, I think."

Akitada got to his feet and stretched those limbs that seemed well. He yawned. "Yes, go get us both a snack. Then we'll discuss progress on the two cases."

"Yes, sir!" cried Tora enthusiastically and dashed off.

Akitada resumed his place behind his desk. The scroll Tora had been reading was the *Tale of Ise*, an illustrated poetry collection. He had probably been attracted by the many scenes of a man and a woman meeting in romantic settings. The poet Narihira had been a famous lover. The text was elegantly written, but the brush style was beyond Tora's skills. Akitada rolled up the scroll and tied the silk ribbons.

Prince Atsuhira had been compared to this same poet. Perhaps he had eventually tried to live up to him. Or had he compared himself to Prince Genji, the fictional son of an emperor who had traded succession for the life of a rake? Akitada did not know the answer, and it struck him that the prince's character was not the issue. It was far more important to understand Lady Masako. What had caused her to commit such a flagrantly scandalous, foolish, and disloyal act as to take a lover so openly while serving His Majesty?

Akiko had been a great help by finding and contacting Masako's companion. The two women had lived together in the imperial apartments, and this Lady Hiroko had probably been in her confidence. Even if Masako had not confided in her, a companion would have been in an excellent position to observe her. He grudgingly admitted to himself that Akiko had done very well. And he found that he actually looked forward to accompanying his sister on their visit to the lady.

Tora returned, carrying a heavily laden tray. His face shone with satisfaction. "Cook has for once done right by you," he announced. "I almost didn't recognize the evil goblin. She was all smiles, gathering the finest morsels for her injured master." He set down the tray. It held a large array of bowls and dishes, containing both hot and cold foods. "Some wine to wash it down with?"

Akitada nodded. He was not particularly hungry, but the food smelled good and he had wanted a cup of wine for a long time.

They drank and ate, reaching for whatever struck their fancy. Between bites, they talked, exchanging observations about the prince's villa, the two caretakers, the doubtful evidence of the *bo*, the equally unreliable signs of a struggle in the villa.

Then Tora made his report.

He told Akitada about meeting Saburo and visiting Genba.

This pleased Akitada. "Has he changed his mind about leaving?"

"Who? Genba?" Tora glowered. "The big lout is as stubborn as an ox."

Akitada shook his head. "It's my fault, I think. He must've taken amiss something I said. What about Saburo?"

"Do you want him back?"

"Yes. Especially now. You didn't mention the note you found."

"Oh. Sorry. It slipped my mind. It was probably nothing."

Akitada knew better, but he did not mention the attack.

"Saburo's found a job and is managing quite well, but I think he misses the children."

This astonished Akitada. "The children? I would have thought he'd have no interest in children."

Tora grinned. "I've watched him. He's shy around them, but I know he buys them sweets and toys, and they like him. It's bribery, of course, but I guess he's lonely. Now there's a man who needs a family."

They both sighed and shook their heads.

"What about Tokuzo's murder?" Akitada asked.

"I talked to Shokichi, I thought maybe she could be relied on to provide useful information to help her friend."

Akitada nodded.

"Well, aside from the fact that nobody liked Tokuzo and that all the women hated him because he beat them, there were only two women who actually died. They were both young. Miyagi grew up in the capital. Her family has moved away, no one knows where. Tokuzo gave her something to get rid of a child, and she bled to death."

Akitada grimaced. "That's barbaric. What about the warden? Did he investigate the death?"

"In the quarter such things are common. The women often swallow the wrong medicine or do things to themselves because they know they can't work when they're with child.

"What happened to the other one?" Akitada asked, shaking his head.

"She was thrown from the balcony to the yard below and died. Shokichi says a drunken and irate customer did it."

"Not Tokuzo then?"

"No, but the girls blamed him anyway. They said he should never have given Ozuru to a brute like that. She was small, frail, and shy."

"Was the man arrested?"

"Yes, but he claimed she stole money from him and when he chased after her, she jumped. Shokichi says Ozuru would never steal money, and the customer was known to abuse the women." I went to see her family. Her father is dead. The mother is very poor. They hold no grudge. In fact, they are grateful to that bastard Tokuzo and sold two more girls."

Akitada raised his brows. "To him?"

"No, but it proves how they feel."

"Yes. What a thing to do to your child! You say both girls were young?"

"Fourteen and fifteen."

Akitada thought of another case, that of the young girl who had been murdered in the brothel town of Eguchi not so long ago. Then, too, he had thought of his own daughter. Yasuko was not the child of poor peasants, but that did not necessarily protect a young woman. Lady Masako was proof of that. He seemed to think frequently about the fate of young women these days. They faced as many dangers as young men who went to war.

"I see." Akitada sighed. "Inconclusive."

A silence fell.

"Well," said Akitada after a while, "talk to Saburo again and tell him what you just told me. Try to enlist his help in identifying the killer. And tell him to come back. We need him. If he cares about the children, he'll come."

Tora nodded. "What about Lady Masako? Do you want me to talk to Lord Masaie's cook again?"

"No. Not yet, anyway. I hope to get the information from her companion."

The next day, Akitada and his sister set out for the Koryu-ji, a small but venerable temple outside the capital. They were on horseback. Akitada wore his brown hunting coat over blue trousers tucked into boots and his sword. To his relief, Akiko, who loved bright colors, had chosen a dark gray silk gown. She also wore the broad straw hat with a veil worn by upper-class women on journeys to holy places.

As soon as they left the busy city streets behind, Akiko threw back the veil with a laugh.

"Oh, how I love this, Akitada," she cried. "What a delightful outing! And it's spring, and the sun shines on us. I'm as free as any young peasant girl to enjoy the day."

Akitada was not having a delightful time. He had woken to aches and pains over his entire body. There were large bruises in places he had not noticed the day before. Of course, the agony of his shoulder might well have canceled out all other discomforts. His body now exhibited the signs of every impact and scrape of his unfortunate tumble. Sitting in the saddle and bumping along at a trot did nothing to soothe his misery.

His irritation mounting, he said, "We have a serious purpose, Akiko. A young woman has died, a woman younger than you who also desired greater freedom. She, too, rode out from the confines of her life in the city, but she rode to her death."

Akiko's face fell. "You always spoil everything." She urged her horse on and galloped ahead.

Akitada bit his lip again and caught up with her. "I'm sorry," he said. "I had no right to spoil your day. Please forgive me. I'm still hurting a little, and the story of Lady Masako has affected me more deeply than I thought."

Akiko slowed down. After a while she said, "Yes, it *is* a nasty tale. But we cannot know for certain what made her behave that way until we speak to Lady Hiroko. I must say, I was surprised she agreed so quickly to meet us. She sent a messenger last evening and suggested Koryu-ji as a meeting place. Very well chosen, I must say." She peered ahead where green mountains beckoned.

Most of the temples and monasteries attended by the people of the capital were in the surrounding foothills and mountains. Here and there, slender pagodas rose from among trees and the curved roofs of a temple or villa broke the greenery.

Akitada agreed. "It's close to the city and a very proper destination for a woman to visit, whether to worship or to meet friends." He gave his sister a smile. "It must have been your persuasiveness that convinced her to speak to us. I expect the palace has warned her not to discuss Lady Masako."

"Yes, I think they would have forbidden it. But perhaps she's just a young and foolish girl who likes attention."

But Lady Hiroko, though young, was not at all foolish. Her choice of a meeting place should have told them as much.

As soon as Akitada and his sister had dismounted at the temple gate and climbed the steps, they passed into a realm of upper-class propriety.

Being close to the northern part of the capital where the nobility had its palaces, Koryu-ji was a favorite of the good people. Women, in particular, liked to come here, especially when the cherry trees blossomed lacy-white among the dark green trees and the age-darkened halls of the temple. The visitors felt as if they moved among celestial clouds that had descended among these venerable buildings, lending this holy world a brief splendor like a blessing from Buddha himself.

Monks passed among the strolling visitors, mostly well-dressed ladies and noblemen. Sounds of religious services floated in the air: soft tinkling of bells, sonorous chants, the murmurs of sutra readings. It was pleasant and very, very proper.

"I feel devout all of a sudden," remarked Akiko, looking about. "It's all so beautiful, so peaceful."

Akitada said nothing. In his mind, the thought of Lady Masako's death warred against such contentment.

A young monk approached. When Akitada asked for Lady Hiroko, the monk consulted a list he carried and directed them to the "hall of tranquility."

They reached this building after a short walk through tree-shaded grounds. The sounds of worshipful humanity receded; there was only birdsong and the rustling of leaves in the breeze. It was cool, and the air was filled with the smell of moist earth and growing things.

The "hall of tranquility" was a very small building of plain dark wood with a roof of cypress. All around the woods enclosed it. A small veranda with a few steps led to the open doors, and in the doorway stood the slender gray figure of a young woman. She was looking up at the sky, but at the sound of their steps, she turned her head.

Akitada bowed, as Akiko called out, "Lady Hiroko? My brother and I have come to pay our respects."

Lady Hiroko inclined her head and murmured something. She was a very plain young woman with a narrow face that lacked even a trace of make-up. Her hair was cut so short it barely reached her shoulders. The court lady had taken the first steps to becoming a nun.

Akitada felt saddened. True, she was not pretty, and true her chances of finding a husband in the palace were minimal, but it seemed to him a waste when a woman as young as this one forsook the world. He wondered if Akiko had known.

They paused at the steps.

"I am honored, Lord Sugawara and Lady Akiko," said the novice in a soft, shy voice. She stepped aside and gestured to the inside of the hall. "Please come in. We will be very private here."

They walked into the single room, dim even on this bright spring day. A few plain cushions lay about and two tapers flickered at their approach. Beneath their feet, above their heads, and on all walls, dark wood enclosed them. Since the doors were the only opening, the room was shadowy and reminiscent of transience and death.

Akitada thought the religious atmosphere along with the young woman's decision to forsake the world would make the coming conversation awkward.

This apparently had not occurred to his sister, who began in a bright voice, "My brother and I wish to make our condolences on your loss of a beloved friend. For a young woman in your position at court it must have been extremely painful to watch Lady Masako lose her heart to a man who wasn't His Majesty."

Lady Hiroko did not answer. She arranged cushions for them and then knelt decorously, raising her eyes only briefly to Akiko's. They took their seats.

"Come," said Akiko briskly, "you must take solace. We've come to help. As I wrote, my brother and I hope to find the man who killed your friend. I trust when we do her soul may rest at last. It's been four months already. Think how terrible she must feel."

Lady Hiroko burst into tears.

Akitada glanced at his sister. "Akiko, please. Clearly, Lady Hiroko feels the death of her friend very strongly. Allow her to say what is in her heart. Then perhaps we may ask some questions."

Akiko sniffed, gave him a look from narrowed eyes, and fell silent.

Lady Hiroko dabbed at her eyes with a sleeve. "Forgive me. This is very difficult. I would not be here, only there was the dream. She came to me in a dream after Lady Akiko wrote to me. It's the dream that decided me. You're quite right, Lady Akiko. I must speak for her and to do so, I must mention things that are forbidden."

Akitada and his sister held their breaths.

Lady Hiroko's head sank a little lower. "Oh, this is so painful. In the dream, Masako spoke to me. She begged my help to find peace. She kept saying, 'Make him confess what he's done.'" She raised her face and looked at them. "She was white as snow and shivered with cold. It was terrible."

Akitada cleared his throat. "I understand your difficulties, but you may trust us. We, too, revere His Majesty. What happened must not reflect on Him."

She nodded and looked at him gratefully. "That is indeed what troubles me. We are forbidden to speak of life in the inner apartments. But in this case . . . well, Masako was so very unhappy. I was assigned as her companion when she first came. It was thought then that His Majesty would make her a favorite. She was very beautiful, you see, and her family is influential. But it did not come to pass, though both Masako and her father did everything they could to promote her

interests. His Majesty's heart had been given elsewhere.
These things happen."

Akitada and his sister nodded. Akiko said, "It must
have been a terrible disappointment."

"For Masako yes. She passed all of last year in grief
and misery. She attended events in her most beautiful
gowns and with her face and hair perfect, but we were
always placed as far away from His Majesty as possible.
There was unpleasant gossip among the ladies about it.
It seems someone overheard His Majesty saying that he
disliked her. Masako wept when she heard. My own
family is understanding and no one expected me to
make much of an impression on anyone, but it was different for her."

Akiko said, "I think you must have looked quite elegant, Lady Hiroko. You have a certain grace."

Hiroko blinked, then shook her head. "You are
kind, but I'm not beautiful. Masako was magnificent,
even if she was taller than the other ladies. She comes .
. . came from a family of tall people. Both her father
and her brother are giants."

A shadow passed over her face as she said this and
Akitada asked, "Did you meet Lord Masaie and his
son?"

"Yes. They visited quite often, especially late last
year." She shuddered. "Their visits were painful for
Masako. You see, they were angry with her that she
had not been noticed by His Majesty. As if she could
have helped it, poor dear."

"I suspected as much," said Akitada. "Lord Masaie
had his heart set on seeing her become empress."

Hiroko nodded again and twisted her hands. "It grieved her so much that her father was angry. They were very close."

Akiko asked, "Were you aware of her affair with Prince Atsuhira?"

Hiroko blushed and lowered her eyes. "Yes," she said almost inaudibly. "I tried to warn her, but she . . . she said he loved her and she wanted to be loved by someone."

Silence fell. Akitada thought that Masako had acted out of loneliness and desperation. The young emperor had cruelly rejected her, her father and her brother blamed and threatened her, and the ladies of the court mocked her. What did she have to look forward to? When that inveterate womanizer Prince Atsuhira had seen the beautiful young woman and courted her, she must have been overcome with gratitude. "How old was Lady Masako?" he asked.

"Eighteen. Older than His Majesty but not as old as His consort." Lady Hiroko blushed and covered her lips. "Oh, I should not have mentioned the consort."

"Never mind," Akiko said warmly. "You must have liked Lady Masako very much. I'm sure her treatment by everyone was very unfair."

Lady Hiroko gave her a grateful look. "I did love her. She was kind to me and I thought her very brave. In my heart, I wanted her to find happiness."

Akiko nodded. "It's surely a most romantic tale: the handsome prince who might have been emperor but for his karma, and the rejected beauty. Who can blame them for falling in love with each other? I take it they met in the palace?"

Akitada shot his sister a warning glance, and Lady Hiroko blushed rosy red again. "It was very proper. I was there, and so were others. It was only later that Masako left the palace to meet him." She twisted her hands again and looked down.

Akiko smiled. "You helped her, I take it?"

Akitada said quickly, "It doesn't matter now. What matters is to find out who knew about their assignations. You said the other ladies were less than kind to Lady Masako. Did she have enemies among them?"

Lady Hiroko looked shocked. "Oh, nothing like that. Not murder." She paused. "Could it have been a madman?"

It was an interesting thought. The killer had been furiously angry, but he had also been coldly calculating.

Akiko gave Akitada a questioning look, and he shook his head slightly. "The possibility of an accidental meeting with a dangerous stranger is remote," he said. "Given her story, someone must have considered her an obstacle to his plans or desires. It must have been a person who knew of these secret meetings. Can you think of anyone like that? It need merely be a matter of gossip being passed around."

The novice looked at Akitada directly for the first time. "Late last year there was some gossip. I don't know how it started and who may have heard. By then, Masako had already planned to leave the palace for good. You see, there was no chance of hiding the relationship any longer."

Akiko said bluntly, "Because Lady Masako was with child."

The young woman nodded.

"Could she have been desperate enough to consider killing herself?" Akitada asked, thinking of the letter the prince had mentioned to Kobe.

"Oh, no. She was very happy when she found out. It was her future, she said. Their future together, for the prince also wanted it. For her, the child was her whole life. Her life was only just beginning."

Akitada was moved by this. "I see." He did not add that she had fallen in love with a man who had not deserved such a sacrifice.

"You will find out who did this?" Hiroko asked anxiously.

"Yes."

"Oh, yes," echoed Akiko.

Hiroko nodded and reached into her sleeve to pull out a slender booklet. "I brought this. I wasn't sure if I had the right to let anyone see it. Now I think perhaps you should read what she wrote. You may find something that tells you who did this. It's Masako's journal."

Akiko gasped. "Her journal? Oh, that is excellent, isn't it Akitada?"

Akitada looked at the thin volume of fine paper in its brocade cover. He was also flabbergasted by the good luck. "It may indeed hold some answer," he said. "Thank you for your trust, Lady Hiroko. You will not regret it."

"You will return it? It is all I have left of her."

Akiko cried, "Of course."

The homeward journey was filled with Akiko's loud chatter and frequent demands to stop and have a peek at the journal. When a rather silent Akitada refused, she spent the time on various theories about what it might contain. They were almost home before Akitada had the heart to spoil her pleasure.

"It may not contain anything useful. If it did, Lady Hiroko would have told us. I doubt Lady Masako knew her danger. She would not have made the lonely journey to the villa, knowing that someone wished her dead."

Akiko was silent for a moment. Then she raised her chin. "Well, in that case we must read between the lines. I have a knack for that sort of thing. I always knew ahead of time what the characters in Lady Murasaki's novel were going to do next."

27

Spies

Tora waited for Saburo in front of Mrs. Komiya's little house. He passed the time charming Saburo's landlady, who had noticed him and come out.

"I knew right away he was good man," she said to Tora after he had introduced himself. "I got a feeling for that sort of thing. And I have a big heart. The poor man looks terrible, and people are unkind or fearful. They believe they see goblins and *oni* everywhere. Me, I've never seen one of those, so I'm not afraid."

Tora regarded her with surprise. He had never really seen any apparitions either, but he believed in their existence with every fiber of his being. He said cautiously, "Well, Saburo's had some bad luck. And you're right. He's a good man. I can testify to that."

She smiled and nodded. "And you're his friend. I must say you two couldn't be more unlike." She chuckled. "Hell and paradise, you might say."

Tora shook his head. "You should look past the outside of things. That's what Master Kung-fu-tse said."

"I know, I know. But it's what people think when they see you two together."

Tora humphed and wished her gone. Fortunately, Saburo appeared around the corner at that moment, his scarred face breaking into one of his twisted smiles.

"Tora. Mrs. Komiya. You've met, I see."

"Your friend's a very handsome fellow." Mrs. Komiya ogled Tora.

"Unlike me," remarked Saburo, "but he's a good sort for all that."

This made her laugh, and she left them to their business.

"I only have a small room," said Saburo. "Maybe we'd better talk while we're strolling down to the river."

"Suits me. The sun's still high and a walk along the Katsura should be pretty this time of year."

"Yes. The cherry trees are blooming. But you have news?"

Tora related recent events, making his own role in the rescue a fairly hair-raising feat."

Saburo was suitably impressed. "I'm glad your master wasn't badly injured."

"Your master, too," reminded Tora. "He sent me to tell you he wants you back."

Saburo frowned. "I'm no use to him. I'm not even a good secretary. All I do all day long is to keep the accounts. It only takes an hour here or there."

Tora stopped. "Don't forget you have other useful skills."

"Those are the ones he doesn't approve of."

Tora said, "He'll come round. He always does."

"I know he's kind, but his position makes it impossible for him to allow the sort of things I do."

"As long as you don't kill anyone or cause a scandal, he doesn't need to know precisely how you get information. He wants you to help me clear Genba."

Saburo said nothing.

They took up their walk again. Long stretches of greenery hinted at the open countryside. Dotted about were occasional vegetable gardens with fruit trees in bloom and a shrine or two.

They reached the river and stopped under one of the flowering trees. Ducks paddled near the shore. The Katsura River would join the Kamo River south of the capital, and together they would become the Yodo and end up in the Inland Sea. They had both been there, working together and almost dying. It was then that Saburo had joined the Sugawara household.

"Remember Naniwa?" Tora asked.

"Yes."

A long silence fell, then Saburo sighed. "I think what you propose may be possible, but I dislike concealing my activities from my master."

Tora burst into a shout of laughter. "That's surely a lie, my friend. Your whole life's been dedicated to hiding what you do."

Saburo's lip twitched. "Well, yes. You got me there."

"Anyway, that's why I'm here. The master wants us to find Tokuzo's killer, and it looks like he's one of your kind. You're a spy, and so is he probably. Who better to find him than you?"

Saburo shot Tora a glance. "You make it sound so easy. Do you have any proof he's a *shinobi*?"

"I think he's the man Genba encountered just before the murder. The one who dropped the assassin's needle. And surely he's the one who knocked you out inside the brothel and took back his needle?"

Saburo grunted. "It could have been coincidence."

"Don't be an idiot. You know I'm right. Someone paid him to kill Tokuzo. The master and I think it may have something to do with Tokuzo's treatment of his girls."

Tora explained about the deaths of Miyagi and Ozuru. "I don't think Ozuru's family is at the bottom of this, but I haven't been able to get hold of Miyagi's people. Their name was Satake. The neighbors say the old people moved away and died, but you never know. The master wasn't satisfied. Maybe you could find out what happened to them?"

"Yes, but it could still just have been a robbery gone wrong. Tokuzo had all that gold in his place. Maybe he interrupted the robber."

"You mean the guy Genba ran into was a robber?"

Saburo sighed. "No. If he was a *shinobi*, he wasn't there for robbery. There could be someone else involved."

Tora grinned. "Well, you should know. Will you look into it?

Saburo nodded.

They stood a while longer, watching the ducks and some boats on the river. Above them, the blue sky shimmered through the blossoms of the cherry tree. Then they parted, Tora to return home, and Saburo to begin his search.

Saburo wanted to prove himself. His self-respect had suffered severely when he was dismissed. But he faced a dilemma with this case. In spite of his words to Tora, he was convinced the killer had been a trained *shinobi*, a shadow warrior, as he himself had been. He had no proof of this, except the reasons Tora had cited and a strong suspicion about his identity.

Instead of going to the address Tora had given him, Saburo decided to talk to Shokichi first.

Shokichi was at work at this hour. At the Sasaya. Steeling himself, Saburo walked to the Willow Quarter and the late Tokuzo's brothel. His arrival there caused consternation. The customers sitting around drinking stared at him. Saburo called the waitress, a plain girl who turned pale and pretended not to have heard.

"Hoh!" shouted Saburo again. "Service!"

No reaction.

"You there! Girl! Come here. What does a man have to do to get a drink in this place?"

Tokuzo's mother put her head through a door to see what the shouting was about. The girl finally came, but she avoided looking at him.

"So," sneered Saburo, "I'm not to your taste, am I?"

She shuddered. "What can I bring your honor?"

Saburo still smarted from her behavior. "How much for a night with you?"

She started shaking. "Twenty coppers," she murmured so softly he could barely hear her.

"Too much for someone like you," he sneered. "Where's Shokichi?"

The girl turned and ran to the back door where she told the old woman who gave a nod and disappeared. Soon, another girl appeared. She was older than the first and approached him calmly, sitting down across from him.

"You asked for me, sir?" She found his good eye and smiled at him.

Bad teeth and a few pockmarks, thought Saburo, but not unattractive. Still, he was not here for that. "You're Shokichi?" he asked. "Ohiro's friend?"

Her eyes narrowed. "Yes."

"I want to talk to you. Suppose we go upstairs?"

"That will cost you twenty coppers."

He reached for the money. She bowed, rose, and took his hand, leading him to the backdoor, where the old woman waited. Shokichi passed her the coins. She counted, nodded, and disappeared into her room. Shokichi led him to the backyard and up the stairs to a room at the end.

There she placed a couple of dirty cushions on the floor and gestured to the bedding rolls. "You've paid. Do you want to make love first?"

"Thank you, no." The offer pleased him. "You're not frightened by my face?" he asked.

"No. I'm sorry you were hurt."

Saburo did not know what to say. He had never met a woman who had offered herself to him in such a matter-of-fact manner. He looked at her silently and found her even more attractive, but he caught himself and said, "You're back working here. Why? You tore up your contract like the others, didn't you?"

"I sold it back to the old woman. I needed the money, and she needed someone who knows the business. Things are better. I look after the women."

He said nothing to this. "I'm trying to help Genba and Ohiro. Tora told me about the two women who died. Miyagi's parents are gone, and the house now belongs to strangers. Is there anything else you might recall?"

"I didn't know her family left. They were her grandparents. Her parents died. Miyagi loved her grandparents and went to see them often, taking them what money she could. I think after she died, they had nothing to live on. It's sad. They were good people who'd come down in the world." She looked angry.

So Miyagi's death had caused further misery. Perhaps the old people had also died because their only source of income was gone. "Was there anyone else?" he asked.

"She had a brother. He was a soldier up north. When Tokuzo mistreated her and she cried, I used to tell her to write to him. Miyagi could read and write a little. I don't know if she did, but she never got any letters, and no brother ever came."

"What was his name?"

She looked away. "She must have told me, but I don't remember it. Sorry." When Saburo said nothing, she added, "I expect he died a long time ago in the fighting. Or else he took a wife up north and won't come back."

Saburo looked at her steadily until she started fidgeting. "There must be someone else who killed Tokuzo," she said nervously.

He shook his head. "I don't think so. Thank you. You've been a lot of help." He got to his feet.

"Help? How?" she asked, looking up at him.

"I don't know yet." He hesitated, then said in a rush, "Perhaps some day when you're free, you'll allow me to buy you a meal somewhere?"

She blushed. "Maybe, but we're not supposed to meet customers outside. You could come back here."

"No," said Saburo, with a glance around. "You deserve better."

He left disappointed and strangely stirred by the encounter. She had told him what he wanted to know, even though she had not intended to do so. She had lied about not knowing the brother's name, and he admired her for it.

It was a bad situation all around.

He went next to the city administration for the western wards. There he asked for the property lists of the ward where the Satake family had resided. He found them quickly: grandfather, grandmother, father, mother, two children. Father and mother had died the same year four years previously, perhaps during the epidemic. The grandparents had remained with the grandchildren: a boy, Narimitsu and a younger girl, Nariko. Nariko must be Miyagi's real name. The property had changed hands last year, a few months after Miyagi died.

So far, he was no closer. He had merely confirmed what Shokichi had told him. And yet he was certain she had lied about something else.

What if the brother had returned to the capital after all, only to find his sister dead and the family home sold? It would surely make him a prime suspect in Tokuzo's murder. But how was he to prove this? And where would he find the man?

In Akitada's household, Saburo had learned to be meticulous. He made another search, this time for the whereabouts of Miyagi's grandparents. This produced nothing and suggested the old people had left the city. Since he did not know where they might have gone, consulting tax registers was pointless.

It was time to change to another tack. Late that night, Saburo visited a small monastery in the northern foothills. He had to walk and did not reach his destination until well past the hour of the boar. He hoped to get his information and set out on the return journey in time to reach the capital at day break and steal a few hours sleep before reporting to his employer, the rice merchant.

The monastery was too insignificant for elaborate walls and gates, and it did not bother to lock people out. There was nothing to steal here. The monks who lived in this small outpost had other gifts.

As he passed between the wooden buildings, his steps mostly muffled by dewy grass, he looked for a light somewhere, a sign that one of the monks was awake even at this hour.

Instead, the hair on the back of his head suddenly tingled, and he jumped aside. The jump caused him to slip on the wet grass and come down hard on one knee and a hand. A black figure loomed momentarily, blocking out the starry sky. Then its weight crashed down on him.

Saburo grunted and struggled to free himself. In vain. The other man was bigger, younger, stronger. Giving up the unequal contest, he gasped, "Monkey on the roof."

The other relaxed his grip slightly. "Shinobi?" he asked.

The voice was young. Feeling depressed by the difference between them, Saburo said, "Yes."

The other jumped up and grasped Saburo's wrist to pull him upright. In the darkness they faced each other. Their features were shadowy, but Saburo saw that the other was much taller and broader than he and felt a bit better.

His attacker reached for his face. "Mask?" he demanded.

"Ouch! No." Saburo slapped the other's hand away. "Mind your manners," he growled.

"Sorry." The young monk sounded contrite. "Didn't know. What are you doing here?"

"I need information."

"About what?"

"Let me speak to the abbot. Is it still the Reverend Raishin?"

"Yes. Come along then."

They walked past several shadowy buildings and came to a smaller hall. All was dark inside, but the young monk stepped up on the veranda and cleared his throat. After a moment, a voice from inside asked, "Yes, what is it?"

"It's Kangyo, Reverence. There's a visitor here."

They heard the sound of a flint, and then a soft golden glow seeped through the cracks of the door and a shuttered window. "Come in."

Saburo followed the young monk through the door he held open. For a moment he blinked against the light, then he saw an elderly monk of astonishing size peering up at him. The abbot must easily be of Genba's build, though in his case, his shoulders and chest bulged with muscles rather than fat.

"It's you!" the abbot said, his eyes widening.

"It's me," Saburo agreed.

"Leave us, Kangyo. He's one of us."

"Yes, Reverence. So he said." The young man hesitated, looking from the abbot to Saburo and back. "Will it be all right? Should I stay close?"

Abbot Raishin frowned. "No, no. Get back to your rounds."

They waited until Kangyo had closed the door behind him. The abbot said, "Sit down, Saburo. You look tired. I've often wondered how you are managing."

"Thank you. I manage," Saburo said drily.

"But not easily, I bet. I grieved over what happened, but we had no choice."

"I know. Once people see my face, they remember."

"Yes. Why have you come?"

"A friend of mine is in trouble because of something done by a *shinobi*. I came to get information about the man."

"You know I cannot give you information about our people."

"I think this man may not be one of ours."

"I see. That's different. Tell me about it."

Saburo told Genba's story from his encounter with the stranger and the dropped needle to his being arrested for Tokuzo's murder. Then he waited.

The abbot had listened with a lively interest. Now he smiled and said, "That was very careless of him."

"To be fair, he probably didn't expect to collide with a wrestler," said Saburo. "There's more. I also encountered him. At least I assume it was the same man, because we both had taken an interest in Tokuzo's place. I got there before him and took the women's contracts. When I was leaving, he jumped me in the dark hallway. When I came to, the contracts and the needle were gone."

Abbot Raishin frowned. "It could have been another burglar."

"He found the needle, though I carried it in the seam of my jacket. Only someone in our business would know where to look."

"Perhaps. Still, it's not proof. If this Tokuzo was as evil and as wealthy as you say, he could well have had several enemies."

Saburo's heart sank. "It's all I have, except that Genba remembers the man smelled as if he'd just come from a bathhouse."

Raishin sat up. "A bathhouse? Now I wonder. Needles. Hmm."

"Yes," said Saburo, hope rising again. "It occurred to me also. I agree it's far-fetched, but there's a link." He told the abbot how he had ended up in the beggars' guild and how none of the beggars had wanted to answer his questions or Tora's.

The abbot nodded. "We have taken note of this person. He's not been here long. The first reports reached us a few weeks ago. He received his training in the north. But I must tell you he doesn't seem to be an assassin. A *shinobi*, yes, but he hasn't killed anyone to our knowledge."

"Do you think it's possible he killed Tokuzo?"

The abbot spread his hands. "All things are possible. I wish I could be more helpful."

Saburo bowed. "Thank you, Reverence. I think I'll take a closer look at him."

Raishin said, "It's a difficult issue, this question of justice. I don't envy you."

Saburo nodded and got to his feet. He was almost out of the room, when he heard the abbot say, "Most likely the killer has a very troubled conscience himself."

28

The Journal

The ride to Koryu-ji had been more than Akitada should have undertaken so soon after his fall. When they reached his home, he slid from the saddle and clung to it while waves of pain washed over him. The worst of it was that he would not have been in condition to fight off another attack or protect his sister.

"What's wrong?" asked Akiko, sounding irritatingly chipper as she got down from her horse.

"Nothing. I'll be all right in a moment."

"Here comes help," she said. "I'll run in and see Tamako."

Tora appeared by his side, and then, to his surprise, Genba. They also wanted to know what was wrong.

Akitada pushed himself away from the horse and took a deep breath.

"It's just some soreness from the fall. Genba? I'm so glad to see you, but what happened?"

Genba regarded him with moist eyes. "Superintendent Kobe let us go, sir. I expect we owe you our thanks." He bowed.

"It wasn't my doing. We haven't found the killer yet. Saburo is working on it. Kobe must have decided his case against you wasn't strong enough." Akitada embraced Genba. "Welcome home," he said, then stepped back to look him over.

Genba wiped his eyes and smiled, speechless at this reception.

"Well," said Tora, clearly embarrassed by all this emotion, "I think it was high time the superintendent realized you're innocent. And what about all those floggings?"

Akitada said, "Yes, I'm sorry about all you've had to suffer. How are you?"

Genba grinned. "It was nothing, sir. I'm very well. But what about you? Tora told me what happened."

"I'm also very well . . . now that you're back," Akitada said happily, patting Genba's shoulder. "We really missed you."

"Thank you, sir. Let us help you into the house."

Akitada walked leaning on Genba's strong arm. In his study, he got behind his desk. "Sit down, both of you. Genba, what about Ohiro? Is she free, too?"

"Yes, sir. She's gone to stay with Shokichi." Genba shot Tora a glance.

"But I thought you and she . . . I was under the impression . . . ." Uncertain, Akitada stopped.

"Well . . ." Genba looked to Tora for help.

"Genba thinks it will be best if he visits her in the city." Tora was clearly uncomfortable.

"Oh." Akitada looked from one to the other and frowned.

Tora bit his lip. "We thought you wouldn't want another woman from the amusement quarter under your roof."

"What nonsense! Another woman? You mean Hanae?" Tora nodded, and Akitada snapped, "You were wrong. Hanae is part of my family, as are both of you. You are like brothers to me. How could I deny either of you the joy of raising a family? My fortunes aren't great and my future isn't promising either, but if you'll settle for what we can offer, Genba, and if you wish to take a wife, I will welcome her and your future children into my house. The same goes for Saburo. If I have given you a different impression in the past, I'm sorry. I tend to worry about the company you keep, but you're both grown men, and I have no right to interfere in your lives as long as you respect my family."

They both gaped at him.

When nobody said anything, Akitada smiled. "Are you happy here, Genba?"

"Yes, sir, but . . . are you sure? Ohiro . . . I love her dearly and she's a sweet and good woman, sir, but she did work in a brothel. Hanae never did."

"I've learned a few things lately about how young women end up in places they shouldn't be, sold by their parents to men who mistreat them. Ohiro's not to blame for what her life was like in the past, as long as she will be a devoted wife to you." Seeing Tears well up in Genba's eyes again, Akitada added quickly, "And now you two had better go and see about living quarters for Genba and his bride."

They left grinning, with Genba muttering his thanks over and over again.

Having thus arranged his household to his entire satisfaction, Akitada stepped out on his veranda and stretched. The garden was peaceful in the afternoon sun. Sighing with pleasure, he drew Lady Masako's journal from his sleeve and went back inside.

It was tastefully bound in pale green brocade with a pattern of golden shells and white cherry blossoms. He undid the darker green silk ribbon and opened it. The paper was of the finest quality, and the lady's brush strokes proved she had a good education. The journal was short and tended to skip days.

He settled down at his desk and started reading.

The entries were dated by the year and month, and it appeared she had started the diary soon after she had entered the palace. As was customary, she referred to herself in the third person and never by name. This device made the diary read like a tale about an imaginary character and was, no doubt, meant to protect the author's identity.

It occurred to Akitada that he had no proof this was Lady Masako's journal except for Lady Hiroko's word. He would have to read the entries carefully, looking for internal evidence of the author's identity.

The first pages described the season—it was spring, and the writer grieved at not seeing the cherry blossoms of her former home—but soon she mentioned incidents: visits from a father, then from a brother, court festivities, seasonal observations, more parental visits. Interjected poems began to suggest first melancholy, and then sadness: "Alas, each day brought deeper grief; each week another lament," and "In sorrow her days passed without comfort."

After the initial introduction to His Majesty, which dwelled in detail on the lady's gowns, there were no more references to the emperor. To Akitada this implied that her hurt at being rejected by the young monarch was too great to allow her to make the slightest reference to Him.

Akitada had progressed this far, when quick steps approached. Then the door opened, admitting Akiko and his wife. The ladies were wide-eyed with curiosity.

"There you are," said Akiko. "And you're reading it. Why didn't you wait for us?"

Akitada frowned. "I intend to absorb the contents in peace and quiet. I can't think when women chatter in my ears."

Akiko hissed. "Shameful! When I was the one who got the journal for you. You are the most ungrateful creature."

Tamako smiled and came to sit across from him. "You look tired, Akitada. I had the water heated for your bath. It will soothe your aches and pains."

He looked at her gratefully. "Thank you. I'll bathe as soon as I've had a look at this."

"What about us?" demanded his sister. "You cannot keep it to yourself."

Tamako said, "She has a point, Akitada."

Akiko sat down beside her, her chin in the air. "I'm not leaving until I've read the journal."

Akitada sighed. "Very well. I'll read it out loud. But don't interrupt constantly."

The ladies smiled triumphantly and settled themselves comfortably on their cushions. Akitada turned to the beginning and started reading. They listened, sometimes exchanging glances and nods, but remained quiet. It was not until he was well past the middle of the diary and had reached a passage where a page arrived and passed a branch of flowering orange to the lady that his sister spoke.

"A note from Prince Tametaka? Who is that? There is no Prince Tametaka."

Akitada gave her a reproving look. "She probably means Atsuhira; she's hiding his true identity."

"Oh! How fascinating!" Akiko clapped her hands.

Akitada ignored this and continued. It seemed to him Atsuhira had pursued Masako rather early in her career at court, but he said nothing of this.

The writer passed over the incident of the flowering orange branch or the note attached to it, only composing the conventional poem in response. However, the poem was certainly suggestive: "The scent of orange flowers is welcome to one whose sleeves lack such perfume."

The ladies gasped. Akiko said, "That's an invitation."

Tamako merely looked shocked.

Akitada was beginning to enter into Lady Masako's frame of mind. The rejected young woman wrote of her loneliness. No wonder she longed for love.

The affair began soon after. The prince called on her and spoke to her through the lowered reed curtains. His poems suggested they make their dream a reality. She responded, "I dream sweet dreams; my sleeves are wet with tears. If I take the dark path alone, we will meet in paradise."

A few nights later, he slipped into her room, and they became lovers. He marked the occasion with a poem on the meeting of their souls. She told him, "The cuckoo's song was full of pain; now it is summer and he sings with full-throated joy."

He paused. Had Lady Hiroko known of the forbidden meeting inside the palace? More than likely. And summer would soon be over.

Akiko sniffed. "Hurry on. We still have nothing to point to murder."

Entries followed about more shared nights and exchanged poems. The meetings in the palace were deemed too dangerous, and the lady arranged outings so she could meet him in his villa. He talked of marriage. She worried about scandal. And still the time spent in the imperial palace hung heavy on her hands. She had no friends except Lady Hiroko, who appeared in the journal now and then as Lady Sakyo. Her father stopped his frequent visits but sent angry letters. At some point, he demanded she return home. She obeyed, but the journal contained nothing about the visit. It picked back up late in autumn, when she was back in the palace.

At this point the tone changed. She had made up her mind to leave her service to the emperor in order to live with the prince. However, there appeared to be difficulties. Lady Masako did not specify what they were, but they seemed to have to do with the prince's household.

Having got this far, Akitada paused again. "My throat is dry. Let's have some wine."

Tamako rose quickly to get it.

Akiko said, "It seems strange nobody in the palace caught on. He managed to creep into her room a number of times, and then she was always going off on excursions. It must have been very dangerous. If he was so eager to take her to wife, he should have done so much sooner."

Her brother nodded. "Yes. I thought so, too. Prince Atsuhira has played fast and loose with young women before. Perhaps he got cold feet?"

She nodded. "Men are such cowards."

"Not all men, surely."

"No, but there are enough of those like the prince at court. If you ask me, Masako was a fool. Even at eighteen, a girl knows better than to listen to such honeyed words."

Akitada thought back to his last encounter with the prince. "He seemed very distraught over her death. I wonder if it was Lady Kishi who found out about their plans and made difficulties."

"Kishi would have done more than make difficulties. She would have gone to the emperor."

"Really?" Akitada was surprised by this and wondered what might have happened if she had done so. But, no, he did not believe the palace would engage assassins.

Akiko said, "No. Kishi doesn't love her husband. You have to love a man madly to cause a scandal like that."

Tamako came back, followed by her maid with a tray containing a wine flask and three cups. The maid set this down and poured, then left again. Akitada drank thirstily and refilled his cup immediately. The ladies sipped.

"Akitada thinks Kishi might have informed the emperor of the affair," Akiko told Tamako.

"Surely that would simply have meant sending Lady Masako home in disgrace," Tamako remarked.

"Exactly," nodded her husband. "Still, might she have written to Masaie?"

They pondered this but found no answer.

"Go on with the reading," urged Akiko. "If she did, we'll find out soon enough."

In the middle of the Gods Absent Month, Lady Masako went home again. Akitada paused, looking at the women.

"Strange," murmured Tamako. "She couldn't expect anything but more harsh reprimands from her father, yet it sounds as though she requested permission to travel."

Akiko cried, "I have it. She found out she was with child. It's the only possible explanation. She couldn't stay in the palace in that condition."

Akitada said mildly, "It wouldn't have been noticeable under all those gowns you women wear."

Akiko snorted and Tamako smiled. "There are other signs," she told her husband.

He flushed. "Oh, but would anyone know beside herself and her companion?"

Akiko said, "Certainly. In the imperial palace, there are ladies assigned to taking note of such changes."

Akitada was embarrassed and decided to go on with the reading rather than pursue such matters.

As it turned out, Lady Masako returned to the palace a week before her death in the Frost Month. The entries were even shorter now. She noted the arrival of winter, perhaps because her visits to the mountain villa became more arduous. Somehow, Akitada sensed that a decision had been made.

"I try to read your heart," she wrote in one poem to her lover, "while snow falls on my melancholy days."

"It sounds as though she realized too late she couldn't rely on him," commented Tamako. "He's not a good man. Could he have killed her?"

Silence fell as they considered this.

Akiko nodded first. "I like it. He's never had a conscience when it came to women. I think he did kill her. How will you prove it though? Go on and read the rest. What does she say just before the day she died?"

"If he killed her, he didn't try to cover up the affair," Akitada reminded her. "It got him in all this trouble."

Akiko pursed her lips. "The trouble happened because your friend insisted on going to the police."

"True." Akitada reluctantly gave Akiko credit for having seen this. "But his behavior seemed to be the reaction of an innocent man who was profoundly shocked by her death."

"Oh, you're just stubborn. Go on and read."

There was not much more. Some court observances at the beginning of the Frost Month were briefly mentioned. The prince sent a note. She responded, "Are you also thinking of the moon over the mountain's edge, lamenting how the days drag on?"

The decisions had been made, Akitada thought. And he read the final entry.

"'Oh winter storm! Your voice is thunder and my sleeves are soaked with tears.'"

"There!" cried Akiko.

Akitada said, "There is no more. She didn't write another line."

"A storm. It means a bitter quarrel. She quarreled with the prince." Akiko's voice filled with excitement. "They quarreled, Akitada. She wanted marriage and he refused. So she threatened scandal. He made an appointment to meet her, and then he either killed her himself or sent someone to do it. There's your proof."

Tamako looked troubled. "She doesn't use his name. There is no real proof."

Turning the journal in his hands, Akitada nodded. "Yes, Tamako is right. There is no real proof, just suspicion."

Akiko jumped up. "Oh, you're both blind. Can't you see he's the obvious one? What was simpler than to send her up to the villa and stage a suicide while he could claim to have been with Kosehira?"

"It could have been as you say," said Akitada. "But this must have happened while she was still supposed to live in the palace. It could also have been someone else." He sighed and put down the journal. "And now I think I'll go and have a nice long soak in the bath."

He did not mention that he had recognized a line in the journal.

29

The Bathhouse

Saburo was aware that his suspicion could be wrong and an embarrassing waste of time. Even given the two pieces of information which supported it, they could fit any number of different people. Yet he could not shake the feeling that he was right.

He spent every free minute watching. This was complicated and expensive because he did not want to attract notice and scare his suspect off. He sat outside a wine shop to keep his eyes on a door farther down the street, hoping his man would emerge or enter. Eventually, he had to abandon his watch to go to work before he laid eyes on him.

The following night, he was back at his spot, and this time he was in luck. His quarry emerged and walked away down the street. Saburo followed at a distance, watching, waiting for the other to make a mistake. Once or twice he thought he did, but he could not be sure.

The next day, he met with Tora and Genba.

He was surprised to see Genba free. They embraced and then walked to a nearby restaurant to celebrate.

Genba and Tora took turns filling him in on all that happened since Genba had been released.

"I don't mind telling you," said Genba, his face shining with joy, "I was flabbergasted. The superintendent himself came to set me free. It was almost like he meant to tell me how sorry he was except, of course, he didn't do that."

Tora broke in, "He should've apologized. He had no business treating you or any of us who work for our master in this fashion."

"Well, I was glad enough, except there was Ohiro. I hardly dared ask about her, but I did, and he said to wait outside and she'd be with me. And it wasn't any time at all before she came, looking just as confused as I felt. I can't tell you how good it was to see her."

"So what are your plans?" Saburo asked, wondering if Genba really intended to make a prostitute his wife.

"Oh, that's the best part," Tora said. "The master made her welcome. We're on our way now to hire the carpenter. Genba will need a separate place for his wife and children. We'll use part of the stables. There's plenty of room there, and the master's given us his blessing. Genba and Ohiro will have a cozy room or two with a small kitchen, just like Hanae and me."

"Ah, in the stable?" said Saburo, thinking this would mean losing the room he and Genba had shared.

"Well, it's the best place, and the two love birds can move in within a week. But I haven't told you about the master's accident yet."

Tora related the frightening hours spent on the mountainside. Genba spoiled the suspense by saying too quickly, "But the master's fine. Just a pulled shoulder joint and some bruises."

"Don't forget the cut on his head," Tora pointed out. "He was unconscious for hours, lying there on that narrow ledge. I talked myself hoarse, telling him not to move."

Saburo shook his head. "A terrible accident . . . if it was one."

Tora frowned. "Of course it was. He says e slipped."

"Hmm. Did you and the master find out who killed the lady?"

"Not yet, but we will. He has her diary. What about you? Any progress on Tokuzo?"

Saburo hesitated. "Yes and no. I have an idea that's pretty vague. Still it keeps nagging at me. I've taken to following someone."

The other two looked blank. "What are you talking about?" Tora asked

Saburo explained.

Tora said, "I know him, and I don't believe it. He is what he is. And that means he couldn't have killed Tokuzo."

Saburo glowered. "Really? Why not? For a *shinobi* it's the best disguise in the world."

They gaped at him. Genba nodded slowly. "There was that smell. And I had hold of the guy. He was very strong and very quick. But I don't see how anyone could get away with it for long."

Saburo said, "He mostly goes out after dark. One night I nearly ran into him. He stopped first. That's what gave me the idea."

Tora said, "It proves nothing. Their hearing is very good."

Saburo sighed. "I know. It does make sense, though, especially when people are so used to seeing them about. I did check out the Satake family. They'd come down in the world and, in my experience, people like that have a good deal of pride. After the parents died, the grandparents raised the two children. The girl's name was Nariko, and the boy's Narimitsu. Shokichi said Miyagi could read and write."

"Didn't do her much good," Tora observed dryly. He still had trouble reading and his writing was nearly illegible.

Saburo gave him a look. "What I meant was the son must've hated having his sister earn their living on the street. It explains why she didn't write her brother until it was too late."

Genba asked, "You think he got her letter and came home only to find her dead? And then decided to kill Tokuzo?"

Saburo nodded.

"That would do it for me," observed Tora. "But how do we prove it?"

Saburo said, "We must confront him. He'll deny it, of course, but I don't see another option."

"All of us?" Genba asked, perhaps thinking of their errand and the waiting Ohiro.

"It's best. If I'm right, he's dangerous and will be desperate."

Tora nodded. "Let's go then. You know where he is?"

"At work."

The Jade Arbor was doing a good business after hours. People usually came from work to relax before their evening rice and sleep. Or perhaps they planned a visit to the amusement quarter.

They paid their fee to the woman at the door and walked toward the steamy rooms with the communal tubs. Smaller rooms opened off the corridor, their doors either open or closed for privacy. The bathhouse offered specialized services and kept a staff of masseurs and attractive women for this purpose.

In a room with shelves and benches, they stripped, handed their clothing to the attendant, a youth wearing nothing but his loincloth, his skin beaded with moisture from the steam in the next room. He stared when he saw their scars and became very accommodating.

In a larger room filled with a hot white fog, three big wooden tubs served the bathers. Heads showed above their rims. Tora, Genba, and Saburo took small pails and bags of rice chaff from a shelf and crouched on the slatted wood floor to scrub themselves clean. Then they climbed into one of the tubs, muttering greetings to the two men who already soaked in the hot water.

Nearby was a tub full of chattering and giggling women, but their two companions were content to doze with their eyes closed.

Genba muttered, "This will be difficult."

When Saburo said nothing and Tora merely grunted, Genba fell silent. They sat, letting the heat loosen their muscles and relax their tension.

The two men eventually left, and Tora said in a low voice, "We have to risk it, Genba. He'll hardly agree to a meeting in some lonely grove someplace."

"Then let's get on with it," said Genba, heaving his huge bulk out of the water.

The attendant brought dry hemp kimonos. They wrapped themselves into these and asked for the masseur.

"All of you with the same masseur?" asked the youngster.

"Yes. Bashan. He's said to be the best. We'll take turns."

The boy directed them into one of the small rooms where a narrow raised platform awaited customers.

Saburo took off his kimono and lay face down on this, while Tora and Genba crouched against one of the walls.

After a short wait, they heard Bashan's staff tapping along the corridor. The door was pushed open.

"Gentlemen?" Bashan asked, his half-closed eyes seeming to scan the room as he waited for a response. Saburo lay with his head turned to the wall.

Tora said, "There are three of us. You can start with my friend. We'll take turns."

Bashan bowed in his direction. "Just a regular massage or a treatment?"

"Just the massage."

Bashan approached the platform, tapping with his staff and then leaning it against the wall. He set down the bamboo case he carried in the other hand, and touched Saburo's naked back. "Do you wish me to give special attention to any part?" he asked Saburo.

Saburo grunted, "No. Just the usual."

Watched by Tora, Bashan bent to remove a stoneware flask from his case. He poured oil on his hands, then began kneading and rubbing Saburo's back from the neck to the waist.

Genba moved quietly to the door, blocking it with his bulk.

Tora said, "I know they call you Bashan. What's your real name?"

"My name is Bashan."

"I think your family name is Satake. You're Satake Narimitsu."

Bashan froze, his body suddenly tense. "I don't understand."

Tora got to his feet. "You had a sister called Nariko, didn't you?"

"I have no sister."

Tora watched the man's back. It had the stillness of a coiled snake. "You can stop what you're doing. We really came to have a chat with you. Turn around."

"I'm paid to give massages to customers. If you don't want me to do that, I'll leave." Bashan fumbled for his staff. Tora snatched it away.

"You don't need this. I believe you can see as well as anyone."

Bashan finally turned. He moved his head from side to side as if trying to locate Tora. Genba grinned and flexed his muscles. Saburo sat up and put on his kimono.

"What do you want?" Bashan said, inching toward his case. "I can call for help."

"I'd better take charge of this," Saburo said, taking Bashan's case and moving it away from him. "Can't have you reaching for your needles."

Bashan turned his head. "You!"

"I told you he can see," Saburo said with great satisfaction. "You recognize me, don't you, Bashan?"

"I recognize your voice, you ungrateful cur," snarled the masseur. "Is this the thanks I get for patching you up?"

"Thanks? After you nearly cracked my skull?"

A brief silence fell.

Tora and Genba flexed their hands. Saburo looked frustrated.

Bashan abruptly sat down on the platform. "I suppose," he said slowly, "there's no point in going on with this game. I was getting heartily tired of it anyway, but it's a way to earn some money. What do you want?"

Tora made introductions.

Bashan stared at Genba. "Are you the one they arrested?"

"Yes," snapped Tora. "You let them arrest an innocent man and woman. They tried to beat confessions out of both of them."

Bashan grimaced. "Sorry," he muttered. "It wasn't my doing. Fate put you in the way of the ignorant police. How is it that you're free?"

Genba said, "They let us go. No proof."

"No proof?" Bashan smiled. "Yes. There was none in your case, and there won't be any in mine either."

Tora glared at him. "We can't leave things the way they are. There's been a murder. What if the police arrest someone else?"

Bashan said, "It isn't likely, is it? Or are they even stupider than I thought?"

Saburo straightened up. "Why are you still here? If your only purpose was to avenge your sister's death, then you should have left for the north days ago."

"You think it was just revenge? That would merely have been a selfish act."

"What else could it be?" Tora growled. "You're Miyagi's brother, aren't you? You see, we know who you are and what made you do it."

Bashan suddenly looked tired and pale. "Yes, I'm Nariko's brother. I left them to seek my fortune with the army. They starved until Nariko was sold to that animal. I didn't know any of it, but I should have looked after them. All those years, Nariko never once asked for help, until her last letter. I'm not making excuses, but that is what happened. By the time I got back, she had died and so had our grandparents." He raised his head and looked at each of them in turn. "Do you understand now? All of it was my fault. I hoped to make up for my sin."

Genba, always softhearted, said, "I think I understand. You decided to do something to help others like your sister, and so you killed Tokuzo for abusing the women who worked for him."

Bashan nodded. "I had learned the use of needles and *moxa* from some monks in the north, and massage is easy enough. It turned out to be a useful skill in the army. When I needed a disguise, I added blindness and became a masseur."

Tora snorted. "Saburo said you're a hired killer. I don't buy your story."

Bashan drew himself up. "I'm a soldier. The needle I dropped was meant for Tokuzo. If I hadn't lost it, nobody would have known it was murder. My colliding with Genba was fate." He pointed to Saburo. "And fate brought him to the brothel that night."

Genba said, "I picked up the needle and gave it to Saburo. He did say it was an assassin's needle because he knows about such things. I don't mind admitting that shook me up a bit."

Bashan studied Saburo and nodded. "I see. It all hangs together now. What will you do?"

They looked at each other. Tora said, "The master won't like this."

Genba shook his head. "The master's a good man but he serves the emperor. We cannot just let you go."

"You've trained as a shinobi, I think," Saburo said. "Do you plan to stay and work here?"

Bashan looked shocked. "No. I told you, I only did what I did to help those poor women."

"It was you who returned the contracts to them?"

"Yes. It's why I went back after I killed him. I was upset that night. It was a botched job."

Tora said dryly, "It may interest you to know that almost all the women sold themselves again. Some went back to work for Tokuzo's mother."

"At least the old one doesn't treat them badly. I've stayed to keep an eye on her."

Someone pounded on the door of their room. "Hey, Bashan? What's taking so long? You've got a customer waiting."

Saburo straightened up. "Nothing will be solved to-night. I suggest we all go and think about what is best to be done. We'll meet again tomorrow. Where, Ba-shan?"

Bashan did not answer right away. He looked at Saburo, then at Tora and Genba. "Yes," he finally said softly. "That will be best. Let's meet after sundown at the beggars' temple. It may be that the priest Kenko has a solution."

The others nodded and left one by one, Tora abandoning the staff and Saburo returning the case to Ba-shan. The attendant met them outside to collect three fees for their massages.

When they were back outside in the street, Tora said, "He'll run."

Saburo nodded. "Oh, yes."

Genba pondered for a moment. "I don't think his running solves our problem."

The other two looked at each other and sighed.

"Let's go get that carpenter," Tora said.

30

The Horse

Akitada slept deeply after his bath and woke refreshed and quite clear-headed. He lay, watching the shafts of sunlight that entered through his shutters. Tiny sparks danced in them, dust particles so small they floated. He pondered the nature of light and of knowledge. They made visible what darkness and confusion had obscured.

Darkness was the time when human trickery was most active. Saburo could testify to that.

The murder of Lady Masako had probably happened in darkness, or at least at dusk. If the prince had not been so late that night he might have prevented what happened.

Or died himself.

Since the attack on him, Akitada had suspected that the killer haunted the place. Was his conscience troubled, or were there other forces at work? There had been Lady Hiroko's dream. Even in the telling, it had seemed strangely vivid with a sense of the cold and snow and night that were part of Lady Masako's final moments.

Night fell early in winter, and it must have been overcast that day. New snow had fallen and obscured the murderer's tracks. Riding or even walking those mountain paths at night must have been difficult. Still, the prince had chosen to make the journey, perhaps not realizing snow would soon make things even more difficult. Surely it was proof he cared for Masako and his unborn child.

Akitada sat up abruptly. The old woman had seen and recognized the prince. How was this possible if he had arrived long after dark? Surely by then, both old people had gone to bed. And how could she have seen him clearly enough to recognize him?

It must have been his horse she had recognized, a familiar horse with a white blaze on its forehead. Something was not right about this.

He got up quickly, threw on his old robe, and walked across the courtyard to Tora's place. Trouble came limping from the stable, wagging his tail and pressing his cold nose into his hand. Akitada patted him absent-mindedly. A pile of boards and timbers lay outside the stables. Soon he would welcome another member into his family. Would Ohiro fit in? Whatever the situation, he would make the best of it. He owed it to Genba.

On Tora's veranda, he whistled softly. All was quiet inside. They must have worked late to get Genba settled.

Tora appeared in his shirt, yawning and scratching his head. "Morning, sir. Is something wrong?"

"No. Can you get dressed and come to the house? I'd like your opinion on an idea I just had."

Tora nodded and disappeared inside. Akitada strolled back, followed by Trouble. Someone was knocking at the gate, causing Trouble to bark and start into a lopsided run. The stable boy shot out of the stable, chewing a rice cake. He unlatched the small side gate and admitted a very old man who tottered in, weighed down by a large satchel he handed to the boy.

Akitada recognized the old carpenter. Tora had hired him outside Lord Sadanori's residence, and he had later repaired the earthquake damage to the Sugawara house. He was surprised the old man was still alive, though perhaps only barely so.

Calling out a greeting, he startled both the boy and the ancient one.

"Is it the master himself?" the carpenter croaked, blinking against the morning sun and bending his creaking back into a bow. "Amida's blessings on you and yours, Your Honor."

"Thank you. And the same to you and your wife."

"The old one's gone. She wasn't up to much anymore."

"Very sorry to hear it. How do you manage by yourself?"

I. J. Parker

"My daughter cooks and cleans. That's what a man has daughters for."

Was it? The thought depressed Akitada who suddenly saw himself as a doddering old man waited on by Yasuko. He shook off the image.

"I see you've come to build a home for another couple. Have they told you that Genba is taking a wife?"

The old man chuckled. "He's old enough to know better."

"Perhaps, but as you say, women are useful creatures to have about the house."

The carpenter pondered this. "They talk too much," he finally said.

Tora joined them. "Ho, Juro," he greeted the old man. "Bright and early, eh? Genba and Saburo are still sleeping."

"I'll get them up." The carpenter tottered off toward the stable, followed by Trouble.

"Sorry I overslept, sir. We stopped off for wine after our errands. To drink to Genba and Ohiro's happiness."

Akitada smiled. "Yes, of course. But come inside. I thought of something."

In his room, he threw open the shutters. They sat down on the veranda, and Akitada said, "You remember that old woman on the mountain? When I talked to her about the night of the murder, she told me she'd seen both Lady Masako and the prince arrive. They were on horseback and passed her house on their way to the villa."

Tora's brows rose. "Together?"

"No. Lady Masako came first."

"Right. That's what we've known all along."

"The old woman recognized the prince's horse by the blaze on its forehead."

Tora frowned. "So?"

"The prince has said all along he was very late that night. It was getting dark when he left the capital, and it was nighttime when he reached the villa. How did she see him?"

"Oh. That *is* strange. But she's old. She probably got the days mixed up."

"I don't think so. I think she saw the murderer arrive right after Lady Masako."

Tora's eyes widened. "But what about the horse?"

"A horse with a white mark on its head isn't a rarity. And I bet she didn't see very clearly. It had started snowing. She simply assumed the horseman was the prince because she expected him."

"But who was it then?"

Akitada reached for Lady Masako's journal and held it up. "The last thing Lady Masako wrote was, 'A winter storm! Your voice is that of thunder and my sleeves are soaked with tears.'"

"Was there a storm?"

"No, Tora. Young ladies are given to express themselves poetically. She quarreled with someone."

"Right. Who with?"

"She doesn't say."

"But it wasn't the prince?"

"No, I don't think it was the prince."

Tora thought. His face brightened. "Remember how Lord Masaie's cook said her master was in the capital then? I bet he went to talk to his daughter again."

Akitada nodded. "Perhaps. It would make sense. I think it's time we found out what Masaie was up to."

Tora got up. "I'll have another talk with the cook," he offered.

"No. We'll talk to his lordship himself."

"Even better, sir." Tora looked pleased, but then his face fell. He cleared his throat. "I have news. We know who killed Tokuzo, sir."

Akitada was not at all sure if this was good news. "You do?"

"It was Bashan."

"Bashan?" Akitada was at a loss. "You mean the blind masseur who put my shoulder back?"

"Yes, only he isn't blind."

"Really?"

Tora nodded.

Akitada thought about it. "It's possible. Men will do strange things to earn a living. But what makes you think he killed the man?"

Tora sighed. "Genba said the stranger smelled like a bathhouse."

Akitada did not laugh. Recognizing a smell had once before led them to a suspect. "Explain!"

Tora did so.

Akitada was impressed by their accomplishment. "That was extremely well done," he said warmly. "How do you plan to proceed?"

"We . . . er . . . proceeded already, sir. We confronted him."

"Oh? He denied everything, I take it."

"At first, but he could see we knew all of it." Tora looked distinctly uncomfortable now and shifted from one foot to the other.

"Don't make me ask a thousand questions. What happened?"

"We've arranged to meet him tonight to discuss what is to be done."

Silence fell.

Akitada decided they had let the killer go because they approved of his actions. Truth to tell, they had not had many options. They could have taken their story to Kobe, who would not have given it any credence. Or they could have come to him. Thank heaven they had not. At least he had not been faced with making that choice.

He sighed. "I see. Well, I don't suppose he'll show up for the meeting. He'll be miles from the capital by now. You'd better inform Kobe at some point."

Tora gaped. "You aren't angry?" he asked.

"Not angry, no. But I hope you're right about Bashan. If he's a professional killer, he may practice his craft on an innocent person next time."

Tora hung his head. "We're pretty sure he was telling the truth. And he knew we had no proof he was the one who killed Tokuzo."

"Everything considered, not a very satisfactory solution. Kobe won't like it either." Akitada shook his head. "But it isn't all bad. We have Genba back, and some of the women in the Willow Quarter have a better life."

They smiled at each other.

Akitada was anxious to settle the murder of Lady Masako, but he had a living to earn. He was late getting to the ministry where his pronounced limp and the stiff way in which he held his bruised body served as an excuse.

Kaneie was in and had heard of his mishap.

"There you are," he cried, eyeing Akitada sharply. "You don't look too bad. People said you suffered a terrible injury."

"Good morning, sir. I took a tumble in the mountains two days ago. I suppose the fact they had to bring me back on a litter caused some talk. I'm quite well again, just a little stiff, and my left arm is still sore. Nothing to stop me from dealing with work, though."

"I'm relieved it wasn't worse. Nobody knew what to make of it. I just heard this morning, or I would have stopped by."

"Thank you, sir. You're very kind." Akitada smiled at Kaneie. They liked each other, and he thought it very likely that Kaneie would have visited.

"You fell in the mountains? Not by any chance at Prince Atsuhira's place?"

Akitada flushed. "I'm afraid so."

"I knew that business would get you in trouble. Well, I hope the effort wasn't a total disaster."

"I hope not, sir. Speaking of the matter, do you happen to know if Lord Masaie is in town?"

Kaneie's eyebrows shot up. "You haven't had enough yet? Yes, Maseie and his son are in the capital. Is he in trouble? Never mind answering that."

"I thought he would have left the capital after the scandal with his daughter."

"He did, but he's a proud man. His son was dismissed from the emperor's guard, and Masaie has come back to protest the matter."

"Surely they could not dismiss Masanaga without cause."

"With Masanaga there was always plenty of cause. He's a drunkard and a troublemaker. In the past, his sister's position protected him."

"I see. Well, if you have no new instructions for me, I shall get to work."

The long break enjoyed by officials meant the first day of the week was busy as everyone tried to catch up. Akitada got home well after dark. He had time only to pour himself some wine and step out on his veranda to look up at a starry sky and smell the fragrance of some flowering shrub before Tora joined him.

"You're late, sir," he said. "I've been waiting. Lord Masaie and his son are both at their residence."

"Yes. The minister told me the son lost his post in the guard. I thought you'd be meeting with Bashan."

"Saburo went. Their lordships will be in a foul mood."

"I don't feel very good about this myself."

"It's a terrible thing if he did it. A terrible thing!"
"Yes."

I. J. Parker

They were silent for a span, then Akitada sighed. "Well, we might as well go."

They walked together through the streets. Tora kept one step behind. It was easy to converse this way, but they both remained quiet.

The Minamoto residence was lit up, and the gates stood partly open. They were admitted and followed a servant into a reception room in the main house. Both of them felt tense. Tora paced, while Akitada weighed once again what he must tell Maseie.

They knew Masaie had a bad temper, but neither of them wore a sword. Weapons were frowned upon when making calls on the nobility.

Masaie came quickly, and Akitada was shocked to see the change in him. The big man seemed to have shrunk in the week since he had last seen him. His shoulders slumped, and his face was an unhealthy gray color.

"What is it now?" he demanded in a tone that was at least reminiscent of past belligerence.

"It is still about your daughter's death," Akitada said. "It is time you accepted that she was murdered."

Masaie stared at him, then gestured at Tora. "I won't speak to you with your servant present."

Tora opened his mouth to protest, but Akitada said, "Wait for me outside. It's all right."

Tora left reluctantly, and they sat down. Masaie ran a hand over his face. "Why do you trouble me again? What is her death to you?" he asked. "Do you think I care about your friend Kosehira? Or about the swine who seduced my child?"

So Maseie had begun to grieve for his daughter after all. Akitada said more gently, "I think you care about her memory."

Masaie stiffened. "Her memory? Do you know what they called her? They called her the emperor's woman! As if she'd been some harlot brought in from the streets or the brothels to amuse the Son of Heaven. My daughter! Masako is descended from emperors. Her bloodline is better than that of the Fujiwara hussy who is to become empress. The insult to my house is not to be borne."

For a moment, he was the old Masaie, Lord of Sagami, undisputed ruler over his lands and his clan.

Akitada sighed. "I came to speak to the father, not to the clan chief. I was told you loved her."

Masaie turned his head away. "I loved her like my life. No, more than my life."

"When I was here last, you said she was dead to you already. Perhaps pushing her off a cliff wouldn't have mattered much to you."

Masaie looked up. "You think *I* would do this?"

"No. I thought so once, but I know better now."

Masaie paled, but he said nothing.

After a moment, Akitada continued, "She was very lonely at court. Nobody liked her, His Majesty least of all."

Masaie remained silent.

"She tried to obey you. It wasn't her fault she didn't find acceptance, but you turned your back on her in her misery. Her whole family turned against her. Is it any wonder she looked to Prince Atsuhira for support?"

Masaie turned a ravaged face to Akitada. "How dare you? I can have my guards cut you down like a dog."

Ignoring this, Akitada continued, "Your daughter did not jump. Let me tell you what happened the night Masako died. She arrived at the villa in the afternoon of that winter day, expecting to meet the prince and accept his protection." Masaie made a sudden move, but Akitada raised a hand. "No, let me finish. Your daughter was with child. Atsuhira's child. He intended to make her his wife, but he was detained that night, though perhaps it wouldn't have mattered. Someone else followed her up that mountain road, someone who had quarreled bitterly with her earlier that day. I'm not sure if he intended to kill her or the prince, but it doesn't matter. Her killer was riding a dark horse with a white blaze on its forehead. The caretaker mistook his horse for the prince's. I don't know what happened in the villa, but there must have been another quarrel. I found signs of violence, a few blood stains, some long hairs, and a few blue silk threads from the gown she wore. I think the killer struck her with one of the wooden staffs kept in the room. Perhaps he thought he had killed her and panicked. In any case, he carried her to the promontory, where he pushed her over the edge, hoping people would believe she had committed suicide. That is what happened."

Masaie had listened with his head lowered. He sat very still.

In the silence, the opening of the door sounded like a thunderclap. Both men started.

Masanaga closed the door behind him and walked toward them. His face was flushed, hi eyes bloodshot, and beads of perspiration glistened on his face. He wore his sword, and his right hand gripped it. His eyes fixed on Akitada. In a shaking voice, he said, "It's a story you've made up. Another lie." His voice broke, then rose. "It's nothing but lies. I warned you!" The hand on the sword shook convulsively.

Akitada said calmly, "It's no lie. Yes, you tried to warn me away and then attempted to kill me when I got too close to the truth."

In the silence, only Masanaga's heavy breathing could be heard.

Then Masaie staggered to his feet and took a step toward his son. "We'll speak later. Get out now," he said, his voice hard and final.

Masanaga hesitated a moment, then turned and left.

Akitada also got up, gritting his teeth. His body still resented sudden moves. He said, "I brought your daughter's diary so you should read what your ambition caused." Taking the journal from his sleeve, he extended it to Masaie.

For a moment, he thought the big man would dash it from his fingers, but then Masaie took it with a trembling hand. He opened it, and tears began to well up in his eyes.

"I'll leave you now, my Lord," said Akitada.

There was no answer, and he walked out.

He was half afraid that Masanaga would lie in wait for him, but the anteroom was empty, and Tora waited at the outer door.

When they were back on the street, Tora said, "What happened? I saw the son go in and almost followed."

"Not much. I returned Lady Masako's journal to her father."

"Weren't you supposed to give it to her companion?"

"A grieving father has a greater right."

"Even if he killed her?"

"He didn't kill her, Tora. I brought him more terrible news."

"What? I don't understand anything. I thought you meant to accuse Lord Masaie of murdering his daughter."

"I did think at one time he was guilty, but there was someone else who had a stronger motive and fit the image of a killer much better."

Tora kicked at a rock on the street. "I'm a fool. I'll never learn this business."

"You're not a fool."

They walked in silence, Tora kicking more rocks from time to time. Suddenly he stopped. Akitada turned and saw a curious expression cross his face. "The cook," Tora said. "She as much as told me." He hit his forehead with his palm. "She didn't like him either. She said he was bad."

Akitada watched him. "Well?"

"The brother?"

Akitada nodded. "Yes. Only three men could have known where she had gone, the prince, her father, and her brother. And whatever his character, the prince isn't the type to commit such a violent act. We'll know soon enough. I think Maseie already knew or suspected as much, and this time he will not forgive Masanaga."

For a moment Tora was silent. Then he said, "The cook did say the boy was always resentful because the father preferred his daughter. But it all feels so unfinished."

"Sometimes it's better to stand back and allow events to correct themselves."

31

Loose Threads

Saburo met them when they returned. He bowed formally to Akitada and said, "I regret to report, sir, that the man called Bashan did not come to the agreed meeting. I must assume he feared arrest and fled."

"Thank you, Saburo. It's as good as a confession. Are you back to stay?"

Saburo contorted his features into a smile. "Yes. And thank you and your lady."

Akitada liked that he made no apologies and spoke with self-assurance. He returned the smile. "Good. I was wrong to dismiss you without weighing your reasons and shall try to act more fairly in the future."

Saburo bowed again and headed off to the stable where they could hear hammering. "You aren't taking his room, I hope?" Akitada asked Tora.

"No, of course not."

As they watched, Trouble came out of the stable to greet Saburo. Saburo petted the dog and suddenly did a little jump and dance of joy that the dog joined in with a happy yelp.

Tora chuckled, and Akitada heaved a deep sigh of contentment.

After changing into his comfortable robe, Akitada went to report to his wife. He found her with Akiko.

His sister glared at him. "There you are, you traitor. Why didn't you take me along to see Maseie?"

"Because it was too dangerous."

She pouted. "Evidently it was safe enough. What happened?"

Akitada reported what he had told Maseie about Masanaga. Tamako looked subdued and shook her head, but Akiko cried, "You gave him Masako's journal? How could you? You promised Lady Hiroko that you would return it."

"*You* promised. I did no such thing. Her father has precedence. But there was another reason."

"Nonsense. He treated his daughter abominably."

"You're right, and I thought it important to have him ponder his actions. For all his reprehensible behavior, Maseie really loved his daughter. He still loves her. In time he'll come to understand his own role in her death."

Akiko snapped, "I doubt it. And what about the detestable Masanaga? You'll just let him escape?"

"Detestable, yes. But because of the delicacy of the situation, which involves His Majesty, he cannot be arrested and tried. I think his father had already realized what Masanaga did. We must wait and see what action he will take."

Tamako asked, "Will you inform Prince Atsuhira?"

Akitada sighed. "I suppose I must. I no longer like him very much. He is as much to blame as Masaie and his son."

Akiko's eyes flashed. "Men! All of them. Women will always be at their mercy. It will always be this way."

Lady Kishi had said something very similar. At the time she had astonished Akitada because she was one of the most powerful women in the country. He did not argue against his sister's point. Not only Lady Masako's fate, but also Genba's story had made him very aware of the injustices suffered by women.

Tamako saw his face and said, "Not all men are like that. Neither your husband nor mine nor your sister's would treat their wives or daughters badly."

Akiko sniffed. "I for one shall always be on my guard." She glowered at Akitada.

He said humbly, "I'll try to be a better brother, Aki-ko," and smiled at her.

"Well," she said mollified, "I hope that means you'll consult me on future cases."

Akitada and Tamako laughed.

The following morning, Akitada emerged from the house on his way to the ministry. Another hot bath had eased his remaining aches and pains, and he felt quite well again.

Waiting in the courtyard were Genba and a young woman. They stood side-by-side, smiling shyly and bowed very low. Genba straightened up, but the young woman remained bowing.

"Sir," said Genba, "I brought Ohiro to pay her respects. She promises to be faithful and work hard."

Akitada saw she was a sturdy-looking girl and would surely be a big help in his household, but that was not why she was here. He went up to them. "Welcome, Ohiro. Please feel at home here. We think much of your husband and are happy that you're making him happy. He's been far too lonely all these years."

She gave him a huge smile and bowed again. "Thank you," she said softly. "Genba is very good to me."

Genba blushed. "It's the other way around, sir."

"Have you introduced Ohiro to my wife?"

"Not yet, sir. Should I?"

So there was still some shame. Well, they couldn't have that. "Come along," Akitada said briskly and headed for Tamako's pavilion.

There the introductions went very well indeed, especially when Ohiro showed immediate affection for the children.

Akitada departed for the ministry, feeling content in his world and satisfied with the way he had handled his domestic affairs.

His good mood did not last. He still had to speak to Prince Atsuhira, and that was something he did not look forward to. He left the ministry early and walked to the prince's palace. There he demanded to see the prince with important news.

The servant returned, saying the master was seeing no one.

Anger seized Akitada. How dare Atsuhira deny him after all he had done for him in the past and more recently. He said "Thank you," in an icy tone, then walked past the servant and into the house. He knew the way to the prince's room and strode ahead, followed by the protesting servant. Throwing open the door to the prince's study, Akitada walked in and slammed it behind him.

"Your man brought your message but I chose to ignore it," he snapped. "We have some matters to discuss, and when I'm done I hope sincerely I'll never have to trouble with you again."

Atsuhira, who looked pale and disheveled, stared up at him from a seat near a brazier. He was leaning on an armrest and had been reading. "I have nothing to say to you," he said.

"I have some things to say to you, so be quiet and listen."

Atsuhira opened and closed his mouth as if he were snapping for air but came up with nothing.

"The murder of Lady Masako is solved. Her brother Masanaga found out she was leaving the palace to join you. No doubt, he realized this would mean the end to his own career, particularly since he had already made a bad name for himself. He went to speak to her at the palace, where they quarreled. Lady Masako noted this in her journal. It was her last entry. I think it was then Masanaga decided to kill you. He followed her to your villa, where they quarreled again and he struck her with one of your *bo*. He probably waited for you to arrive, but you were very late, and she may have regained consciousness. In any case, he panicked. He carried her to the promontory and pushed her over, hoping that her death would be taken for a suicide. Then he left."

The prince was pale and shuddered. "Masanaga murdered his own sister?"

"Yes. According to her companion, she loved you and looked forward to raising your child. I'm curious. Why did you tell the superintendent that Lady Masako intended to end her life?"

The prince frowned. "I don't know. I don't remember. I wasn't myself."

"In her journal, she copied down a poem she had sent to you. It read, 'I dream sweet dreams; but my sleeves are wet with tears. If I take the dark path alone, we will meet in paradise.' By any chance, is that what you remembered when she was found?"

"Yes. I was trying to account for what she had done."

"The poem is dated months earlier, at a time when she was distraught over her father's anger. In other words, there never was any indication that Lady Masako intended to die that night at the villa, was there?"

"Oh." Atsuhira wept. "No, there wasn't. Oh, what a relief! Thank you. Thank you for telling me. I have been in agony. I blamed myself."

Akitada said coldly, "As to that, you will know best what your responsibility was in seducing a young and inexperienced girl who was one of the emperor's women. Your behavior is inexcusable in my eyes. I had to intercede once before when one of your careless affairs nearly precipitated another succession scandal. Your uncle, the late Bishop Sesshin, asked for my help on that occasion. I had hoped you had learned your lesson then."

The prince dabbed at his eyes. "I see why you're so angry at me," he said. "But you must believe that I truly loved Masako. We couldn't help ourselves. Our love was stronger than everything. I don't want to be emperor, but the way my cousin treated Masako angered me. He didn't deserve her."

Akitada glared at him. "So you shared your feelings about His Majesty with Kosehira and involved him. I expect you to go to the regent to clear his name, apologize for your behavior, and ask his help in settling the matter of the succession once and for all. You may wish to take vows afterward. Nothing short of becoming a monk will convince people that you don't want to be emperor." Without waiting for a response, Akitada turned and walked out.

In the following weeks, life in the Sugawara family settled down. Saburo was once again installed as Akitada's secretary. Genba and Ohiro moved into their new quarters in the stable, and Ohiro spent a good deal of her time in the kitchen where she attempted to teach Cook new ways to prepare foods. Cook had never been more than passable in her skills, and the household fare was uninspired. Now some very tasty dishes appeared. As a result of this interference, Cook departed in a huff to the secret joy of the members of the household. Ohiro took over her duties.

Not long after this, his friend Kosehira returned to the capital, cleared of all suspicion and eager to celebrate with his friends and supporters. However, in spite of his contentment, Akitada felt restless.

One morning, Tora voiced the reason for Akitada's dissatisfaction. "You know, sir," he said, "two people have died violently and nobody got punished. It doesn't seem right."

Akitada nodded. "You're right. It doesn't. Not that we had any choice in the matter. Bashan, that slippery fellow, left no proof of what he'd done, and Lady Masako's killer could not be revealed or arrested because it would have involved court matters. But it troubles me also."

Bashan, or Satake Narimitsu as he was born, disappeared into the northern provinces, and nothing else was heard of him. But Morinaga's fate became known soon after this conversation. The minister, Fujiwara Kaneie, conveyed the information to Akitada one morning.

"You recall the death of one of His Majesty's ladies last winter?" he asked.

"Yes. She died of some illness, didn't she?"

"Yes. A bit odd that. People have been saying she lost a child. The palace, of course, won't confirm such rumors. However, it's not the young woman who is being talked about but her brother."

Akitada became alert. "Minamoto Maseie's son?"

"Yes. It's shocking. First the man loses his daughter before she can become a consort of the emperor, and then his only son dies. A hunting accident, apparently. It happened in Sagami, right after Maseie and Masanaga reached their home. Mind you, the young man had a poor reputation while he was here. The regent dismissed him from his post in the guard." The minister shook his head. "Maseie's karma must be very bad."

Akitada nodded. He wondered how Maseie had managed his son's death, but there would have been many opportunities. The father had avenged the daughter's murder, but at what cost to himself?

For a moment, he lost himself in imagining the man's pain and despair, uncomfortable with his own role in bringing it about. Yes, karma explained it very well. Maseie, as well as his children, must have earned these tragedies by having committed evil deeds in their past lives. One must accept one's fate and strive to earn a better future.

Historical Note

The time of this novel is 1028 in the Heian period and predates the centuries of shoguns and samurai warriors. Though there certainly were wars and warriors, life was more peaceful and orderly than in later centuries. An emperor and a central government controlled the people from the capital city of Heian-Kyo (later Kyoto). Additional provincial administrations along with a well-organized transport system made for a mostly stable government. Most institutions and customs followed those in T'ang China, but the Japanese had long since broken off relations with that nation, and the meritocracy of the Chinese government had made place for promotion by rank and influence.

Control of the central government eventually passed into the hands of a single large family, the Fujiwara. Through marriage politics, senior Fujiwara officials held all the highest positions and controlled the emperor. They became the fathers-in-law, uncles, grandfathers, and cousins of ruling emperors. By encouraging the early abdication of emperors in order to replace them with more easily controlled children, they protected their power. Perhaps the most powerful man of the time was Fujiwara Michinaga, who ruled for many years, either as chancellor or as regent, being the father or grandfather of chancellors, empresses, and emperors. By 1028, he had died, but his power had passed to four of his sons

We know a great deal about life in the imperial palace. The court ladies of the time were avid writers and produced novels, diaries, and an abundance of poetry depicting their lives and those of the courtiers. Lady Murasaki's *Genji* is the most important of these works. It describes the events in the life of an imperial prince who was also a famous lover. Then there are the diaries which deal with real events and real people at court and around the person of the emperor. Among these are Sei Shonagon's sharp-tongued commentary, Lady Murasaki's account of her service as lady-in-waiting to one of the young empresses, diaries of women like Izumi Shikibu, the *Kagero Nikki,* and the *Sarashina Nikki.* We learn from these not only about court observances, but also about the manners and mores practiced in this setting. Love affairs were common and fraught with grief for many of the women. Access to pretty young girls serving the emperor was apparently easy, and courtships/and affairs were pursued with alacrity by the gentlemen who served at court. The best and most accessible scholarly account of life at court may be found in *The World of the Shining Prince* by Ivan Morris.

With the administrative power almost exclusively in the hands of the Fujiwara family, whose daughters were usually empresses and consorts, emperors tried to rule briefly before resigning under pressure from their in-laws in favor of sons who were minor children and ascended the throne under the guardianship of a Fujiwara grandfather. Political uncertainties about the imperial succession could ensue when there were several claimants to the throne. Invariably, the choice of a crown prince was in the hands of his Fujiwara relatives but affected all the lives and careers of officials. Hence, in this novel, the seriousness of the alleged plot by Prince Atsuhira and the efforts of Minamoto Maseie to introduce his daughter Masako into the emperor's bed.

Marriages for the upper classes were polygamous, that is, a husband could have several wives in addition to casual lovers. The wives differed in status, depending on their backgrounds and the birth of sons. A marriage could be dissolved on the husband's word. But women of the eleventh century could own property. That fact and the influence of their fathers protected upper class women to some extent. Lady Kishi in the novel has considerable power even though her husband prefers others over her.

A commoner had rarely more than one wife, and she was usually a hardworking partner in the business or on the land. Poverty put women at great risk as families struggled to feed all their children. The Confucian ideals of obeying and honoring one's parents forced them to work in near-slavery or to sell their bodies to support them.

The Willow Quarter mentioned in some Akitada novels has no solid historical sources. This is probably largely due to the fact that contemporary accounts were written by the upper classes who rarely referred to prostitution. But noblemen do speak of taking pleasure cruises to the brothel towns of the Yodo River, and one of the diaries mentions how the writer met a group of female entertainers while on the road to the capital. Female entertainers were not only talented performers of dance and song, but they were also available for sexual services. It stands to reason that the capital would have had prostitutes, and that they would have occupied a specific part of the city. For an account of the sex trade in early Japan, see Janet Goodwin's *Selling Songs and Smiles.*

The references to bathhouses, blind masseurs, and various treatments of wounds and diseases rely to some extent on later sources, though an early treatise on medicine (Yasuyori Tamba's *Ishimpo*) mentions acupuncture and *moxa* treatments and all sorts of odd herbal concoctions. In general, medical knowledge was rather primitive.

By the end of the Heian period, a guild or association system developed for trades. This included some of the outcast (*eta*) such as beggars and certain occupations thought to be unclean in terms of Shinto taboos (those who touch dead people and animals). Such brotherhoods usually existed under the protection of a temple and conducted themselves by their own rules.

The references to *shinobi*, the shadow warriors and forerunners of the *ninja*, can also be supported by contemporary accounts of the use of specially trained spies in times of war. Saburo learned his skills from monks, but Bashan trained with the northern army.

Law enforcement at this time was in the hands of a police force (*kebiishi*) and city wardens. Wardens supervised each ward of the capital and kept the peace in their own area. The imperial police investigated serious crimes, arrested criminals, and jailed them in two city jails. They worked closely with judges who heard the evidence and pronounced sentence. Flogging was a part of the gathering of evidence. Occasionally, mediums were called in to speak for the victim. Punishment consisted of incarceration or exile to labor camps. Executions were rare because of Buddhist laws against taking lives. Periodically, emperors would grant freedom to all prisoners to appease the gods in times of disasters and epidemics. Ranking police officers were trained warriors, and the top administrators, like Superintendent Kobe, belonged to the aristocracy.

About the Author

I.J. Parker was born and educated in Europe and turned to mystery writing after an academic career in the United States. She published her Akitada stories in *Alfred Hitchcock's Mystery Magazine,* winning the Shamus award in 2000. Several stories have also appeared in collections (*Fifty Years of Crime and Suspense* and *Shaken)*. The award-winning "Akitada's First Case" is available as a podcast. Many of the stories are collected in *Akitada and the Way of Justice.*

The Akitada series of crime novels features the same protagonist, an eleventh-century Japanese nobleman/detective. It now consists of ten titles. *The Emperor's Woman* is the latest. Most of the books are available in audio format and have been translated into twelve languages.

Her historical novels are set in twelfth-century Japan during the Heike Wars. The two-volume *The Hollow Reed* tells the story of Toshiko and Sadahira. *The Sword Master* follows the adventures of the swordsman Hachiro.

The Akitada series in chronological order
The Dragon Scroll
Rashomon Gate
Black Arrow
Island of Exiles
The Hell Screen
The Convict's Sword
The Masuda Affair
The Fires of the Gods
Death on an Autumn River
The Emperor's Woman

The Collected Stories
Akitada and the Way of Justice

The Historical Novels
The Hollow Reed I: Dream of a Spring Night
The Hollow Reed II: Dust before the Wind
The Sword Master

For more information, please visit I. J. Parker's web site at http:www.ijparker.com. You may write the author at heianmys@aol.com.

I. J. Parker

Books may be ordered from Amazon and Barnes&Noble. Electronic versions of the novels are available for Kindle and PC. The short stories are on Kindle and Nook. Please do post Amazon reviews. They help sell books and keep Akitada novels coming.

Thank you for your support.

32662293R00233

Made in the USA
Lexington, KY
01 June 2014